Praise for *Lost, Found, and Forever*

"Like the proverbial dog with a bone, I devoured this book in almost one go. It's the adorable tale of a movie-star dog at the heart of a rescue doggy custody battle . . . which is actually a love match rescue. Pure delight!"

—Julia London, *New York Times* bestselling author of *You Lucky Dog*

"The most charming love triangle of the season. It's a good thing one of them has dog sense. I especially loved the inside peek at moviemaking with the cutest canine ever. Spencer will steal your heart."

—Shelley Noble, *New York Times* bestselling author of *Imagine Summer*

"For everyone who has loved a dog—or a human—this warm and fetching story is an absolute delight. With a charming and intimate small-town setting alongside Hollywood glamour, a winning romance, and one precocious pup, all wrapped up in a bighearted tale of a woman's journey toward passion and purpose, *Lost, Found, and Forever* is a real treat."

—Phoebe Fox, author of *A Little Bit of Grace*

Praise for *Who Rescued Who*

"Move over Marley and Enzo—there's a new dog in town! Chock-full of heart and humor, anyone who has ever been redeemed by the love of a dog will treasure this uplifting, bighearted novel. A treat from start to finish!"

—Lori Nelson Spielman, *New York Times* bestselling author of *The Star-Crossed Sisters of Tuscany*

"A charming fish-out-of-water story about finding your heart and home in the place you least expect. After reading this book, I wanted to adopt a puppy and relocate to rural England. I absolutely adored it." —Sarah Smith, author of *Simmer Down*

"Once again, Schade comes at us with her trademark smarts and humor to deliver a story with everything to love. . . . A winner."

—Kristine Gasbarre, #1 *New York Times* bestselling author of *How to Love an American Man: A True Story*

"The engrossing, evocative prose whisked me away to an utterly charming British chocolate-box village, where I would have loved to stay. *Who Rescued Who* is certainly a special treat for dog lovers, but also for anyone who enjoys a multilayered story about finally finding a family in every sense."

—Evie Dunmore, author of *A Rogue of One's Own*

Praise for *Life on the Leash*

"Charming and heartfelt, *Life on the Leash* will delight readers. The perfect book for dog lovers!"

—Chanel Cleeton, *New York Times* bestselling author of *The Last Train to Key West*

"Even cat lovers will get wrapped up in this delightful story of girl, girl's best friend, girl's best girlfriends, and a couple of guys. Cora's canines in training will steal your heart. I couldn't wait to see what happened next!"

—Shelley Noble, *New York Times* bestselling author of *Lucky's Beach*

"*Life on the Leash* is the novel you've been waiting for all year—a strong, funny, bighearted heroine to cheer for in life and in love, plenty of 'I've-been-there' dating moments, and adorable, endearing, sometimes mischievous dogs to love on every page."

—Nicolle Wallace, dog lover, author, and MSNBC host

"A bighearted and witty debut from a writer with remarkable insight into the minds of dogs and those who love them. The winsome cast of characters will have you hooked on *Life on the Leash* from the first page."

—Meg Donohue, *USA Today* bestselling author of *You, Me, and the Sea*

lost, found, and forever

VICTORIA SCHADE

JOVE
NEW YORK

A JOVE BOOK
Published by Berkley
An imprint of Penguin Random House LLC
penguinrandomhouse.com

Library of Congress Cataloging-in-Publication Data

Names: Schade, Victoria, author.
Title: Lost, found, and forever / Victoria Schade.
Description: First edition. | New York: Jove, 2021.
Identifiers: LCCN 2020046447 (print) | LCCN 2020046448 (ebook) |
ISBN 9780593098851 (trade paperback) | ISBN 9780593098868 (ebook)
Subjects: GSAFD: Love stories.
Classification: LCC PS3619.C31265 L67 2021 (print) | LCC PS3619.C31265 (ebook) |
DDC 813/.6—dc23
LC record available at https://lccn.loc.gov/2020046447
LC ebook record available at https://lccn.loc.gov/2020046448

First Edition: March 2021

Printed in the United States of America
1   3   5   7   9   10   8   6   4   2

Cover photo by Nicole Mlakar / Offset Shutterstock
Cover design by Rita Frangie

For Frances O'Neill,
my very own fairy godmother

chapter one

Justine Becker held the base of the foot-long oblong pink dog toy in her fist, like she was swishing a sword at her employee. Her dog, Spencer, dropped into a play bow at her feet with a tongue-lolling grin, ready to give the new product a test-drive.

"Sienna, seriously?"

Sienna Fisher looked up from the packing slip and spit out the end of her dirty blond braid. "What? Dogs love that thing. USA made, no phthalates, natural rubber . . ." She trailed off when Justine started stroking the toy with an unmistakable up-and-down motion. "Oh my God, how did I miss that?"

"Yeah, I guess Tricks & Biscuits is now stocking dirty stuff with the dog toys. Remind me again why I let you take over ordering?" Justine laughed and shook her head as she peered inside the box and quickly counted the penis-shaped toys. "*Two dozen?* We have to sell twenty-four of these things? What will Mrs. Zwyicki think?"

Spencer stood on his hind legs and placed his front paws on the edge of the box, his feathered tail thumping against the bright blue counter as he leaned in and tried to grab one of the toys.

"Don't you worry, I'll sell the hell out of these. Give me a chance and I'll make them go viral," Sienna said.

"I know you will, and that's the only reason I'm not returning the order."

Sienna whistled to Spencer. "Hey, Spence, you wanna take some PG-13 pics?"

Justine peeked at the invoice total and felt a wave of relief wash over her when she saw the "net 30" stamp. She'd stretch it to "net 45" with apologies and promises to be better next time, but she'd make sure they eventually got paid, like every other vendor. Three years in business and she'd become an expert at juggling funds that didn't exist. She felt lucky she could afford to have Sienna on the payroll for twenty hours per week. The boho twentysomething's Birkenstocks and flowy skirts camou-flaged a talent for CEO-level strategizing, and her growing pet-sitting business, Like Family, almost kept her busy enough to not need the hours in the shop.

"Are you ready to talk about my big plans yet?" Sienna asked with an overwide smile on her pretty, angular face. "T&B will be so much more profit—" She stopped abruptly and cleared her throat. "We'll have more, uh, more growth, if you go for it."

Justine leaned back against the exposed brick wall next to the leash and collar display and crossed her arms. Sienna kept pushing her to move to all-natural product lines and add an online shop, convinced that the changes would be enough to reverse Tricks & Biscuits' flatlining. But her suggestions didn't come cheap. Natural products meant higher price tags, and cre-ating an e-commerce site would set Justine back a few grand that the store didn't have. She was embarrassed that her employee was more gung ho about profitability than she was, but Sienna didn't know the tap dancing Justine was doing behind the scenes at T&B. The three nearly maxed-out credit cards and the past-due calls she occasionally got from her dog food distributor kept her awake at night, but she didn't want to burden Sienna with the details.

"Can we talk about it later?" Justine asked. "I'm starving; I'm going to run to Monty's real quick."

"Are you bringing it back or eating there?"

Justine could tell by Sienna's expression that she was eager to start brainstorming, what with the steady rain outside and the lack of humans or canines walking in the door. It didn't matter what she was about to suggest they try; Justine would still feel like she was using a teaspoon to bail out her sinking ship.

"I think I'm going to eat there. Maybe the rain will let up by the time I get back and we'll actually get some customers in here. Want me to bring you something?"

"Nope, I've got my famous quinoa-and-broccoli bowl." Sienna paused when Justine grimaced. "Oh yeah, the smell. I totally forgot. I'll light a candle, promise." She held three fingers in the air like a Boy Scout.

"The vanilla one, please. Vanilla makes people hungry, and hungry people buy dog biscuits." Justine paused. "If anyone would come in."

"The rain is going to stop; I can feel it in my bones," Sienna said, wiggling her fingers in front of her like she was casting a spell. "And this little lag means I'll have a chance to get everything unpacked for the weekend. There are two more boxes in back. I went a little crazy because you can't sell what you don't have. And I'd love to get my hands on your messy office. Hold on—maybe I'll *sage* the place too! That's even better than a candle."

"Whatever you think is most important, do that. I trust you."

Justine felt a wave of gratitude for Sienna the witch goddess. Her positivity was the only thing keeping Justine from flipping the CLOSED sign for good. That and the shop's core of loyal supporters, who told her, in one way or another, that the little dog-friendly shop was their happy place. Every time she imagined shutting T&B, she pictured customers like lonely widower Frank Mancini, who held court at the counter every Saturday morning with an everything bagel and his Yorkie named Flossie. Or Miranda Leahy and her son Brandon, who at seven was still nonverbal, but who chattered his own language with every dog that walked through the door. The shop was in free fall, but no one, from her customers to Sienna, had a clue.

"Hey, I forgot to tell you that Seth stopped by looking for the lease. Have you signed it?" Sienna asked.

Justine shook her head. "Not yet."

Putting her signature on the lease meant three more years of financial gymnastics. Three more years behind the counter.

And three more years of trying to figure out what the hell she was actually doing with her life.

"Spence, c'mon," Justine called to her dog, who was still halfway in the box eyeing the questionable new toys. He hopped out in a single bound and trotted to her.

"Seth didn't seem mad or anything, but he wants to talk to you," Sienna added. "Is everything okay?"

Justine flushed, remembering how she'd asked her landlord

for a payment extension the prior month. He probably wanted to revoke her option to renew.

Which wouldn't be the worst thing.

"Everything is fine," she lied as she clipped the leash on Spencer and grabbed her Dalmatian-print umbrella. "I'll be back in a bit. Good luck dealing with the crowds." She gestured around the empty store with the tip of her umbrella.

"I'll run it like I own it!" Sienna replied with a salute.

chapter two

Spencer trotted along glued to Justine's side beneath the umbrella, doing his best to avoid getting hit by a single raindrop. It was one of those cold early fall days that were a coming attraction of the ugly season to come. Justine wished she was in bed under a down blanket with a book, a mug of hot tea, and Spencer curled behind her knees.

"You love to swim; why do you hate the rain so much?" Justine reached down to scratch her dog's scruffy head. He looked adorable in her friend Ruth's latest creation, a navy bow tie with a tiny repeating hedgehog pattern. Spencer glanced up at her and held her gaze for a few steps, and Justine's heart swelled Grinch-style. "Spence, you are the most amazing dog. Do you know that? How did I get so lucky?"

He wagged back at her as they paused beneath the awning outside Monty's.

"Shake off, bud," Justine said. Spencer obliged, getting rid of any rain that had settled on his fur and making it stand up in little peaks all over his body. She nodded at him. "Better. But you still need a bath and a trim. You're a mess."

Sometimes, when the wiry fur above his eyebrows and the wisps of his beard got too long, Spencer looked like a friendly wizard. People always tried to guess what he was and suggested everything from an Irish terrier mix to an obscure German breed called a Kromfohrländer. Justine was occasionally tempted to do a DNA test on him, to try to figure out where his soulful black eyes came from, and which breed was responsible for his mix of tenacity and goofiness. But in the end she decided that she liked not knowing. All that mattered was that they belonged to each other.

Their love affair had begun a year prior when she'd found Spencer's Petfinder post, after losing her beloved but anxiety-ridden shepherd mix, Flynn. Justine hadn't been actively looking for a dog, but he'd found her just the same.

I'm yours, his expression in the photo seemed to say. *Meant to be.*

At their first introduction he'd run to her like they were meeting at the top of the Empire State Building at midnight, like he *knew* that Justine was his person. Even the volunteer from the rescue had been shocked by the immediate connection between them. It wasn't love at first sight; it was flat-out mutual obsession.

Justine fumbled in her pocket for the quarter-sized key fob to unlock the door to the private dining club as a couple with a child in a stroller approached her tentatively.

"Is this Monty's?" the woman asked, pointing to the old brick building. "I read that there's no sign outside, but I think this is the place."

"It is," Justine said with a winning smile. "Are you a new member?"

She shook her head. "No, we're just visiting for the weekend, but we were hoping we'd be able to eat here. We've read such wonderful things about it."

"Oh, so sorry. Monty's is a members-only club for locals. But Sweet Oven is wonderful." She pointed to the restaurant half a block away.

Having to turn away weekenders at Monty's locked door was a regular occurrence, since Rexford bridged several worlds. First there were the crunchy, tree-hugging locals who had claimed the area as an artistic retreat in the 1960s. Then there were the tourists, who hogged parking spots, crowded the hiking trails, and kept the restaurants busy every weekend. And more recently, the "escape from New York" new-money folks who built weekend "cottages" and infused the area with artisanal bread shops and higher property values. It was a delicate ecosystem, but it worked.

As much as Justine loved her adopted hometown and was tempted to put down real roots, sometimes it made her feel claustrophobic. Anytime she wanted to gossip in public she'd crane her neck to make sure no one was within eavesdropping distance. Her mailman Bruce's wife was the receptionist at her gynecologist's office, so when Bruce dropped off Justine's mail he'd put her annual pap appointment reminder postcard on top of the stack, wink at her, and say, "Going to see Phyllis soon, are ya?" Rexford was like a cooler, more diverse Hallmark town, but it still felt like it wasn't enough for Justine.

It was her mom's fault. Four states before she'd even hit high school meant that she had wanderlust in her blood. Justine had loved trying on new locations together to see if they'd finally found "the one." East Coast, Midwest, West Coast; they found something to love in each state. Her mom's final move to Phoenix had happened while Justine was in college, and at first she was bummed that she couldn't experience desert life, but her visits there convinced Justine that she was an East Coaster through and through. Their magical time together in Connecticut during her elementary school years had left an imprint on Justine's heart, and she knew she needed the change of seasons to feel at home.

She just wasn't sure that Rexford was her forever.

Justine peeked around the mostly empty restaurant and spied Monty herself seated at a table in the corner with two other people, deep in conversation. Luis waved his spatula at Justine from the open kitchen. She could smell something smoky and oniony on the griddle.

"Hey, Luis, we just need a quick lunch; I know it's late."

"No problem, Justine, sit," he said, pronouncing her name with a soft *hus*. "Nice bow tie, Spencer. How's he doing?"

"Soaking wet. Sorry, we're going to stink up the joint."

"I just burned the boss lady's fish tacos. I think wet-dog smell is better."

Luis met her at the counter and Spencer's tail thumped in anticipation of getting something greasy from him. "What can I make for you?" He slipped Spencer a piece of bacon.

"Falafel wrap, please. We're going to eat here. Your girlfriend is holding down the shop."

Luis closed his eyes and sighed. "If only . . ."

"Why don't you just ask her out already? You've been in love with Sienna since the day you came to town. She's single; you're single. It's getting stupid, Luis."

"I will, I will. I just need to be ready, okay?" He widened his eyes at her like she was asking him to cliff dive instead of asking out a woman who was secretly just as hot for him.

If she wasn't on a dating hiatus and was just a few years out of college like Sienna, Justine would pounce on Luis herself. His black eyes and full sleeve of tattoos on a ripped arm made him look like he was the naughty boyfriend in a telenovela, but he was teddy-bear sweet. Add in his skills in the kitchen and he was basically the perfect man. Justine had held true to her promise not to tell Sienna that Luis was pining for her, but her patience was running out.

"Have you taught him anything new?" Luis nodded at Spencer.

"Always. Check it out." Justine stood up and sped Spencer through a series of tricks, including an impressive "pawstand," which was a handstand on paws. As she finished she noticed that Monty and her tablemates were watching and realized that one of them was Monty's daughter, Taylor.

"When did Taylor get to town?" she whispered to Luis when she sat down again.

"Yesterday. And that's the director of her new show, Ted-something," he whispered back. "That prohibition series she's doing. They're staying at Monty's farm for the weekend." He walked into the kitchen to start her lunch.

Monty Volkov had been a model turned muse for the Sonic Dukes in the early '80s, when Russian glamazons dominated magazine covers. She'd let her chestnut hair go silver, but her cheekbones were still as sharp as her wit, and no one could mistake the green eyes that cemented her place as rock-and-roll royalty. She'd claimed a writer's credit on the band's most successful song, "Her Eyes," and used the money she made from it to open her first restaurant in SoHo. A well-deserved Michelin two-star award and twenty years later, Monty decamped to a sprawling lavender farm in Rexford to simplify. Her daughter had thankfully inherited more of her mother's genes than her meth head–skinny rocker father's and was a rising star in Hollywood. She found her way back to Rexford after breakups and in between projects.

"Impressive," Monty said in her commanding voice from the table in the corner. The man in a baseball cap and sunglasses sitting with her nodded. "What else can he do?"

Even though Justine considered Monty an acquaintance-friend, she still got a little nervous when the Russian wolf singled her out, especially when she was with her famous friends and family. She ran her hand over her hair self-consciously, pissed that the chin-length bob wasn't growing out fast enough. Whenever she was around Monty and her people she felt like a bumpkin.

"Tell me what you want to see and he'll do it," Justine said with a smile.

"Show her how Spencer does that bell trick." Luis jogged from the kitchen and placed a deli bell on the edge of the counter. "Do it, she'll love it."

Justine felt silly interrupting what was surely some sort of important strategy session with Taylor but knew she couldn't refuse. "Hey, Spence." He looked up at her. "Service, please."

Spencer stood on his hind legs and danced in place, trying

to gauge if he was tall enough to reach the bell with his paw. When he realized he couldn't, he sat down for a second, then launched himself onto a stool, placed one paw on the edge of the counter, then delicately rang the bell with his other.

"Woo-hoo," Taylor hooted and clapped like she was at a hockey game. It was easy to forget that five-ten creature was only twenty-two, until she suddenly acted her age. "Good boy!"

Justine was still totally starstruck by Taylor, as was the rest of Rexford. Seeing her in person was like being in the presence of an endangered animal you'd only ever seen in photos; she was taller, skinnier, and more luminous than any camera could rightly capture. Even though Taylor had always been friendly when they'd run into each other around town, the air around her felt different. In Rexford she was a blue blood surrounded by a sea of normals.

The man wearing sunglasses inside leaned close to Monty and said something softly to her. She nodded.

"Justine. Bring Spencer over and sit with us." Monty gestured to the empty chair at their table. It wasn't a request.

She'd shared lunch with Monty before, but it was always a casual "I'm here, you're here, let's sit at the counter and eat" situation, not a formal invitation to join Hollywood royalty. She ran her hand over her hair again and walked Spencer to the table.

Monty grabbed a piece of crust off her plate and fed it to the gleefully wiggling dog, then thrust her chin at Justine. "Ted, this is Justine. She owns the little dog shop here in town, and obviously this handsome boy is Spencer."

Justine waved at Taylor, who flicked her eyes up from her phone for an instant and beamed her showstopping smile at her. Justine gave her palm a stealth-wipe on her leg, then reached out to sunglasses man. "Nice to meet you. Spence, say hi." Spencer cocked his head and raised his front paw in the air to wave at them. He looked like a kindergartener on the first day of school.

"Wow, he's incredible," the man replied in a soft voice as he shook Justine's hand. "Such an expressive face. What else can he do?" He managed to tear himself away from watching Spencer to look Justine in the eyes. Or at least she thought he was looking at her eyes, since all she could see was her distorted reflection in his aviators. "I'm Ted Sherman, by the way."

That's why he looked familiar. Ted Sherman was in the business of directing blockbuster movies and TV shows. "Nice to meet you. Spencer can basically do anything. He takes requests . . ." Justine trailed off and looked around the table.

"High five!" Taylor shouted. "Do a high five."

Justine held her hand out. He sat back on his haunches and slapped her palm, then waited for her to do the down-low position and slapped her again.

"Can I try?" Ted asked. He finally pulled his sunglasses off and stared at Justine.

"Yup, put your hand out."

Ted opted for the down-low position.

"Spence . . ." Her dog turned to look at her. "Go do." She pointed to Ted's outstretched hand. Spencer dashed to Ted and smacked his hand like they'd done it a million times, and Ted held on to Spencer's paw for a few moments.

"How about play dead?" Monty asked.

"Sudden or prolonged?"

"You mean he has *range*?" Ted asked with awe in his voice.

"Make it dramatic!" Taylor said.

Justine made a soft clicking noise with her mouth and Spencer snapped to attention. She placed her palms together like she was praying and pointed her hands at Spencer for a moment, then flipped them apart like exploding jazz hands.

Spencer staggered for a few steps like he was dazed, then slowly lowered himself to the ground on one shoulder. His entire body telegraphed pain.

"Oh my God," Ted whispered.

Spencer paused, panting hard with his eyes squinted, then flopped to the ground on his side. He closed his eyes and let his head drift, his four legs drooping.

No one moved.

"Spence, end!" Justine said cheerfully.

He jumped up and wagged his tail as they exploded into applause.

"That brought a damn tear to my eye," Monty said. "He really looked dead!"

"Why does he know how to do so many tricks? Are you a professional trainer? And why do you opt for hand signals instead of saying the commands?" Ted asked Justine. He was staring at her with an intensity that made her palms sweat.

She leaned into the barrage of questions. "I'm a hobby trainer, not a professional. It's just something fun we do together because he loves learning. And I do hand signals because it's easier for dogs to learn them." She shrugged. "You caught me; I'm lazy."

"I wouldn't say that," Ted replied. "Does he ever have trouble performing? Do loud noises or strange people scare him?"

They were all watching her carefully, and it felt like both she and Spencer were being sized up. She opted to edit her answer and leave out the dicey part of their shared history.

"Not that I've seen. I mean, I've only had him for a year, I'm not sure about everything he went through before I adopted him, but as far as I know he's pretty bombproof." She reached down and scratched the side of Spencer's neck. "Nothing really fazes him."

Except the one thing that *did* faze him.

Luis dropped her lunch on the counter and all she could think of was shoving the warm garlic pita into her mouth.

"Do you know how to read a script?" Ted asked.

"Um, yes?" It wasn't a lie; she'd once dug up an old *Living Single* script online to win a bet with Sienna.

Ted nodded. "Would you feel comfortable giving me your contact info?"

"Sure." Her heart sped up. What was happening?

"I'm going to send you the pilot script of the show we're working on, *The Eighteenth*. Focus on the parts labeled Ford. That's the main character's dog. Read it and tell me if you think it's all doable."

"What's a pilot script?" She wanted to know exactly what she was getting into even though something in her bones told her that it was going to be good.

"It's a test episode for a proposed series, to see if the show is marketable. FilmFlix wants the pilot plus two extra episodes, so as it stands we've got a three-show run. But if audience reaction is strong we'll get a full series."

"This might be a dumb question, but what, uh, how do you mean, read it?" Maybe he wanted her to do some sort of feasibility study, to check if the tricks and behaviors were something most dogs could do? A sort of editing pass before they got started?

And would she get paid for it?

"It turns out the dog we picked to play Ford isn't quite right. He's not 'of the era.'" Ted made air quotes. "He's an incredible dog, but he's just not doing it for me."

Justine's heart thudded. This sounded like more than just an editing pass. She swallowed hard. "Okay."

Ted leaned across the table to study Spencer. "It's a lot. Ford plays a huge role in the first three episodes. And Spencer is a novice so I might kick myself for even suggesting it, but read through the script and tell me if you think he could play the role. I'll want to see him perform some of the tougher stuff, and if he can do it before we head back to the city on Sunday we'll move on to a chemistry test with Anderson. That is, if you want to give it a shot."

He didn't even have to say the last name. Ted was talking about Anderson Brooks. Not just Hollywood royalty, but inter-galactic royalty for the past thirty years. The leading man who had transitioned from young stud into grizzled and wrinkly but still handsome territory.

Justine stood with her mouth hanging open.

"Speak, woman," Monty urged.

"Yes, okay! I'll do it. Yes, that sounds great!"

She gave Ted her email address, said her good-byes, and went to the counter to tackle her falafel. Monty and company had forgotten they'd asked her to sit with them, though she didn't think she would've been able to eat while they pinged her with questions about Spencer's skills.

"What's going on?" Luis asked quietly as he stacked dishes under the counter.

Justine looked down at her dog, who was licking up crumbs from the last customer.

"I think Spencer just paid my rent."

chapter three

Before heading back to Tricks & Biscuits, Justine detoured to Love Letters, her friend Ruth's card shop. She had two red velvet cupcakes from the local bakery and she wanted to dissect every bit of the Ted Sherman encounter with someone who knew her way around a rehashing session. She caught her reflection in the window on her way in. Most of her strawberry blond bob was plastered to her forehead, except for the cowlick behind her ear, which mocked her no matter how much product she used. The shoulders of her sweatshirt were drenched despite the umbrella. But it wasn't as if she'd have to see customers on such a crappy day.

"Excuse me, do you sell birthday cards here?" Justine yelled as she walked into the store once she confirmed it was empty. "It's me, I need to tell you something."

She dropped Spencer's leash and he parkoured onto the houndstooth-patterned chair next to the counter so he could get closer to Ruth's Chihuahua, Freida, who was dozing in her little pink bed by the cash register. He startled her awake with a woof, and she wagged her tail when she realized her boyfriend was visiting.

"Very funny," Ruth said as she swished through the curtain separating her workspace from the rest of the store. They both loved their customers, but sometimes they couldn't resist making fun of some of the ridiculous stuff people said to them. "Is it still raining?"

"It's getting biblical out there." They leaned in for a quick hug. "Why don't you join me in the world of athleisure when the weather is this crappy?" Justine did a slow runway turn and pointed to her snakeskin-print leggings like a game-show model. A tiny part of her wished that she were still using them for their intended purpose out on the trail, but she just wasn't ready.

"Never." Ruth shuddered. "I don't even wear that stuff to bed. I keep hoping I'll rub off on you." Ruth smoothed the front of her navy striped A-line skirt, which she'd paired with a crisp white blouse and navy kitten heels. Ruth Vernon's wardrobe was a few degrees from 1950s housewife cosplay. Everything she wore was as cheerful as a handful of confetti, just like her rainbow-colored shop.

"Listen, your life is sitting at a desk with paper, scissors, and pens. My life is on my knees with saliva, fur, and poop. I'll keep my leggings, thank you." She paused. "I have news. *Big* news."

Ruth's face clouded. "I do too. I need to show you something. I've been waiting to do it in person. Come here." She started walking to the computer behind her counter as her phone rang. She fished it out of her pocket and squinted at the screen. "Crap, that's my bride. Hold on for a sec."

Justine busied herself checking out her friend's handmade cards as Ruth talked yet another bridezilla off the ledge about her save-the-date postcards. She was the craftiest person Justine had ever met, from bespoke wedding invitations to hand-crafted parasols made out of flamboyant fabrics from India to the replica of the *cave canem* Pompeii mosaic she'd created for T&B's front step. Ruth Vernon was a one-woman art show.

"Okay, she's happy," Ruth said as she hung up. "You should see what I did for her. I think it's my best yet. It's a hipster wedding. She wanted octopi; I gave her octopi. What she doesn't know is I had octopi hidden among the flowers on *my* wedding invitations fifteen years ago, so she's hardly breaking new ground. Anyway!" She clapped her hands. "Why don't you tell me what you were going to tell me; then I'll go. Based on your expression, your news is way better than mine."

Freida interrupted with a sassy yip, so Ruth placed her on the floor near where Spencer was standing. Then the game was on with the tiny Chihuahua dashing around and Spencer in barky pursuit. The shop echoed with the sound of dog play as they raced across the harlequin-patterned cement floor.

Justine couldn't hold in her excitement for another second. "I just met the director of Taylor's new show at Monty's, and he thinks Spencer might be able to play a part on it! He's sending me a *script*. Like I have a clue what to do with a script!"

"What? No *way*!" Ruth stared at her with her jaw hanging open. She moved her black-rimmed glasses onto her forehead for extra dramatic effect.

Justine nodded. "But it's not a sure thing, I have to audition him, and if he passes, check this out: we get to meet Anderson goddamn Brooks!"

Ruth staggered a few steps, clutching her heart. Justine could always count on her to give important moments the reactions they deserved.

"That's big-time! Will you remember me when you're rich and famous?"

Justine laughed. "Spencer is the one about to get rich and famous; I'm just his bitch."

"Seriously, that's incredible news. Congrats!" Ruth said as she settled herself in front of the computer, already half-focused on what she had to say. "When is it all going down?"

"Soon. It's going to happen so quickly that I won't have time to get nervous." She paused a beat. "Okay, that's a lie. I'm definitely going to be nervous."

"Stop, you're both going to do amazing." Ruth pursed her lips. "Okay, can we shift gears for a sec? I've been sitting on this since yesterday and it's killing me."

"You've got me a little freaked out. Is everything okay?"

"I don't know; you have to tell me. So, I was on Facebook and I saw a photo that someone posted in my makers' group. The subject looked *awfully* familiar." She dragged her red nail down the touchscreen dramatically, scrolling to find the photo in question. "There it is. Look."

She swung the screen to face Justine.

"Weird. I've never seen that photo of Spencer." It was a close-up black-and-white image that looked like a professional modeling shot. "That's definitely him, though. He's got the one white ear with the polka dots. Maybe the rescue took it?"

"Nope. Read it." Ruth stepped aside.

"You're making me nervous. What's going on?"

"Just read it."

It was one of those posts that had been forwarded and shared so many times that it was hard to tell where it had originated. Justine leaned close to read the text.

"My name is Griffin McCabe and this is my dog, Leo. It's been over a year since he went missing, so the chances of finding him are low, but I'm hoping that if this photo gets shared enough we might be able to get him home to me. I miss him every single day. He was my best friend. Leo, if you're out there, know that I'll never stop looking for you. I'll love you forever, doggo."

Justine looked at Ruth in slack-jawed horror, then over at her dog.

"Oh my God," she whispered. "Spencer isn't mine."

chapter four

I found his work number," Sienna said, not looking up from her phone at her spot behind the counter. "It's right here. Griffin McCabe, platform planning and deployment manager at Vendere."

"What? How is that even possible? I just told you about him like three minutes ago."

In the flurry of the discovery, Justine hadn't even mentioned the audition. Ownership rights to Spencer seemed more pressing than a moon-shot audition. She'd given Sienna the details about Spencer's past in a breathless download before she was due to leave to care for a geriatric cat client. Reaching out to the guy who had posted the photo didn't even seem like an option, yet as always, Sienna was pushing her to step way outside her comfort zone.

Sienna shrugged. "I'm a supersleuth. I've spent some time on the dark web, picked up a few unauthorized search techniques. No biggie."

"Are you serious?"

"*No*, I'm not serious. I looked him up on LinkedIn. Which, if you'd listen to me and set up a profile, you could've done your-self." Sienna reached into her pocket, then tossed Spencer a treat. He caught it in midair. "And even though it's not the best photo with the profile, I can tell he's hot," she continued. "I mean, Spencer wouldn't have just any old dude on the end of his leash. Would ya, bud? You had a DILF for sure."

"It's not like that matters. Hiatus, remember?" Justine said primly as she dug through a shipment of new leashes she prob-ably couldn't afford.

Sienna placed her hands together and bowed to Justine. "And I honor your hiatus. But would a quickie with a DILF count?"

"Yes, it would count. I need to get the Nick-stink off of me before I get out there again. I'm not even thinking about dating, *especially* someone who might try to steal my dog. Which means I'm not calling him."

"Yes, you are," Sienna replied as she packed her things to leave. "You knew you were going to reach out the second you figured out what happened with Spencer."

"Why would you say that?"

"Because I know how you operate! I've read your tarot cards enough to see your primary energy vibration is empathy. I can tell by the way you're trying to keep busy over there that you're thinking about how you'd feel if it happened to *you*. How you'd feel if you lost Spencer." Sienna paused. "Am I right?"

"I don't know." Justine frowned and shrugged. "No. Maybe. But what if Spencer ran away from him on purpose? What if he was a terrible dog dad and he kept Spence in a crate all day?" She warmed to the idea. "What if it was a prison break?"

Sienna pursed her lips. "Or what if something spooked Spen-cer and he slipped off his leash and just got lost, accidentally? I mean, the dude is still looking for him a year later. He obviously loved him."

Justine glared at Sienna. Common sense was so overrated.

"Fine," she huffed. "But I don't want him to know who I am and where I live. He might try to steal Spencer back or something; you never know. I could send him an anonymous letter with a photo to let him know that Spencer is okay and leave it at that. Proof of life, like a kidnapper."

"A *paper* letter with an actual printed photo? And, like, a stamp? Sounds like a lot of work."

Justine sighed. "You really are young, aren't you?"

"Yeah, and you're a totally decrepit, what, thirty-year-old? Anyway, just call him." Sienna leaned against the door and pushed backward, still focused on her phone. "Texting his number now. Bye."

The bell above the door jingled as Sienna left, and Spencer peeked out from behind the counter.

"Pavlov's dogs got nothing on you, buddy."

The rain hadn't let up, which meant that shoppers were unlikely. Maybe a few quick food pickups, but she wasn't going to luck into a new-puppy parent eager to spoil their little one. There was still plenty of work to be done, most of it of the accounting variety, but given the dreary day, the last thing she wanted to think about was her store's soul-crushing bottom line.

But she didn't want to think about the Leo/Spencer situation either.

Justine glanced at her phone. The text from Sienna was just Griffin McCabe's number with paws, hearts, and prayer hands emojis next to it.

"I shouldn't, right?" she asked Spencer as she walked over to where he was getting ready for his afternoon nap. "He'll want to take you back because you're so amazing."

Spencer gave a swish of his tail and dipped his shoulders into an exaggerated downward dog, closing his eyes as he stretched on top of his navy corduroy dog bed. He straightened up and dragged his paw along the fabric.

"Make your bed, bud," Justine encouraged as she sat on the floor next to him. His elaborate pre-sleep process was one of her favorite rituals.

Spencer dug at the bed rhythmically with one paw, then switched to the other. He dragged his nose along the bed a few times, then went back to digging at it. He turned in circles a few times, then collapsed on the bed so that he was flush against her body with his head resting on her thigh, like he was an anchor that would keep her from drifting away. He sighed.

Justine massaged Spencer's shoulder and he moved even closer to her, stealing her warmth in the drafty, high-ceiling space.

For a moment she allowed herself to experience what Griffin McCabe might have felt when he discovered that his dog was missing. Did he stay out all night looking for him? Did he put up LOST DOG posters with Spencer's photo? How long did he keep hoping he'd turn up? Did he cry?

Her heart twisted as she realized that Griffin's "missing" dog was resting safe and sound beside her and he had no clue. Based on the Facebook post, he hadn't given up hope, even after a year with no leads. She closed her eyes in defeat.

Damn it, she had to do it, and it had to happen now. If she

waited, she'd find a million reasons not to call. But now, on a dead-end day when she could feel his loss in the pit of her belly, she could allow it. It wasn't fair to let the stranger continue to wonder if his dog was dead or alive.

But . . . but what if he was an a-hole and demanded that she give him back? And who *actually* owned Spencer? Was there a statute of limitations on pet parenthood?

Justine felt herself getting preemptively angry at Griffin.

"No matter what he says, he's not getting you back." She twirled Spencer's fur into little peaks on the top of his head. "But do I text him or call him? What's safer?"

She tried to envision how she'd phrase what happened in a text.

"I have your dog"?

It sounded like she'd kidnapped him.

"Your dog is alive"?

Kidnapped, again.

"I have something to tell you that might come as some surprise . . ."

She realized that she needed to hear his voice. It would be the only way she could gauge if he'd been good to Spencer, back when he was Leo. She'd keep the call short, the details sparse, so he wouldn't be able to figure out anything about her.

The more she thought about how to choreograph the call, the less confident she felt about placing it. But Justine braced herself for the weirdness to come, took a deep breath, and dialed.

As the phone rang and rang, she realized that he probably wouldn't answer an unknown number. She was about to hang up when she heard his voice.

"This is Griffin, may I help you?"

He sounded friendly and upbeat, almost like he'd been expecting her call. It knocked her off-balance for a second. She wasn't ready for him to sound *pleasant*. For an instant her brain started creating a face to match the voice, but she stopped herself before she could humanize him too much. She needed to keep her guard up. What she was doing was risky, no matter how warm and inviting he sounded.

"Hi, my name is Justine. Do you have a couple minutes to talk? Did I catch you at a bad time?" She kicked herself for not organizing her thoughts before calling.

"Not at all. I have a few minutes." She could hear the smile in his voice. "What's going on? Is that update giving you problems? My phone's been ringing about it nonstop."

"No, actually this is about—"

"Wait, don't tell me." He chuckled and she involuntarily smiled at the sound of it. "You locked yourself out. Don't worry, it happens! I'm here to help. Are you in front of your computer?"

He sounded so genuinely kind that her nerves dropped to a manageable level. "This isn't about business. I'm sorry, is it a bad time? Are you busy?" Her finger hovered near the phone, ready to hit the disconnect button.

"Oh. Yeah, I have a minute." A wariness replaced the happy tone. "How can I help?"

Justine took a deep breath.

"I don't know how else to say this, but . . . your dog, Leo, is here with me. I mean, his name is Spencer now, and I've had him for a year, and I adopted him, officially. I have the paperwork and everything. But I wanted you to know he's okay." The words came out in a rush. It was important for him to understand that his dog was fine, but also that Spencer was no longer *his* dog.

"Wait, what?" Griffin went silent for a moment. "You have Leo? How did you find me? Where are you?"

She hesitated. Once she answered, there was no going back. "I saw your Facebook post." She wanted to stop there, but she inexplicably opened her stupid mouth and continued. "We're in Rexford."

"Oh my God, you're only two hours away! I'm in Brooklyn. He's okay? Leo's healthy?" Griffin's voice went up an octave, like he didn't believe what he was hearing.

Spencer stirred and for a second Justine wondered if he could hear and recognize Griffin's voice. Regret flooded through her.

And worse, jealousy.

"He's great," Justine answered confidently. "He's amazing. And happy. So happy." And she knew it was true. Her dog was *her* dog and he was exactly where he belonged.

"I'm in shock. I've been waiting for this day..." Griffin's voice broke. He paused to collect himself and Justine found herself moved despite the simmering ugly feelings that were making her want to hang up. "To be honest, I actually never thought this day would come. Thank you so much for tracking me down. I'm sorry, what was your name again?"

It felt like a power move, especially considering she couldn't get his name out of her head.

"I'm..." She considered giving him the wrong name since he couldn't remember how she'd introduced herself. "I'm Justine."

"Justine!" It came out in a whoop, like he was toasting her.

"You made my day. You have no idea. Leo was my partner in crime since he was a tiny puppy. We spent nearly every day together for two years. I am so fucking *happy* right now!"

Justine calculated how her year with Spencer compared to Griffin's two before she answered. "I'm glad to hear it. Listen, I just wanted you to know he's okay, so—"

"When can I meet you to pick him up?"

Justine almost dropped the phone. Suddenly her butt felt numb from sitting on the cement floor. "Wait. What?"

Griffin was silent for a moment.

"Isn't that why you called me?"

"I thought I told you . . . he's, uh . . . S-S-Spencer is my dog." She stammered.

He didn't respond.

"I adopted him, paid the three-hundred-dollar fee, signed the official paperwork, and everything," Justine continued, her voice strong. "I've had him for a year. He's . . . *mine*." She felt like a grown-up version of Veruca Salt.

"Well, I have papers that say he's mine," Griffin said slowly.

They both paused, and the only sound was Spencer snoring softly beside her.

Justine went for his jugular. "But you *lost* him. He ran away from you."

"Wait, wait, wait, hold up. That's not how it happened. I need to explain the whole situation." Anger seeped into his voice.

Justine realized she'd made a huge mistake by calling Griffin. He was treating her like she was someone who answered a LOST DOG poster, not the rightful owner of the dog in the photo on the telephone pole.

"You know what? I've gotta run," she said in a rush. "I just wanted you to know he's okay."

"Wait, can we set up a time to meet and talk this out? I'm going to be home—"

"Sorry," Justine cut him off. "I'll call you back later." She hung up the phone abruptly and tossed it on the bed next to Spencer.

It was official. She'd just made a huge mistake.

chapter five

Justine gazed out at the acres of lavender plants as she drove up the driveway to Monty's house a day later. Everything was happening so quickly that she barely had time to process the stress. At least the audition would keep her from thinking about the guy with the customer-service voice who wanted to steal her dog.

Monty's lavender field was the very reason she'd ended up in Rexford, and Justine felt a pang as she remembered cutting her way down the rows of purple flowers with her trusty wood-handled sickle. It was backbreaking work during the hottest weeks of the summer, when the sun was so relentless that even taking breaks beneath the trees that bordered the fields didn't provide relief. But the camaraderie with her fellow harvesters and the beauty all around her made the hard work bearable. She loved going home at the end of the day with a feeling of accomplishment, exhausted in a way that no desk work could touch, then kicking off her lavender-scented sneakers and finding blossom pods trapped in them. Working in the fields had been a perfect transition from her old life to her new.

Prior to landing in Rexford, she'd been a rising star at the Good Market, a small regional all-natural grocery chain in Watertown. She'd been hired right out of college as an assistant category manager in the nonfoods wellness and pets departments and quickly jumped to full manager. Justine loved her job until the powers that be started pushing price over quality for their furry consumers, assuming their human shoppers wouldn't notice. When her boss told her that they were discontinuing her passion project, bringing small, regional natural pet brands into the store in favor of more chain products, she quit without a safety net. Justine heard through a friend of a friend that someone in Rexford needed seasonal harvesting help, and what was supposed to be a stopover turned into a summer in the blazing sun in Monty's fields and, eventually, Tricks & Biscuits.

Her heart pounded when she got closer to the sprawling stone farmhouse and saw the low-slung black Mercedes with New York plates. "You ready for this?" she asked Spencer.

Justine wasn't. Everything felt itchy. She was wearing slim-fitting jeans and a lilac T-shirt with a wide boatneck that kept slipping off her shoulder, forcing her to constantly yank it back up. Her hair was annoying her too, settling on the back of her neck and making her feel sweaty even though she wasn't. Her hair had finally grown out to the point where she could make a sad little spiky ponytail, but she still didn't feel ready to pull out her elastic bands quite yet. Whenever she gathered her hair at the nape of her neck, she was brought back to the reason she'd cut off her hair in the first place.

The script for *The Eighteenth* was more complex than she'd realized when she said yes to Ted Sherman. Spencer could do cute better than most dogs, but much of what they needed on the show was so subtle that they didn't even feel like tricks. They didn't want Ford the speakeasy dog to sit pretty or wave; he needed to do things that normal dogs do in everyday life, like look around, stand still, or walk from point A to point B. And Spencer wasn't known for subtlety.

When they set up the trial at Monty's farm, Ted suggested that they try "riffing" on the script rather than focusing on specific behaviors, which made practicing for it even tougher. But working with Spencer kept Justine from thinking about Griffin McCabe and the fact that her beloved dog was actually a lost dog named Leo. Every time her phone buzzed she worried that it was Griffin.

"We're back here," she heard Monty's voice call out. "With the chickens!"

Justine turned and saw that Monty and Ted were behind her at the chicken coop. Her heart fell when she saw that the chickens were milling around outside their cage.

"Shit. Free-range." She quickly pulled a thin leather leash out of her back pocket and made a silent plea to Saint Francis as she clipped it on Spencer. "*Please* don't chase them, okay? Don't blow it before we even get started."

Justine felt a stage-mom level of stress. Part of her wanted to try to enjoy the process, but she knew exactly how much was riding on Spencer's performance.

She waved and led Spencer down the hill to meet them. It didn't feel right to call it a chicken coop since the building that housed Monty's array of fancy-breed chickens looked like a tiny stone replica of her main house, complete with shuttered windows. As always, Monty was perfectly staged for the moment with her silver hair knotted in a red bandanna on top of her head, wearing worn chambray and denim, with a wildflower-filled basket at her side. Based on Taylor's Instagram feed, Justine knew that she was in California taping an appearance on a late-night show, so she had one less observer to worry about.

Ted sized up Justine and Spencer as they approached, once again unreadable in his baseball cap and aviators.

"Hello there. We're going to have some fun today," he said, sounding like a dentist comforting his root-canal patient.

Monty dropped to her knees and Spencer greeted the keeper of bacon and other meaty delights with appropriate gusto. Justine breathed a sigh of relief when an oversized black rooster strutted close to them and Spencer ignored it.

"We're ready and excited. Thanks so much for the opportunity." She gripped the leash tighter when she noticed Spencer zeroing in on a hen running toward the coop. A slow rooster stroll was one thing; a full-tilt chicken run was another. Spencer peered around Monty with the locked-on focus that usually meant he was weighing his options: run for fun, or stay for the pats. His recall was impeccable *if* he wasn't chasing after something furred or feathered. For a second Justine imagined him taking off after the chicken and not stopping when it dashed into the woods bordering the property.

Maybe that was how Griffin McCabe lost him?

"Let me tell you a little bit about the show before we start," Ted said in his quiet, self-assured manner. After reading the script, Justine knew exactly what the show was about, but she wasn't about to correct him. "The title refers to the Eighteenth

Amendment, which established prohibition. The show focuses on a New York speakeasy run by Anderson's character, Izzy Malone. Taylor plays his girlfriend, chorus girl Ginger Costello."

She stifled her gag reflex. Anderson was closer to Monty's age than Taylor's. She sneaked a look at Monty, but she didn't seem fazed by the casting choice.

"Izzy's dog, Ford, is the mascot and lookout for the speak-easy. As written, Ford is in every episode in the first season. If we get picked up it's a big role."

"Wow," Justine said quietly, half listening to the conversation and half stressing about Spencer's chicken obsession. The cluck-ing and scratching weren't helping with his focus.

"I'd like to get started now, if you're ready." Ted made it clear that there was no other answer than yes.

Justine moved away from the coop as casually as she could, trying to make it seem like she was motivating her dog instead of preventing a literal game of chicken. "Of course, let's try it."

Monty sat down on the ground and a black-and-white chicken with a bouffant and sliced-almond feathers settled into her lap.

"Luella wants to watch too," Monty said, stroking the bird.

Justine pulled Spencer a few steps closer to her and gave him a quick shoulder massage. He was so focused on Monty's cluck-ing lovefest that he barely even acknowledged her.

"I'm going to play Anderson's part," Ted said. "I want to see how Spencer interacts with someone he doesn't know. We're go-ing to do this cold, with no contact between us before we try."

It was the absolute worst way to start the audition.

"I'm going to walk toward that tree over there." Ted pointed to a towering oak far away from the chicken coop and Justine whooped internally. "I'll start walking alone; then I want you to send Spencer to walk with me when I signal with my left hand, and when I stop walking, I want him to sit next to me."

Justine knew exactly which scene they were trialing. It was the last shot of the first episode, where Anderson/Izzy is walking in the alley behind the speakeasy after having a fight with Taylor/Ginger. It was tough enough in regular circumstances, but add in the chickens and she worried that Spencer was about to nose-dive. Justine grabbed a handful of the fabric draped on her arm and yanked it up to her shoulder.

"Ready?" Ted asked.

Justine nodded and gave Spencer a hopeful pat. He finally looked up at her, and they exchanged the knowing glance that meant they both understood that they were getting ready to do something major together.

Ted walked away from them with his hands clasped behind his back. After a few feet he raised his left hand briefly.

"Spence, side!" She pointed to Ted and gave Spencer an encouraging nod, her heart ricocheting in her chest as she envisioned all the ways things could go wrong the second she unclipped his leash.

Spencer paused, looked at Justine for a millisecond, then locked his focus on Ted. He took off running and caught up to Ted, falling in step beside him. They walked along together, Spencer peering up at Ted every few steps, his tail low and wagging slowly.

"Oh my God, he's acting," Monty said with awe in her voice. "He looks like he's worried about Ted!"

It was true. Spencer was connected to Ted with an invisible tether, like the two of them were weathering an emotional storm together. Justine got so caught up in her dog's skills that she barely noticed when Ted came to a stop.

"Spence, *sit*!"

He tripped and looked over his shoulder at Justine. She nodded exuberantly and did her version of a hand signal for *sit*, holding her hand above her head with her fingers splayed then clenching them into a fist.

He moved into position and gazed adoringly up at Ted.

"He nailed it," Monty whispered. "They have to cast him."

It was true. Spencer had been almost flawless, despite not having a practice run and being surrounded by feathery distractions. Justine wanted to puff up her chest and cluck too.

Ted walked back to them with Spencer dashing playfully around his feet, a smile on his normally unreadable face.

"I like this guy," he said. "That's not exactly how it would go on set, but it still gave me a feel for his abilities. I'd also like to do some smaller reaction shots. Some facial expressions, maybe?"

"Of course, Spence is up for anything."

Ted slipped his phone out of his breast pocket and filmed Spencer as he asked for a variety of poses and behaviors. Justine felt the tension in her shoulders ease as Spencer aced every request from the head tilt to the sad expression to the startle take.

"Clearly this dog is a gifted actor. Are we finished here, Ted?" Monty asked, bossy as ever.

Justine fiddled with the leash and clasp and watched as Spencer eyed a shiny black rooster that was pecking near where they were working.

"We are," Ted replied. "Justine, can you bring Spencer into the city next week? I want you both to meet Anderson. A quick chemistry test and we should have our answer."

She swallowed hard and did a few quick calculations about how early they'd have to arrive in the city before the meeting to cope with Spencer's car sickness. She couldn't have Spencer puking on the biggest action star in the world.

"We can be there; just name the date."

chapter six

W ell?" Sienna stopped stocking the treat shelf the second Justine and Spencer walked into the store after the audition. "I've been dying over here."

"Guess who's got a beard, four paws, and a hot date with Anderson Brooks in New York?" Justine paused, then pointed at Spencer. "This guy!"

"Yay!" Sienna clapped and jumped up and down. "I want all the gossip. I *knew* you could do it!"

"It's not a sure thing yet; he still has to charm Anderson. And I didn't do a thing—Spencer did all the work," she answered as she let him off leash. Spencer dashed to Sienna for congratulatory pats.

She leaned into Spencer's kisses. "Ah, you're a self-taught genius, Spence. Is that how it works, mister? Lots of book learning?"

Justine laughed. "Fine, it was a team effort. Anyway, I'm hoping you can cover the store next Friday while I go into the city. Is that possible?"

"Of course, happy to." Sienna focused on petting Spencer,

who had collapsed onto his back in an effort to direct all of her attention to his belly. "And I bet you'll be happy to get out of here for the day."

Justine stopped in her tracks. "What do you mean by that?"

"Nothing, never mind." She shrugged. "Anyway! Details, please. Start from the beginning: were you nervous?"

"Yeah, I was pretty shaky at first. And Monty's chickens were—" Justine's phone interrupted her. When she looked down at the screen she froze.

She'd added his number under the name "Jackass McAhole" and used the poop emoji as his photo after she'd hung up on Griffin McCabe a few days prior. It made her giggle like a third grader at the time, but seeing it flash up on her screen made her realize that there was nothing funny about it.

"No!" Justine exclaimed with her eyes wide.

"Who is it?"

"Shit-shit-shit!" She jogged in place. "It's that guy who lost Spencer!"

"Answer it. See what he wants."

Justine stared at her phone and didn't say anything.

"Come on, answer it and get it over with," Sienna said in a way that made it sound like it was no big deal.

She took a breath and answered. "This is Justine."

"Hi, Justine, this is Griffin McCabe."

"Yes?"

"I'm Leo's person," he continued.

Justine couldn't think of a thing to say back to him.

"Are you there? Hello?"

"Yeah, I'm here, hi." Justine galloped to the stockroom and slammed the door behind her.

"Hi. You said you were going to call me back."

The kind voice she remembered was gone, replaced by a tone that sounded more like he'd been waiting on hold with the cable company for too long.

"Did I?" she fumbled. "Sorry, I've been super busy. And to be honest I didn't think there was anything more to say." She paced in the narrow space between the baker's racks filled with dog food bags.

"I think there's *plenty* more." He exhaled quietly. "But before we get into that, I was hoping we could reset and start over. I got a little overexcited the last time we talked. I hope you understand why."

His voice got softer, which made Justine's heart rate slow a few BPM. Maybe it wasn't going to be a war?

"I do. You were happy that he's okay. I get it." She wished Spencer had followed her into the stockroom so she could use him as an emotional support dog during the call.

"Thank you. One of the reasons I'm calling is because I feel like you need to know how Leo got lost."

The way he phrased it took any responsibility out of what had happened, and it irked her like those "I'm sorry if you were hurt" faux apologies.

"Okay." She stretched the word out for several seconds.

"And I'd like to see Leo, too," he continued. "I was hoping that we could set up a time for me to drive to Rexford to meet you guys somewhere. I don't have to come to your place or anything, since you don't know me. Stranger danger and all that. I'm out of town right now, but I'll be back in the city next week, so maybe we can do it then?"

She stopped pacing. "Really."

"Yes, really. I just need to see him. Put my hands on him. Make sure he's okay."

Justine didn't respond. How dare he imply that her dog might *not* be okay? She glared at the wall and let the silence on the line stretch on. The sound of the Grateful Dead's "Sugar Magnolia" drifted under the door.

Griffin heaved a sigh. "I was worried it would come to this. Okay, Justine, I'll beg you if that's what you want. Can I *please* see my dog?" It almost sounded like his voice broke for an instant. "I just wanna see my dog."

"My dog," she replied with an unmistakable edge in her voice.

"Listen, I don't want to fight with you. I'm sure you're a wonderful person. But the fact is that for the past year I've pictured Leo dead on the side of the road, or stuck in a test lab with tubes in his stomach, or losing his mind in a kennel in some backwoods shelter. Leo was my baby, Justine, and not knowing what happened to him almost broke me. I just need to see him so I can get those nightmares out of my head." His voice went soft. "Does that make sense to you?"

She could envision every scenario as he listed them, and the visuals hit too close to home. There was no way she could deny him at least a quick visit. She cleared her throat to collect herself before she responded.

"Of course, yes. I get it. You can see him. But you don't have to drive to Rexford. I have to be in the city for a . . . thing with Spencer on Friday. We can meet you somewhere after if you want." She wasn't ready to tell him that the dog he lost was a star in the making.

"No, you shouldn't have to go out of your way," he protested. "I don't want to put you guys out."

"I don't mind at all." She *did* mind the idea of him showing up in Rexford and finding out where her store was and where she lived. She wasn't about to open herself up to a potential dog-stalker or, worse yet, dog-napper.

"It would be easier on me if I didn't have to drive, to be honest. I'm pretty road weary."

Justine filed the biographical tidbit away and squeezed a Chuckit ball as a stress reliever.

"I feel like I shouldn't ask you for any more favors, but would you please text me a photo of him?" Griffin asked.

"Yeah, sure." Justine mentally scrolled through the thousands of pictures of Spencer to try to settle on one that showed him living his best life. "I'll text you my schedule, too, and we can figure out when and where to meet. I won't have much time, though," she added quickly.

"That's fine, I'll take what I can get."

"Okay. I'll text you," she repeated.

"Justine," Griffin said, his kind voice back. "Thank you. I mean it."

"You're welcome." She stopped fidgeting and forced herself to say something nice. "I bet he's going to be really happy to see you."

They hung up and Justine took a few minutes to scroll through her photos. Her finger hovered over an image of her with Spencer on the couch, both wearing huge grins, taken by her ex-boyfriend, Nick. Then she remembered the time frame for the photo and kept scrolling. She finally settled on an arty cropped photo of Spencer sitting in profile in the grass with his head cradled in her palm, her fingers gently curling up from under his chin. She was just out of frame, and the way Spencer was gazing up at her made it look like he was completely and utterly in love with her. The photo showed off her pretty hand but gave no indication of what she looked like.

Staying incognito was her first power move. She didn't want Griffin using her photo to do recon on her and figure out how to stalk his former dog in Rexford. The less he knew, the better. She had a vague idea of what he looked like thanks to his slightly blurry black-and-white LinkedIn photo, but beyond that single image, Griffin seemed nonexistent on social media. As tempting as it was to text him one of the professional photos the local paper had taken of her and Spencer to help promote Small Business Saturday, in which the two of them both happened to look adorable, he hadn't asked for a photo of *her*. Griffin wanted to see Spencer.

"Arty shot it is," she said, texting just the image.

chapter seven

Anderson Brooks leaned against the table in the conference room and crossed his arms, resting his fists behind his massive biceps so that they looked even bigger. Justine was shocked to realize that even the highest-paid action star in the world seemed to be insecure about the size of his muscles. She sneaked looks at him while he played with Spencer, trying to put her finger on his strange vibe. He'd started growing out his signature black buzz cut for his role on *The Eighteenth*, which made him look like an Anderson Brooks cosplayer who hadn't quite nailed the costume.

"I'm not saying I don't love your dog, Justine," Anderson said with gravitas.

It still blew her mind that he was saying her name. She'd been beyond nervous at first, shaky and a little nauseous to be in the same room as the guy who always ended up in her "kill" category in games of celebrity eff, marry, kill.

Spencer's antics kept the focus on him, so until Anderson started talking to her, all Justine had to do was watch and smile as her dog charmed both Anderson and Ted Sherman. They had

driven into the city a few hours early so that Spencer could recover from his predictable bout of car sickness, which was actually more like extreme car anxiety with drooling, vomit, and
lingering depression. Justine worried that he still smelled like
puke.

She still couldn't believe that she was four feet away from the
actual, real-life Anderson Brooks, who was simultaneously bigger and smaller than she'd thought he'd be. Onscreen he looked
to be about nine feet tall, but in real life he seemed average. The
biggest part about him was his aura; he filled the entire room
with a vibe Justine couldn't quite describe. She tried to pinpoint
what it was so that she could explain it to Ruth and Sienna, but
the best she could come up with was *charisma*, which made
him sound like a cheerleader.

"I mean, I think Spencer is an incredible actor," he continued.

Justine nodded and looked down at Spencer, who was whipping his ball on a rope so hard that it hit him on the sides of his
face repeatedly. Ted stepped out of the way to avoid getting
smacked by it.

"But this role calls for a bond between us that's closer than
lovers. And I'm not sure Spencer loves *me*."

Justine took a second to try to process what Anderson meant
and realized that what was about to go down between them
could mean the difference between getting the part and blowing it.

"Is that so? What makes you say that?" It was the one lesson
she remembered from debate class. Answer an unanswerable
question with another question to buy time. Justine knew Spencer had nailed the chemistry test with Anderson, playing happily with him, posing for photos together, and showing off with

some of his cute tricks. She was afraid to envision what the "lovers" part of the chemistry test might look like.

"Let me tell you a story," Anderson replied, settling against the table. "My granddaddy raised hounds down in South Carolina his whole life, and he taught me everything I know about dogs." His cadence had changed, and he was looking at Justine with his patented Anderson Brooks Smolder™. Justine realized that he was putting on a show for her, like he was doing a late-night TV interview in front of a live studio audience. "One thing he told me, and I'll never forget this, he took his little hand-rolled cigarette out of his mouth and said . . . 'Andy boy, dogs tell their truths with their tongues. If a dog ain't licked ya, that dog don't like ya.'"

Anderson mimed putting the cigarette back in his mouth, still in character.

It took a few seconds before Justine realized what he meant.

"Oh, so you think Spencer doesn't like you because he hasn't *kissed* you yet. Okay, I understand." Her mind raced while she tried to figure out how to fix what had to be the weirdest request in dogdom. Spencer wasn't a licker, but based on some bizarre family folklore Anderson Brooks clearly needed a lick or else he wasn't going to allow Spencer to be cast in the show.

She glanced over at Ted. He lifted the bill of his baseball cap and rubbed a hand over his bald head, his brows knitted. Justine assumed that no one was allowed to question Anderson, not even his boss.

"Okay, let's get some dog kisses going, then!" Justine said gamely. "Mr. Brooks, you're a big guy, so could you get down on the ground? Do you mind?" She asked as delicately as she could, making sure to throw in some flattery.

"Not at all!"

He sat down on the ground cross-legged and looked like the world's least flexible yogi, his jeans and T-shirt straining from the position. Spencer immediately dashed to him. There was no question that Spencer liked Anderson, just not in a way that was enough to win the role as Ford.

So far.

Justine ran to her bag of tricks and turned her back so they couldn't see what she was doing. She squeezed a tiny dollop of canned cheese onto her fingertip and prayed that it was small enough that it wouldn't register, then walked over to where Anderson and Spencer were sitting with her hands gently cupped behind her back.

"Okay, Spencer! Are you ready to give some kisses? Are you ready?" She raised her voice and leaned down to hype up her dog until he was play-bowing and dancing in front of Anderson.

"Mr. Brooks, do you mind if I touch you really quickly? It just helps Spencer know what's allowed and what isn't." She was making it up as she went along and hoped she sounded convincing. "Just right here, by your ear." She pointed to her own ear.

"Of course! I've got no weird rules about that sort of stuff; come get up close and personal. Or should I say, pup close?" He chuckled.

Justine approached him tentatively. Anderson Brooks looked like himself from a distance, but when she got close to him she realized that he looked a little manufactured. His hair had layers more precise than her own. His face looked poreless and slightly plastic, with just a few lines radiating from the corners of his eyes. When she saw the color demarcation at the edge of his chin she realized that he was wearing makeup, and a tiny part of her felt bad for him.

"Okay, I'm just going to ... touch ... your ear ..." She hid her trembling cheese-finger until her hand was out of his line of sight and then pressed her pinkie and ring fingers to the side of his cheek to distract him from the fact that she was smearing cheese on his earlobe with her pointer finger. "See Spencer? Right here. Give kisses!"

It wasn't a cue that she'd actually taught him, but he was hungry enough to go for any morsel of food presented to him. Spencer didn't pause once he realized that Anderson was wearing a cheddar earring and went in for a PG-13 kiss, tilting his head back and forth and essentially consuming Anderson's entire ear.

"Ted, are you getting this?" Anderson giggled and put his beefy arm around Spencer as the dog continued to deep throat his ear. "Ted, take pictures! Ted! I knew I hadn't lost my magic touch. This dog loves me!"

Ted pulled his phone from his back pocket and snapped while Anderson posed with Spencer. The kisses continued down his cheek, and Justine realized that Spencer was licking Anderson's makeup off.

"Yay, Spence, such a good boy." Justine wanted to call him away, but Anderson seemed to love making out with her dog.

"Attaboy," Anderson said, finally moving out of Spencer's striking range and holding him back with chest scratches. "I guess you do like me. Isn't that right, buddy boy? Whaddaya say?"

Anderson's voice had changed almost imperceptibly once again, and Justine recognized that he was using his character Izzy's pet name for his dog.

"How are we feeling, Anderson?" Ted asked.

Anderson didn't say anything, but instead leaned away and studied Spencer. The dog studied him right back, probably trying to decide if he wanted to go in for seconds on his ear.

"I think this cake eater's gonna keep the bull away from our wet goods." Anderson's voice went clipped and slightly nasal again.

Justine couldn't understand exactly what he was saying, but based on Anderson's expression she knew that she and Spencer were about to have the adventure of a lifetime.

"And so it is," Ted said, smiling at Justine. "Congratulations, we have our Ford. We need to iron out some important contractual details with you, and you'll have to hit the ground running since we're well into preproduction, but as far as we're concerned, the role is his."

"Seriously? No way!" Justine squealed, which caused Spencer to run over and play bow in front of her. "Spence, you did it!"

"I'd say it was a team effort," Ted replied, smiling a genuine, non-aviatored smile at her.

"And it all happened because I've got the magic touch with dogs," Anderson added. "When he licked me? That was like he was branding me, like I'm his property. That's what my granddaddy always said; a dog kiss is a contract. We're bros now, Spencer." He held his hand up the way Justine had showed him, and Spencer gave him a solid high five. "Welcome to the swole patrol, brother!"

chapter eight

The featherweight pale blue cashmere V-neck Justine had opted to wear to the meeting with Ted and Anderson was anything but featherweight in the hot fall sun. After the stress of the chemistry test she felt like she was trapped in a terrarium as she speed-walked Spencer to the park where they'd be meeting up with Griffin. Her leopard-print slides weren't helping either; she was a toe clench away from kicking one off at an unsuspecting pedestrian.

But she wanted to smile at every person she passed. Spencer had done it! It barely felt real. She hadn't taken a single photo during the chemistry test so she wouldn't seem like a fangirl, and as she raced to the park with Spencer she tried to commit the entire bizarre situation to memory so she could describe it to Ruth and Sienna. She could swear that some of Anderson's cologne had rubbed off on her when he swooped her into a farewell hug, and she kept raising her forearm to her nose to see if she was imagining it.

Justine glanced down at Spencer as they navigated the crowded sidewalks. Despite being a country dog, he wasn't bothered by the bustle of the city. He walked close enough to Justine that his shoulder occasionally grazed her calf, just like he did in Rexford. But Spencer barely glanced at a homeless guy staggering toward them and didn't react when a French bulldog in a puffy camo vest barked a hello. Then she remembered that Spencer had clocked two years of city-street walking before he'd found his way to Justine. It killed her to admit that he had more history in Brooklyn than in Rexford.

Even though Rexford was just a two-hour drive from New York, Justine didn't go in as often as she'd have liked. She used to visit her friends from college who had settled in the city, but nearly all of them had downshifted to the suburbs when their lives started to include diapers.

Justine couldn't imagine ever getting tired of city life. She loved everything about New York. When she visited she felt . . . *possibility*. Every food she could ever want within a five-block radius, eyebrow threading at ten o'clock on a Friday night, pole classes next door to meditation retreats, and people who were always willing to lend a helping hand despite the way movies depicted them. The lights, the pace, the vibe . . . Justine couldn't wait to pretend to be native a few days a week while they shot *The Eighteenth*.

They walked in step and Justine let her mind wander, going over the details of the meeting with Ted and Anderson and laughing to herself about putting cheese on the world's biggest action hero's ear. When they got to a corner she peered at the street sign to make sure they were still headed in the right direction. Suddenly the sidewalk was less crowded with people and more with overflowing bags of garbage and stacks of flattened cardboard boxes. They dodged puddles of murky liquid in the shadows of run-down buildings. Justine picked up her pace and Spencer went from a trot to a canter beside her.

The prickle on the back of her neck and cold feeling of dread shot through her body before the sound even reached her ears. Footsteps, running at a distance but getting closer fast. Justine's heart sprang into action, pumping hard enough to convince her that it was happening again, and she needed to be ready-ready-ready for what was about to go down. She clenched her toes in her ridiculous shoes but was ready to kick them off and run through the disgusting puddles if necessary.

Spencer pressed closer to her as if he could feel her fear swirling around her. Justine held on to his leash tightly, so that her fingernails dug into her sweaty palm. No matter what happened, Spencer would be there beside her, strong, devoted, and ready to unsheathe his teeth on anything that needed to be kept away.

The pounding footsteps were gaining on them, and it sounded like a herd. Justine kept walking in a way that she hoped conveyed a "don't fuck with me" vibe, even though her guts had turned to Jell-O. She didn't want to look over her shoulder to see what exactly was about to come up behind them. Spencer did it for her, and she watched his body language closely as they jog-walked to gauge his reaction to the terror that was now only a few feet away.

His softly wagging tail made her heart slow half a measure, and she sidestepped at the exact moment a trio of high-tops, sweatshirts, and flailing arms sped past her.

"Kids," she said in a shaky voice to Spencer. "They're just kids."

She held her hand to her heart and bowed her head, willing

her heart rate to slow to a normal pace. Spencer bumped his nose against her other hand, and she knelt to acknowledge him.

"We're okay, right?"

He shifted his weight and bumped his shoulder into her in agreement. Spencer's tail spun in its typical circular wag, and his wide smiley pant got her to half grin back at him.

Justine ran her hand down his wiry fur. "I'm being stupid, aren't I?"

It took her fight-or-flight reptile brain a few blocks to finally agree.

When they were surrounded by people again and close to the park where she was supposed to meet Griffin, Justine pulled Spencer into an alcove and reached into her bag for a mirror, expecting to see a pale face and sheen of sweat. Instead, the face that greeted her in her Scottie dog compact was the exact same one she'd seen in the bathroom mirror that morning. Pink cheeks, clear blue-green eyes, and the product-resistant cowlick behind her ear. She clicked the compact shut, then knelt to have another chat with Spencer.

"You're looking good, my friend. The new stripy collar is bad-ass; you're still soft from your bath." She ran her hand down the side of his body. "Hey, Spence? I need to tell you something. I'm sorry I'm springing it on you now. I didn't want to give you too much notice, since you don't have a concept of time and if I had said we're doing this major thing 'tomorrow' you might have thought I meant 'now.'"

Spencer shifted from one foot to another and tilted his head at Justine as if he were digesting what she was saying.

"We're going to see your old . . . dude. The guy you used to live with before we met. Do you remember him? Griffin?"

She probably imagined it, but it seemed like Spencer alerted at the mention of Griffin's name.

"I know it's going to be weird, seeing him again. Maybe he'll explain why he let you go. Don't be mad at him, okay? What happened wasn't your fault. But no matter what he says, I want you to know that you're still my dog. You're still coming home with *me*."

Spencer wagged his tail and pressed closer to Justine as if he understood.

"You ready?"

He wagged again, and they set off for the park.

chapter nine

Griffin said he'd be waiting near the Kensington Dog Run in Prospect Park with a large, bright green snake toy—Spencer's favorite back when he was Leo—and that he'd be hard to miss. Justine wanted to spy on him for a few minutes before she brought Spencer over to him, so she kept her distance from the entrance, lurking in the shadows of the public restrooms, looking for anyone with a toy that resembled a snake. She knew firsthand how much variety there was in dog toys. How large was "large"? Did he mean a giant caterpillar, not snake? Would she be able to recognize the manufacturer? And was it a snake-*like* toy, or an actual representation of a snake, with eyes and flicky tongue?

The park was busy, beautiful, and surprisingly large. The trees were just beginning to show tinges of red and yellow, which felt at odds with the sweltering day. The wide, curved pedestrian walkway that cut through the green spaces was crowded with all walks of life, human and canine, so Justine bided her time by watching the mini dramas playing out around her. She realized that in a few minutes she'd be adding her own to the mix and felt her nerves ratchet up.

"I like your doggy."

Justine turned to see a little blond boy about five years old with his mom standing a few feet away from her. Spencer immediately started wagging his whole hind end.

"Your dog is so cute! Do you mind if my son . . ." The mom trailed off and pointed to Spencer.

"He loves kids." Justine squatted down so that she was even with the boy. "His name is Spencer and he likes to do tricks. Spence, wave!"

He tilted his head and pawed at the air. The little boy squealed with laughter, making Spencer wag harder.

"He's going to sniff you to get to know you first, so just stand still for a second," Justine gently instructed. The little boy didn't move as Spencer checked out his sneakers, then wagged his tail again. Spencer moved closer, then bowed his head and waited while the boy clumsily patted him.

Justine couldn't resist sharing her big news. "He just got cast on a new series," she said to the mom. "With Anderson Brooks. We met him."

"Oh my gosh!" The woman leaned down to her son. "Axel, did you hear that? This doggy is *famous*!"

"Not yet." Justine laughed.

"We're here with a herd of kids. Field trip." The mom pointed over her shoulder. "Better be careful or they'll swarm you two, especially once word gets out that he's a celebrity!"

"Thanks for the heads-up." Justine laughed again. She was so excited about Spencer getting the part that she kept forgetting the other reason why they were in the city.

Mr. Customer Service.

Justine scanned the people and dogs near the park as the pair walked away. Lots of cute kids and pups, but no snakes. She pulled her phone out of her pocket to text Griffin and felt Spencer lurch to the end of his leash at the exact same moment, nearly jostling her phone from her hand. He was making a noise that was half barking, half panting.

Spencer yanked at the leash so hard that he pulled Justine along for a few steps. It was the first time he'd pulled in ages, and the sensation made it feel like there was a stranger at the end of the leash. She scanned the crowd like a secret service agent but couldn't find anyone with a snake toy. Why was Spencer freaking out?

He started galloping in place.

"Spence, what's up? Why are you acting like this?"

Spencer flicked a glance over his shoulder and continued to focus on something she couldn't see.

Justine triple-wrapped the leash around her hand as she felt sweat dripping down the middle of her back. Still no snake. Then she saw it: a group of twenty children running and shrieking in their direction. Spencer seemed fixated on them.

A distractingly tall guy made his way through the river of kids and for a second Justine worried that he was Griffin. She squinted at him and clocked his broad shoulders and confident walk. She couldn't make out the details of his face, but even at a distance Justine could tell the guy was worthy of a second look.

Dealing with someone that hot would throw her off her game, but when she saw that he was snake-free she realized that he was probably just a DILF trying to sort his kid from the masses. Spencer leveled up to a fever pitch, standing on his back legs and air swimming with his front. She tried to get him to walk away with her, to put some distance between him and the children, but he acted like she was an anchor on the end of the leash that he was desperately trying to cut loose.

The handsome young dad was getting closer and smiling at her. Probably the little blond boy's father. But didn't he look a *little* like the guy in the LinkedIn photo? Spencer barked an overstimulated hello as the guy broke into a jog to close the gap between them.

There was no snake.

It couldn't be Griffin.

When the dad was about twenty feet from them, Spencer leaned into a final violent tug and wrenched the leash from Justine's hand, then dashed directly to the guy.

"Leo!"

Spencer launched himself into his arms, knocking him off-balance. They landed in a pile on the ground, laughing, wiggling, and hugging.

Justine's heart fell out of rhythm for a moment as she watched Spencer make out with the second guy that day.

This was Griffin McCabe.

Griffin McCabe was hot.

And Spencer was acting like no one in the world mattered but him.

Griffin finally managed to untangle himself from Spencer after a few minutes of violent kissing. He sat up and hugged the dog while Spencer flopped and jumped in his arms, bucking him around like a rodeo rider.

"Hi, I'm Griffin," he said, holding his hand out to Justine while Spencer frantically covered his face in sloppy kisses, no cheese inducement needed. "And I forgot to bring the snake."

Justine stood frozen in place. She'd just been in the presence of the world's biggest action hero, but she was more starstruck looking at Griffin McCabe sitting on the ground.

His smile.

It was the warmest, most genuine smile that had ever been beamed in her direction. He had perfect teeth, bookended by dimpled cheeks. Brown eyes that were crinkled into joyful half-moons. Wavy light brown hair that was short on the sides, long-ish on top, and looked like he'd just raked his fingers through it to tidy it up, which actually made it perfectly disheveled. Seeing him with Spencer left no doubt that they had once been soul mates. Their happy reunion sent white-hot fear through her.

"I'm Justine," she finally managed to squeak out as she walked over to where he was still sitting on the ground. "Nice to meet you. Obviously, you and Spencer know each other; I won't apologize for his behavior."

"Dude, dude, *dude*," Griffin said as Spencer climbed up on his back like a canine backpack. "Can I please shake her hand?" Spencer leapt in front of him, smashing his outstretched arm to the ground. "Okay, guess not."

Justine hated him on sight.

He was too handsome, too loving with Spencer, and too eager to make a good impression on her. It made her feel small when she finally put a label on her feeling. It wasn't anxiety or nerves or mistrust that was making her insides simmer. It was jealousy. Watching the way Spencer threw himself at Griffin made her realize she was in a distant second place in the best-pet-parent competition.

A crowd of children had gathered around them, watching the handsome laughing guy on the ground getting attacked by an overjoyed dog. They chattered closer, the ring closing in around Griffin and Spencer, and dozens of little hands reached toward the dog. Spencer's panting grew more frantic, and he backed up onto Griffin's lap as he was cornered by the kids.

Justine knew that if she didn't intervene, things were going to spiral. The pressure of the drive and audition plus the happy-stress of seeing Griffin combined with the dozen-headed kid monster closing in on him were way too many triggers. As much as Spencer loved children, the overload of the day meant that he was about to break.

"Um, I think we need to move along." She gestured toward the kids so that Griffin would realize that things were getting intense. "Hey, kids? I think I heard your parents call you!" She cocked her head and pretended to listen. "Yup, just heard it again. Did you?" It was enough to make them pause.

"My parents aren't here!" a little girl in pigtails snapped at her. "Just my chaperone."

"Okay, then your *chaperone* called you, so you better get moving!" The stress of the situation made her sound bitchier than she'd intended. Justine stepped in front of Griffin and body blocked the kindergarten crew from getting any closer.

"You're right, he is pretty scared," Griffin said as he wrapped his arms around Spencer. "Let's bounce."

Justine tried not to roll her eyes at his word choice.

"Shall we?" Griffin stood up and met Justine's eyes, then hitched his head toward the dog park. He was holding Spencer's leash in a familiar easy way that made Justine want to rip it out of his hands and yell, *Mine, mine, mine!*

Instead she replied, "Okay."

They walked to the edge of the gravel dog park just as an oversized Lab started snarl-barking at a golden. The two dogs stood facing each other, having an angry conversation as other dogs surrounded them and egged them on.

"Oh my God, it's mob mentality everywhere today," Griffin said, shaking his head. "I don't feel good about going in there, do you?"

Justine breathed a sigh of relief. She wasn't a fan of unknown dog parks, particularly on days when Spencer had been pushed to his limit. "I'd rather not. Should we just . . . walk around?"

"But then I can't get the full Leo effect," Griffin said. "*Spencer*, I mean Spencer." He squatted next to Spencer and scratched his chest while the dog panted and smiled at Griffin like he was on his knees proposing. Justine felt her cheeks get hot with frustration. She hated herself for being so jealous. It was only natural that Spencer was excited to see his former person, but he was acting like she wasn't even there. Not even a single glance in her direction.

"This might sound creepy, but do you want to come to my place for a little bit?" Griffin asked. "I'm a five-minute walk from here. That way Spencer can have some water and calm down before you put him back in the car. I remember how much he hated going for rides."

Justine didn't say anything. She scanned Griffin quickly, from his perfectly broken-in lace-up boots, to the jeans that fit well but didn't veer into emo-skinny territory, to his lightweight oatmeal-colored sweater with pushed-up sleeves. He didn't look like a serial killer, plus she had Spencer to protect her if Griffin did anything threatening. She knew exactly what her dog was capable of.

She didn't owe Griffin anything more than the five-minute meeting. That's how she'd justified seeing him; it was only to give him a quick opportunity to put his hands on his former dog and see that Spencer was better off with her. Watching them swoon all over each other made her want to say bye, grab Spencer's leash, and disappear for good. Block Griffin's number and never think about him again.

But to deny them a few more minutes together for no legitimate reason other than her jealousy was evil-queen territory. Plus, she wasn't in a rush to get back since Sienna was holding down T&B for the day. And it was only fair to give them a few more minutes together since it was definitely going to be the absolute last time they'd ever have a chance to hang.

"I promise I won't murder you," Griffin added. "At least not right away."

He unleashed his dimples, and Justine felt herself nodding like he'd just cast a spell on her.

"My boyfriend is going to be calling soon, so don't kill me until after that." Better to make him think that she had a jealous boyfriend looking out for her instead of just Sienna and Ruth.

Griffin laughed. "Got it. Oh, here," he said, handing the leash to Justine. "Sorry about that, I got a little overexcited to see him."

She took it and fell in step beside him with Spencer in the middle, like it was something they did every day.

A tiny Asian woman in red shoes pushing a wheeled shopping cart headed toward them as if she owned the sidewalk. Her gaze swept first to Spencer, then to Griffin and Justine.

"Jiātíng," she said, nodding at them with the authority of a block captain.

chapter ten

Spencer dragged them the final block.

"I guess he knows where he's going," Justine said, trying to stay positive. She was holding the leash, but Spencer only had eyes for Griffin. It was mutual. He kept touching Spencer's head and looking down at the dog with moony eyes.

"Yup, this was his home for two years. Did I tell you I rescued him when he was barely seven weeks old?"

"That's pretty young. Why would a rescue let him go that early?" Justine didn't care that she sounded judgy. She tightened her grip on the leash.

"Leo and his litter were found and taken into a shelter. They had them in isolation, but his mom caught a really bad cold and she stopped taking care of them. They had to get the puppies out fast. Someone forwarded me the post with his picture, and I drove out to Hamilton County to get him the next day." Griffin looked down at Spencer. "I got you out of that place as fast as I could, and the rest is history. Who rescued who, right?"

"I think it's 'whom.'"

"Excuse me?" Griffin asked.

"I think correct English is 'who rescued whom.'"

"Okay, whatever," he said with a smile.

Griffin headed up a staircase next door to a pink-striped awning with the name SWEET TOOTH on it.

"You live above a bakery?" Justine asked as she peeked in the shop's window. She spotted rows of pastel-iced cupcakes and drooled. She hadn't eaten anything since she left Rexford hours before.

"Yeah, it's the best, except that's why I'll never get rid of this." He patted his flat stomach as if it were a middle-aged beer belly.

Spencer dragged Justine up the steps and danced in place as Griffin unlocked the front door. Once again the dog nearly ripped the leash from her hand as soon as the door was open.

"You can drop the leash inside." He glanced at Justine out of the corner of his eye. "I mean, that's what I always used to do."

Justine frowned and begrudgingly let go of it.

"He hasn't changed a bit, I see," Griffin said with a chuckle as Spencer raced by him.

"Actually, this is really weird behavior," Justine replied as she tried to keep from staring at Griffin's ass as he took the steps two at a time. "I'm seeing a different side of him since he's with you."

"Sorry." Griffin turned around and frowned at her and nearly caught her ogling his butt. "I'm causing him to regress. When we were together, we were brothers, you know? Walk fast, play hard. He was the best boy, but we never did any real training."

Justine thought about how much Spencer enjoyed training, and how good he was at it. Griffin couldn't give him *that*. She continued to tally up the differences between them, just to make sure that she was still coming out on top as they rounded the corner and headed up another staircase.

"Funny, that's kind of our thing," she replied, trying not to sound like she was bragging. She wasn't sure when she was going to tell him exactly what Spencer's skill sets had just done for them. "He knows how to do a ton of stuff."

The diss rolled off him without registering. "Cool. I always knew he was smart. I hope you'll show off once we finish climbing Everest." He pointed up to yet another narrow staircase.

Justine was panting by the time they reached Griffin's door. Her sporadic workouts were taking a toll. She needed to get back on the trail.

Spencer gave the door an impatient "let me in" scratch and whined.

"Aw, bud," Griffin said, reaching down to massage Spencer's head. "We're home, just like the old days!"

Justine frowned again.

"It's on the small side, but it works," Griffin said as he opened the door and stood back to let her go in first. Spencer zoomed past her and dashed around the place with his nose magnetized to the floor. "Not super homey since I'm hardly ever here. But the Airbnb'ers who stay here while I'm gone don't seem to mind."

The apartment wasn't small at all and it was cool enough to be featured in a Pinterest spread. It had an exposed-brick-and-metal industrial vibe with a ceiling that was at least twenty feet high, with a massive black-framed window that showed off an incredible view. The sitting area near the door had an oversized camel-colored leather couch that Spencer immediately claimed. Beyond it, Justine could see an eat-in kitchen underneath metal stairs that went up to a sleeping area that was filled with sunshine from a skylight.

"So, I'm guessing you travel for work?" She didn't let on that, thanks to Sienna's LinkedIn stalking, it wasn't a guess.

"I do," he replied as he threw his keys on a little table next to the door. "I've got enough frequent flyer miles to get to Mars. Sometimes it sucks not being around much, but it's really rewarding going on-site with our clients and helping them master the software."

"It must be hard to have a life."

He shrugged. "Yeah, it can get a little tough, but I love the fact that my job is different every day. And I'm sort of on a trajectory. It's all part of my big plan." He shot her another devastating smile. "But don't get me started on my career."

She choked back a little envy. Travel, a big plan, a *trajectory*. All she had was a stack of bills and a talented dog who got a lucky break.

Justine glanced around the apartment trying to find photos or mementos that could give her some idea about his level of serial killerness, but it had as much personality as a hotel room. Which was probably a serial killer trait.

Spencer had jumped up on the couch and rolled onto his back with his back legs splayed open.

"Does he still do that all the time?" Griffin asked, pointing and laughing at him.

"Always," Justine said as she settled in next to Spencer on the couch. "Gotta air out the goods, I guess. Such a gentleman."

"Never change, buddy," Griffin said with a grin. "I'm boiling now. It's hard to regulate the heat in here with the high ceiling. Are you hot?" He pulled his sweater over his head and the edge of his gray T-shirt snaked up his body. Justine stole the two seconds to glance at his naked stomach while his head was trapped in the sweater.

So. Many. Abs.

She forced herself to look away just as he finished pulling it off.

Griffin came over and sat on the ottoman, which was close enough to the couch that she had to move down to keep their knees from touching. Spencer wagged his tail and rolled over so he could stare at Griffin, and Justine tried not to do the same. But she needed to make sense of his looks, because she couldn't tell if she was jittery about the fact that she was alone with Spencer's former person, who might or might not be a murderer, or because he was hot.

But he wasn't *conventionally* hot. As a total package he was double-take attractive, but now that she was staring at his features, the individual parts didn't add up. His face was long, and his nose had an impressive curve to it, like he'd taken a punch but shrugged it off. His eyebrows had a slight downward slope, making his brown eyes look a little sleepy.

Bedroom eyes.

Based on how his features were arranged, it absolutely did not compute that he smoldered enough to make Justine have to look away whenever he made direct eye contact with her. But it wasn't just *sexy* smolder. He seemed genuinely nice. It was a contradiction; he had "snolder."

"May I ask why you two are in the city today? I know first-hand that it takes a lot to get Spencer in the car."

"We had an audition today." Justine sat up straighter, ready to brag. "Spencer just got cast on a new Anderson Brooks pilot. He's going to play Anderson's dog." She said it casually, as if it wasn't a big deal.

Griffin's jaw dropped. "Like, *the* Anderson Brooks? Captain Zaltan Anderson Brooks? *Too Fast to Kill* Anderson Brooks?"

She nodded and rubbed Spencer's shoulder.

"Wow. I freaking *love* him. *Galaxy Force* was my show when I was little. I even had the lunch box! How did Leo get the job? Are you a professional dog trainer or something?"

"You mean Spencer," she corrected automatically. "I'm not a professional trainer, but I guess I'm on the way with this gig." She paused, realizing just how much she liked that idea.

She didn't feel like explaining her connection to Monty. Any supporting details about her life would give him clues about how to track her down.

"What kind of show is it? Everything Anderson does is so . . . actiony. Is Leo a bomb sniffer? Attack dog?"

"Spencer," she corrected again. "It's a new thing for Anderson, I guess. Maybe his action days are taking a toll on his body? It's a series about prohibition in New York. Spencer is going to play the speakeasy's guard dog."

"Huh," Griffin replied. He leaned away and crossed his arms. "Is it safe? I mean, are they going to have that 'no animals were harmed' stuff going on?"

Justine's hackles went up. Why was Griffin acting like an overinvolved stage mom?

"Of course they are. The director told me that we'll be meeting with the Humane Federation rep before we start filming. He'll be on set making sure everything is safe for Spencer, plus I would *never* put him at risk." She couldn't resist pushing back. "Do you really think I'd do anything dangerous with him?"

"Well, based on what I've picked up about you in the past thirty minutes, I'd say no. But I barely know you. You haven't even told me your last name."

He activated his customer service smile so that his dimples

appeared, but she wasn't about to let him disarm her with a stupid grin. Her last name was going to remain a mystery so there'd be no chance he could track her down once she walked out of his apartment.

"Aw, no need to worry about Spencer. He's going to be just fine," Justine said, avoiding giving him an answer. She reached over and gave Spencer a pat on the leg.

"Has he gotten over his car sickness?" The way he was studying her made Justine feel like she was in a job interview. Griffin's eyes never left her face. "When he was with me it was pretty bad. It was like car anxiety. Car phobia. Took him forever to normalize after drives. How are you going to deal with going into the city with him?"

"I think we'll be okay, thanks." She locked on to his eyes and smiled in a way that made it clear she wasn't going to say anything else on the subject. But the truth was she was nervous as hell about how her dog was going to handle all the driving. They'd made the journey into the city more than two hours before she was due to meet with Ted and Anderson, but it wasn't something she could afford to do once they were on a regular shoot schedule.

Griffin finally seemed to realize that he was overstepping a touchy boundary and stood up abruptly.

"Hey, Spencer, want a drink?" Griffin said as he walked to the kitchen. Justine watched as he filled a regular bowl, not a dog bowl, and realized that he must have gotten rid of all remnants of Spencer when he lost him.

"Guess not," he answered himself when Spencer didn't move from his spot on the couch. "How about you, Justine? I've got sparkling water, kale and spinach juice, fresh-squeezed orange juice, vodka, or beer," Griffin said as he surveyed his refrigerator. "The beers are perfect because they all have dog names. Imports from a little brewery in England called Lost Dog. I've got a Husky Hefeweizen or a Sealyham Saison."

"I'll have the Husky." Her stomach growled, and she worried how fast the beer would hit her on an empty stomach. She needed to keep her guard up, because she kept glancing at Griffin and finding new angles to admire.

He walked back to the sitting area with pint glasses, his cheerful expression replaced with a furrow. "I'd like to tell you the whole story about what happened with Leo now. And I want to talk to you about something too."

"Um, sure," she replied and took a huge gulp of beer. It was heavier than the wimpy beers she usually drank, and she had to concentrate to keep from gagging. She placed the glass on the floor beside her and put her hand over her mouth, trying to delicately hold back a massive burp-cough.

The second the glass touched the ground Spencer rolled into action. He was on the ground with his nose in the glass before Justine could grab him, slurping the beer so fast that it sloshed onto the floor.

"Whoops, old habits," Griffin said with a laugh. "I always let him have a sip of my beer."

Justine shot him a look and reached for the glass, causing Spencer to drink faster and knock it over.

"Crap, I'm so sorry," she said, trying to hold Spencer's collar to keep him away from the mess. Spencer strained so hard to get back to the beer that his legs slipped out from beneath him, Bambi-on-ice-style, and kicked the ottoman halfway across the room. "Maybe I should take him outside for a quick walk?"

"Good plan," Griffin said. "But please come back, okay? I really need to talk to you."

The intensity in his face freaked Justine out. Was this the part where he tried to murder her?

"Okay," she replied cautiously. "But I have to leave soon. I have plans with my boyfriend later." Fake Nick was more dependable than real Nick.

"There's that boyfriend again, ruining my murderous plans," Griffin said with the dimpled smile. "It won't take too long."

Justine clipped the leash on Spencer and jogged him down the three flights of stairs. The moment they were on the street he reverted to his usual good behavior. Justine watched as Spencer sniffed around trying to find the best places to add his pee signature.

"Do you like it better here with him, Spence?" Justine asked him.

She checked out Griffin's street while Spencer made his rounds marking every vertical surface. His neighborhood felt like a work in progress, where the industrial roots of the past were slowly giving way to new traditions. The outside of Griffin's building wasn't anything special, but she loved the brick warehouse that was being renovated a few doors down, dotted decorative metal stars, huge arched windows, and curved shutters. She could only imagine the gorgeous lofts to come and she tried not to be jealous.

Justine led Spencer back up the steps to Griffin's and he gave a little whine when they reached the door, which landed like a dagger to her heart. She needed to leave before her dog started to think that he was back home.

Once again she was panting by the time they reached the third floor. In their haste to leave, Justine had left the door cracked, so they slipped in quietly. Griffin was on the phone in the kitchen with his back to her.

"Yeah, she's nice." He paused to listen to the person on the other end. "About our age, I think." He grabbed another beer. "I don't know yet. We're about to talk about it." He laughed. "Nooo, she's not my type. She's okay." He paused to listen. "Like a less-cute Reese Witherspoon, I guess."

Justine felt her cheeks get hot. People had compared her to Reese Witherspoon before, but without the "less-cute" part.

Spencer barked at Griffin and he whirled to them. Justine caught a microexpression of embarrassment before his features settled into their usual stock-photography-model expression. He *had* to know how good-looking he was, because he was weaponizing it at that very moment. He waved at them, and Justine nodded back, scanning the room for her bag.

"Okay, I'll catch you later," Griffin said into the phone as he walked toward her. "Yup, bye." He slid the phone into his back pocket. "All good? Did he go?"

"He did," Justine replied in a clipped voice, trying to pretend that his insult didn't matter. "Hey, we have to head out. I didn't realize how late it is and we still have a long drive. But it was really nice to meet you."

"Wait," Griffin replied. "Please give me five minutes. It's important."

Justine sighed and looked at Spencer, who was jumping up and greeting Griffin like they'd been gone for days.

"Please." He gestured to the couch. "Have a seat."

. . .

"I want you to know that I didn't lose Leo. That's not what happened. I would never be that irresponsible." Griffin was on the ottoman staring at Justine with mug-shot intensity and she felt like she had no option but to nod.

"I was dealing with some stuff around the time he went missing . . ." His jaw clenched as he paused. "My dad had died a few months prior, and Leo really helped me through the grief. I was still traveling a ton and I wasn't taking care of myself, so I got the flu. I was basically flat on my back in bed for two weeks except when I had to take Leo out, and he never left my side. Then I left for my first trip after it, and I guess Leo was having a hard time with me being gone. He was staying with his usual dog sitter, Amanda, like he did every time I was away. She let Leo out in her backyard for a final potty trip of the night but didn't realize that someone had left the gate open. Leo took off and we assume he was looking for me. I flew home the next morning and we searched everywhere, but obviously we never found him. That's why when you called, I was so caught off guard. I never thought I'd see him again."

His eyes got misty, and they both looked at Spencer, who was sniffing where he'd spilled the beer.

There was no mistaking the dull ache in her chest; just imagining what he went through, and seeing how it still impacted him, made Griffin's pain hers. She started to reach for his hand to give him a comforting squeeze but managed to stomp down the impulse.

"I'm so sorry to hear about your father," Justine said.

"Thanks. Thank you," he said with a nod. He grabbed his beer and took a huge gulp.

Griffin paused and shifted in his seat, and Justine could tell that there was something else coming.

"I've been trying to wrap my head around everything since you called and let me know he was okay," Griffin continued. "I talked to a bunch of people to try to figure out what to do."

Justine went cold. "What do you mean by that?" she asked slowly.

"Well, my uncle is a divorce attorney, and he said . . ."

"Wait, a *what*?" Justine's tone stopped Spencer in his tracks as he nosed around the room. He trotted back to her with his ears back and tail low, immediately aware that the mood had shifted.

"Just hear me out before you get upset," Griffin said in a way that sounded like he was seconds away from telling her to calm down, which was her second-most hated *c*-word. "It turns out that dogs fall under property laws, and ownership is determined by a few factors like records and microchips."

"Ownership?" Justine sat up straighter. "Wait, you're really going there? Holy shit, you lied to me. You asked me to come here to try to take my dog."

There was no way he was going to steal Spencer back with *paperwork*. She thought of the manila folder stuffed full of his records, and the stacks of papers that surrounded it on the shelf in her home office that included receipts and forms all the way back to her dog Flynn. Then she remembered the loose sheets in the trunk of her car. And a few that migrated to her messy back room at Tricks & Biscuits. She had records; it would just take her a few hours to sort through everything to find specific documentation.

He pushed on, frowning. "There isn't a ton of precedent for this sort of situation, but records help paint a picture . . ." He trailed off.

"Well, of course I have vet records, and *obviously* Spencer didn't have a microchip when I got him; otherwise he would've found his way back to you."

"He actually does have a chip, but if the rescue that found him doesn't have a universal chip reader, they wouldn't know it. Or the chip could've migrated. I did some research and they've been found in dogs' elbows and by their ribs." He was speaking in measured tones, like he was outlining his case for a jury. Was he going to drag out a whiteboard next?

It was possible that the tiny start-up rescue where Justine had gotten Spencer couldn't afford a universal reader. She watched her dog make his way up the metal staircase to the bedroom loft. Even though he was perfectly house-trained, she hoped he'd have a major regression and poop on Griffin's pillow.

"I can't believe I agreed to meet you," Justine muttered, scanning the room for her purse and Spencer's leash so she could leave. "You really think I'm just going to hand over my dog? That threatening me is going to work?"

He leaned back like she'd slapped him. "What did I say that sounded like a threat?"

"Um, everything? Ownership, precedent, vet records, attorney . . . you're like a live episode of *Law and Order*." She jumped off the couch and whistled for Spencer.

"Okay, okay," Griffin sputtered, his nostrils flaring. "Before you go, I just want you to know that based on my research it's an open-and-shut case that he's mine. Any small-claims court would side with me. But it doesn't have to get ugly."

"It's already ugly, Griffin. You tricked me into coming here!" Justine didn't care that she was shouting at him. In that instant she wanted Griffin's entire building to know that he was an asshole. "You wanted to steal Spencer all along; the nice-guy stuff was just an act. Spence, come on. We're leaving."

"Wait." It wasn't a request, it was a command, and his tone caught her so off guard that she stood frozen in place with her mouth hanging open at his audacity. Suddenly the only murderer in the room was about to be her.

"Do you have his dog license?" Griffin asked.

Justine blanched.

License?

She'd done everything letter-perfect with Spencer in the year since she'd brought him home, but she'd totally forgotten about getting his dog license. It was a formality, really, another way to collect taxpayer money and track stats. Dog licenses didn't matter.

Until it came to establishing ownership.

"I didn't think this was going to be a custody hearing, so of course I don't have it with me, for fuck's sake," she huffed, stalling for time as a numb feeling spread out from her core. Her mind raced to figure out whom she could bribe in Rexford to backdate a dog license for her.

Griffin opened a drawer on the end table and pulled out a red folder like he was checkmating her. "Well, I have mine right here. It's a three-year license through New York State. It's still valid. I have all of his important paperwork in this file, all the way back to copies of my receipt when I adopted Leo."

"His name is *Spencer.*" Her shout echoed through the apartment.

Spencer peered down at them from the loft on cue. He was smacking his lips like he'd just devoured something, and Justine hoped whatever he'd discovered up there was important, like Griffin's paycheck. But then she realized that the tidy motherfucker probably didn't have stray paperwork strewn around his bedroom.

"Let's go," Justine called to him.

The dog came bounding down the metal stairs, and it sounded like the building was collapsing. He ran directly to Justine and danced in front of her while she struggled to clip his leash on with shaking hands, then jigged his way over to where Griffin was standing and did an encore for him.

"You're making this harder than it has to be, Justine. I don't want to fight with you."

She turned to him with her eyes blazing. "Did you *really* think that I was going to just hand him over to you? Even after I told you about him getting cast in the show? And with your lifestyle? You're never here!"

He took a step toward her and held her gaze. "I thought that maybe once you heard our history you might rethink keeping him. You've only had him for a year."

"Only a year," she repeated in a mocking voice. She had her own sad backstory, but she wasn't about to tell him what she'd been through with Spencer.

They stared at each other from a few feet apart, Justine scowling with her fists clenched and Griffin with his arms crossed over his chest, still clutching the red file. It didn't even register that he towered over her. Justine was so filled with dog-mom rage endorphins that she felt like she could topple him with a single kick to the dick.

"You lost him," she said quietly, hoping that it made her sound threatening. "The fact is, you couldn't keep him safe and that's why he ran away and ended up with me. And that's exactly why he's going to *stay* with me."

Griffin's shoulders slumped as if she'd bruised an already tender spot.

"Maybe we could work out visitation?" he asked, still clutching the red file.

"I think it's better if we don't. I'm not sure I trust you since you weren't honest about why you wanted to meet me." She headed for the door with Spencer.

"Then I'll be in touch."

It didn't sound like a threat, but it didn't sound friendly either.

"Yeah, good luck with that." Justine snorted, and pulled the door shut behind her.

All he had was her phone number and first name.

She was never going to see Griffin McCabe's face again.

chapter eleven

The first call from Jackass McAhole came as Justine was getting off the George Washington Bridge. She let her phone ring on the seat next to her until it went to voice mail. Then she heard a text. Then he called again. She finally picked up the third time her phone rang.

"What is *wrong* with you?"

"Is Spencer okay?"

"Of course he's okay. Why?" She adjusted her rearview mirror to look at him curled up in the back seat.

"He got into a package of gum up in my loft. I'm pretty sure he ate the whole thing, and it's the kind that has xylitol."

Justine inexplicably slammed on the brakes and nearly got rear-ended. *"What?"*

"He's going to be okay, but you need to get him to a vet, now." Griffin's voice was shockingly calm. "The vet site says, 'The toxic effects of xylitol can occur within ten to fifteen minutes.'"

"Oh shit. What are the symptoms again? Vomiting and what?" She craned her neck and peered over her shoulder at

Spencer despite the heavy traffic all around her. "Being in the car makes him puke anyway. How can I tell if it's from the gum?"

"If he threw up it'll help. They suggest inducing vomiting as quickly after ingestion as possible. Did he?"

Justine looked over her shoulder again and felt her heart sink when she saw how pathetic Spencer looked with his head positioned awkwardly on the armrest and his eyes at half-mast. "No."

"Okay, where are you? I'll find a clinic for you that's close to where you are. You can't wait until you get home."

"I just got off the bridge. Fort Lee maybe?"

Ten minutes later she pulled into the parking lot of a roadside clinic and gently led Spencer out of the back seat of her Mini. He seemed out of it, more so than usual after a brief drive. Once he was checked in and led to the back by a concerned-looking vet tech, she settled onto one of the uncomfortable chairs in the empty waiting room and texted Griffin with an update.

It's been too long to induce vomiting so they're measuring his blood glucose levels and liver values. We're going to be here for a while as they monitor him.

Okay, I'm paying. Call me when you check out and I'll give you my credit card, Griffin texted.

No, I've got it, don't worry about it, she texted back immediately.

But *she* was worried about it. Just walking in the door at the emergency clinic set her back $175 before they even laid a hand on Spencer. The blood work, fluids, liver protectants, and the rest of his treatment were bound to cost more than she could afford, but there was no way she was going to let Griffin pay for it, even if it was his fault.

I'm paying.

Suddenly Griffin's words took on an ominous new meaning. If Justine allowed him to pay, it would be another piece of paper for him to put in his perfectly organized Leo file. Another way for him to lay claim to *her* dog while he was in *her* care.

No way. She wasn't about to let him think that she couldn't afford to take care of her dog.

She kicked numbers around as she waited, trying to envision how much the bill was going to be. Five hundred dollars? Sure, doable with some credit card juggling. Nine hundred? Ouch. But okay, she could make it happen. Anything more? She was going to be pennies from maxing out her personal card, and she wasn't about to put the cost of Spencer's care on one of Tricks & Biscuits' cards. She didn't know when the money from *The Eighteenth* would show up in her bank account.

The dark-haired woman behind the counter stood up. "Excuse me, Spencer's mom?"

Justine leapt up and nearly dropped her phone. "Yes, that's me. Is he okay?"

"He's still getting treatment, but I'm sure he's fine. Can you come over here for a minute? I have to ask you something." She beckoned Justine to the counter. "Someone on the phone says he wants to pay for Spencer's care. Griffin McCabe. We don't normally do that sort of thing without permission from the pet guardian, so I wanted to check in with you before I took his card details. Is that okay with you?"

She felt her face go hot. The *nerve*!

"No, it's not okay with me. Please tell him it's taken care of and hang up."

The receptionist gave her a concerned look and picked up the phone. Justine hovered and listened.

"Sir? I'm sorry but I can't take your payment for treatment. The pet's guardian refused." Her eyes flitted to Justine. "Yes, she's right here. Hold on." She pushed a button on the phone and held the receiver out. "He'd like to speak to you."

Justine backed up like the woman was offering her a flaming turd. "No," she hissed. "Just hang up!"

"Are you okay? Is this person threatening you?"

"No, no, he's fine." She flapped her hand. "I just don't need his help. Tell him I just left the building to go find food." It was a few minutes from being true. The bag of almonds and granola bar in her purse were long gone.

The receptionist nodded and pushed the button again. "Sir? I'm sorry but she just walked out the door to get dinner. She said not to worry about payment." She paused. "Around the clinic? There really aren't any restaurants near here except for a Long John Silver's." She laughed. "Yes, Long John Silver's is still around." She laughed again. "You're telling me! I know. Okay, honey. Um-hm. Will do. Take care."

Justine narrowed her eyes at the woman. Another victim of Mr. Customer Service. "What did he say?" she asked quietly.

"He said he likes Long John Silver's popcorn shrimp."

Justine half smiled at his ridiculousness; then the idea of eating short-circuited everything else. "Is that seriously the only place that has food near here?"

"Not unless you want to drive for a few miles," the woman replied. "It's right across the street."

Justine sighed. "Okay. Do I have time to grab something?"

"You do. He'll be here for a while, so you have plenty of time."

Justine tried not to get killed as she crossed the four-lane road to get to the fast-food restaurant across the street. She was worried about her dog, cold, exhausted, and starving, her feet hurt, and she felt filthy. It was close to seven and she still had hours of waiting ahead of her, which was why she found herself inside the empty bright yellow fast-seafood restaurant.

The skinny young guy behind the counter narrowed his eyes at her. "You Justine?"

She looked over her shoulder in confusion, then pointed at herself. "Me?"

"Yeah, blue sweater. You Justine?"

"Yes?"

"Okay, some dude just called and bought you a gift card." He threw it on the counter in front of him. "Twenty-five dollars. Gave me a really good tip too."

She froze. Damn it, he was good. He'd gambled on her showing up to get dinner and it had paid off. And the fact that he footed the bill for her meal made the $14.29 she spent on various fried delights taste that much better.

"Justine," a comforting voice cut through the haze. "Hey."

She blinked at the fluorescent light and tried to figure out where she was and who was calling her name. Her neck ached and her foot was asleep, and she realized that Griffin McCabe was next to her and staring at her with kind eyes at the River-side Emergency Veterinary Clinic.

She jumped.

"Oh my God, what are you doing here?"

He was looking at her like she was a lost kitten, studying her with his eyebrows knitted and his mouth slightly downturned. She sat up straighter, pulled her sweater so it wasn't rumpled, and ran her hand over her hair.

"I was worried about Leo—I mean *Spencer*—so I decided to come see how things were going. Plus, I thought I might be able to convince Miss Janet over there to use my credit card instead of yours." He smiled his devastating smile, which made Justine want to punch him because Miss Janet had probably already fallen under his spell. Between buying her dinner and showing up in person, it was clear that Griffin knew how to play to win.

"You didn't have to do that," she said, quickly drawing her hand across her chin to wipe away any drool that might have crusted there. "Thanks for all the shrimp, by the way. I meant to text you a thank-you, but I went into a fried-food coma the second I finished."

"Popcorn shrimp, right?" He nodded. "Can't go wrong with those little suckers. So, what's the latest on Le—I mean *Spencer*?"

She shrugged. "No news in hours. I think at this point they're just monitoring him. I'm sure they'd come get me if something was wrong."

"Okay, I guess that's good. Have you been able to see him?"

She shook her head and they both stared at the door that led to the back of the clinic.

"I can't believe you came. You didn't have to do that." Justine blinked. "What time is it?"

He peered at his wrist. "Ten forty-five."

"Wow. I didn't think anyone wore watches these days."

"I'm old-school. I collect them. I have about twenty."

She snorted. "But you only have two wrists."

Griffin huffed and opened his mouth to answer her as a doctor in a white coat came into the lobby. "You're Spencer's people?"

Justine sat forward before Griffin could say anything. "Yes, I'm his person."

"Hi, I'm Dr. Gisemba. I took over Spencer's care after Dr. Doyle left for the night." She reached out to shake Justine's and Griffin's hands. "Spencer is doing very well. So well that Dr. Doyle and I both think he might have vomited the gum immediately after eating it without either of you knowing. Is it possible you both missed it in your home or in your yard?"

"Oh, we're not . . . um." Justine turned to Griffin. "Did you look for vomit?"

He squinted. "I actually didn't. I saw the wrappers and freaked out."

"Well, we're not seeing anything concerning and it's been six hours since he ate it. I wanted to offer you the option of going home and doing a recheck at your regular vet tomorrow morning. To be honest, it's more economical than doing it here."

"Seriously? That would be amazing. I still have a long drive ahead of me."

"Okay, then let's take that approach," Dr. Gisemba said with a nod. "I'll have a tech bring Spencer out to you, and Janet will call you up once I've entered everything in the computer."

"I'm paying." Griffin turned to face her the moment the doctor disappeared in back. "No arguments. It's my fault you're here. You and Spencer have had a really long day."

"Absolutely not," Justine said, grabbing her purse and digging through it for her wallet. "He's my dog and he's my responsibility. Don't worry about it."

She could tell they were headed for a fight at the checkout counter, but it was late, and she was too tired to be truly up for it.

Griffin started to respond when the door opened and Spencer galloped out, dragging a tattooed vet tech behind him.

"There they are," the man said. "There's your mom and dad!"

Spencer seemed overjoyed to see them together and bounded from Justine to Griffin, then back again, as if the past hours hooked up to various drips and monitors hadn't happened.

"Janet will have your checkout info in a minute," the tech said as he handed the leash to Griffin.

Justine was about to snatch it out of his hand when Janet called her to the desk. Griffin was so busy petting Spencer that she was able to sneak away before he realized what was happening.

"Here," Justine said quietly, handing two credit cards to her. "Please split the charge between these two. Do not, under any circumstances, let him pay." She flicked her eyes toward Griffin.

"Got it," Janet said and took the cards. "Do you want your total?"

She frowned. "Is it over a thousand dollars?"

Janet nodded slowly.

"Please tell me it's under three thousand."

"Oh yes, well under."

Justine let out a small sigh of relief. The money from *The Eighteenth* would come soon enough and help her catch up. "Okay, that's fine, I guess. Just run it, please."

Griffin looked up from petting Spencer's belly and realized what was happening at the counter. "Hey! I said I was paying." He reached into his back pocket and strode to her.

"Too late," Justine said gleefully. "All done."

Janet shot him an apologetic smile as she ran the second card. "Sorry."

"I'm not blaming you, Janet," Griffin said, leveling his gaze on Justine. "I still owe you. This isn't over."

"That's what you think," Justine replied, folding up Spencer's discharge paperwork before he could see her address. "Thanks for coming. Bye, Griffin."

chapter twelve

Sienna sat cross-legged on the floor at Tricks & Biscuits sorting through the box of colorful fleece dog vests. Spencer watched her through the gate behind the counter with his face smashed against the rails, so his nose was pushed through. After his pricey visit to the vet the day before Justine wanted to make sure that he didn't regress completely and start eating anything he could put in his mouth. She kept him safely cordoned off with her while she logged on to her credit card account and tried to stop her financial hemorrhage.

Justine sucked in her breath when she saw the balance.

"What?" Sienna asked.

"Nothing, just boring accounting stuff. It's fine."

But it wasn't even close to fine. She could pay for the COD shipment of dog food that was due to be delivered later in the day, but it meant that the invoice she'd been waiting to pay would be even later.

"I can finish putting those vests out," Justine said to Sienna, thinking about how she was also going to need to meet payroll. "You can leave for the day."

"I'm off the clock now; I just want to finish. I hate leaving a job half-done, you know? Five more minutes." Sienna folded the tiny vests expertly, like someone who'd done time at Baby Gap. "By the way, have you signed the lease yet? Seth peeked in looking for you today. He didn't mention it but that's probably what he wanted."

Justine clenched her jaw. "Not yet. But soon. At some point."

Neither one said anything for a few minutes and Fleetwood Mac filled the silence.

"So, what's the latest with the Brooklyn DILF? Is he still texting you?"

"Gross." Justine shuddered. "Please don't call him that."

When she'd shown Sienna the photos she'd secretly taken of Griffin as he walked Spencer, her eyes nearly bugged out of her head. Justine tried to downplay Griffin's hotness but with photographic evidence it was impossible to deny.

"He keeps asking to send me money. I won't give him my Venmo or PayPal. He feels *so* guilty and I'm loving every second of it."

Sienna sat back on her haunches and surveyed her work. "Not that it's any of my business, but wouldn't it help to get some money from him? He is actually at fault."

"No way!" Justine answered too quickly. "Once this gum thing dies down, I guarantee his campaign to get Spencer back is going to ramp up. He'll send me money this week and use the fact that he paid against me in small-claims court next week."

Sienna studied Justine. "Wow, you really don't trust him, huh?"

The bell on the door pealed and both Sienna and Justine looked at it hopefully. They'd only had a handful of customers and they needed a shopper with a new rescue dog and bottom-less wallet who was looking to stock up.

"Where is my sick boy?" Ruth called out as she burst into the store. She was in black pedal pushers and a pale pink sweater, looking like an extra from an old Elvis movie. "I have something to make him feel better."

"Ooh, can't wait to see this one," Sienna said. "What's the theme?"

Ruth leaned over the gate and gave Spencer a gentle rub under his chin, then reached out to hug Justine. "I'm so sorry all that happened yesterday. What a bummer."

"Yeah, the fun of the audition kind of got lost in the mess afterward. I've barely had a chance to think about it," Justine said.

"Our boy is going to be a star! I can say I knew you when, Spence. I hope you'll keep me on as your stylist, since your mom has no interest in the job." Ruth grinned at Justine and handed a little polka-dotted bag to her.

She peeked inside and laughed when she saw what it was. "You are a cruel woman."

It was a white bow tie covered with a repeating gumball machine pattern.

"Please, you can have the honor of reminding him of his trauma," Justine said as she handed the tie to Ruth.

The shop phone rang as Ruth fastened the tie around Spencer's neck.

"Tricks & Biscuits, may I help you?" Justine answered.

"Don't hang up!" the voice demanded.

She recognized it instantly and her heart fell out of rhythm. "*Griffin?* How did you get this number?"

"When you were at my apartment you had a little temporary building pass clipped to your purse. It had your first and last name, so I tracked you down."

"Oh my God, stalk much?" she asked as she realized he'd seen the badge from her meeting with Anderson and Ted.

"I had to, because you won't answer my texts. I still feel awful about what happened, Justine. I want to take care of it."

"You don't have to worry about it," she answered breezily as she fiddled with a basket of collar charms. "He's fine now and I'm moving on. We're done."

"That's the other reason why I'm calling. He's doing okay?"

Justine leaned over and gave Spencer a scratch behind the ears. "He's great. I had him at our vet this morning and they said everything looks perfect. So, we're all set, Griffin. But thanks."

He made a noise that sounded like a frustration growl. "This doesn't feel right to me."

She shrugged and made a noncommittal noise. Both Ruth and Sienna were watching her.

"Maybe I'll drive up to Rexford and hand deliver a stack of cash."

Justine wasn't sure if her heart sped up at the thought of Griffin showing up on her doorstep or the pile of money he promised.

"If you won't take money, I have one final idea about how I can repay you."

"Is that so?" She felt an inexplicable blush creeping onto her cheeks.

"It's so perfect that you'll have to say yes."

He sounded as confident and helpful as he had the first time she heard his voice, and she recognized that he'd slipped into his customer-servicey sales-training persona. He wasn't the guy who wanted to steal her dog away; he was the smiley guy who got paid big bucks to make people more productive.

"Stay at my apartment," he continued. "While you film the show. Stay here during the week so you won't have to commute with Spencer. We can work it out so that I won't be there at the same time, and you'll have the place to yourself."

Her jaw dropped. It was impossible.

It was an amazingly generous offer, sure, but one that had strings. Maybe Griffin would be able to claim eminent canine domain if Spencer started spending time in the apartment again? It didn't matter that, as it was now, she and Spencer were going to have to leave Rexford hours before she was due on set thanks to his car sickness. There was *no way* she was taking him up on it. It was relinquishing too much control, something she refused to do in any aspect of her life.

"No, I couldn't—"

"You know how bad it's going to be for him if you have to go from the car right to the set. I hate the thought of him feeling sick and then getting forced to perform. He might start refusing to get into the car after a few bad trips. That actually happened to me."

"I'm not *forcing* Spencer," Justine protested. She rolled her eyes at Ruth.

"Okay, whatever. The point is you know this is the best option for him. For both of you."

It was true, but she wasn't about to admit it.

"That's a really kind offer, but I don't feel right about staying at your place."

It felt *too* kind. Weirdly so. He was up to something.

"Well, let me know if you change your mind. I'm heading to Salt Lake next week so it would be easy to at least give it a shot. See how it works."

"No, we're good. But thanks again for the offer. I have to run, though, some customers just came in," she lied.

Sienna ran to the door and jingled the bell. "I need help picking dog food, please," she said in an overloud voice.

"Thanks again. Bye, Griffin."

Justine sighed and placed her phone on the counter.

"He's a persistent bugger, huh?" Ruth asked. "He offered you his *apartment*? Are you sure this guy doesn't have a crush on you?"

"Have you seen his picture? I think it might be mutual," Sienna added.

Justine pretended to gag. "Hardly. He's a control freak who wants to steal Spencer and thinks he can fix everything with his money."

"You have a photo?" Ruth held her hand out. "Gimme. Now."

Justine flipped through her phone to find the least attractive photo of Griffin. There were four images, and she thought she remembered one shot that made him look like he had a double chin, but as she scrolled through the photos she realized that he looked good in *all* of them.

"Whatever," she said, showing the photo where Griffin and Spencer were gazing at each other under an arch of yellow leaves, looking like they were posing for their holiday card.

"This is *him*?" Ruth said as she zoomed in on his face. "Woman, what's your problem? First, take this man's money, then steal his heart. Does he have a girlfriend?"

She shrugged. "Maybe."

"A boyfriend?"

"I don't know. Maybe."

Ruth pointed at the photo with her mouth hanging open, then looked at Sienna for confirmation.

"Right?" Sienna agreed. "That's what I said."

"Guys, have you forgotten that he lured me to Brooklyn under false pretenses, then tried to take Spencer back? He's not exactly trustworthy. Plus, I'm not in the headspace to date again, *especially* someone stalkery."

"I don't know," Ruth said, dragging her finger around on the photo to examine the details. "I'd be willing to gamble on an ass like that."

"Okay, enough, we're done here. Sienna, you probably have a pack of dogs to walk, and Ruth, don't you have a shop to worry about?"

"Fine, fine, I'll go," Ruth said with a pout. "What's next for our star?"

"We have a table read coming up, where we go through the first script. And yes, everyone is going to be there."

"You better take notes. I want *all* the gossip. Who's mean to their assistant? Who's had too much work done? Who's still in the closet?" Ruth asked with her eyes shining.

"I'll do my best, but don't forget we have a job to do. A major, important, big-fucking-deal job." Her fingers had actually trembled as she signed the contract the studio had sent over after her meeting with Anderson.

"Psh, he's a natural," Ruth said as she and Sienna headed out the door. "He's going to be great."

chapter thirteen

I'm sorry, bud," Justine whispered as she wiped off Spencer's mouth and chest with mango-scented wipes. "I know you hate this part."

Spencer twisted his face away just enough that he registered his unhappiness with the grooming, but not so much that it was impossible for Justine to take care of it. They were parked on a side street a few blocks from the Brooklyn warehouse that was the main set for *The Eighteenth*. It was the first time she would be meeting the cast and crew for a table read, and instead of calmly reciting "I can do this" mantras, Justine was trying to keep dog vomit off the hot pink Boden blazer she'd borrowed from Ruth.

They'd left Rexford early enough so that Justine could deal with her new-route nerves and Spencer would have time to shake off his queasy feelings, but a rubbernecking delay and a wrong turn meant they were late and frazzled.

When she was satisfied that Spencer would pass Anderson's inevitable kiss test, they set off for the giant warehouse that was going to be the main set. She could tell by the way he was walking with his head down and tail tucked that he was still woozy from car sickness.

Justine's heart started thumping faster when they rounded the corner and she spotted the line of luxury SUVs with black-out windows idling near the brick warehouse. She'd seen the names of the other actors affiliated with the show in the scheduling emails and managed to remain calm, but for some reason the line of fancy cars made it all real for her. She fought off her own queasy feelings.

Justine spoke quietly to Spencer as they got closer to the lime green door. "Spence, no matter what, you've got this. Okay? You're my best boy, and we're going to have fun during this adventure. No pressure to be perfect. Just do your best."

Spencer watched her with wary eyes and twitched his tail in a wag so sad that she almost marched him right back to the car and left. But it would be worse for him to sit through another two hours of travel than go through the table read. All he had to do was look cute while the rest of the cast read through the script, and Spencer was cute even when he was hacking up breakfast in her back seat.

She opened the green door slowly and walked into a swirl of activity. The building had a high ceiling, so the room buzzed with energy and noise, so much so that Justine stood against the wall for a moment to take it all in. She could see a city-street-scene set beyond a dividing wall that looked so authentic, it felt like she'd traveled back in time. There were groups of people clustered together laughing and others running around with worried expressions. A long table dominated the far wall of the building, and Justine could see tented name cards next to bottles of water. She spotted Ted in his baseball cap sequestered in a corner, having a furrowed-brow conversation with two other men. Anderson was holding court in front of a group of people with Taylor standing at his elbow.

"Excuse me," Justine said to a petite, unbelievably pretty brunette woman passing by her. "Do you know where I check in? With him?" She pointed to Spencer, who was alternating between short pants and a closed-mouth worried expression. His ears were plastered against his head.

"Oh, this must be sweet Ford!" the woman replied in a crisp British accent, dropping to her knees next to Spencer. "I'm so excited to meet you." She looked up at Justine and smiled, and Justine realized that her dog was being loved up by none other than the star of a recently ended cable fantasy series *Netherworlds*. It was Claire Cameron, aka the beguiling mermaid Hydranea, who was now playing Anderson's put-upon wife, Myrna.

Justine knew that despite the fact that Claire's perfect face had launched a thousand cosmetic campaigns, she was now a colleague of sorts and she had to swallow her urge to fangirl. She held out her hand and pretended like Claire was just another person on the street who thought her dog was cute. "Yup, this is Spencer, and I'm Justine. Nice to meet you."

She gave a little wave instead of taking Justine's hand. "I'm Claire, lovely to meet you too. Honestly, I'm not sure who you should talk to. It's a bit of a madhouse at the moment, but I did see someone in a Humane Federation shirt over there." She gestured to a long table filled with catering platters. Claire refocused on Spencer. "We have a moment together in the pilot, young man. Make me look good, okay?" She patted him on the head and disappeared into the crowd.

Justine headed toward where Claire had pointed, only to be

stopped every two feet by admirers. Spencer took the cooing and petting in stride, gamely wagging every time someone interacted with him, but Justine could tell that he was still feeling awful. She hoped no one else could tell.

"Hey there, you're the reason I'm here, I guess."

Justine turned around and was greeted by a tall, bald Black man whose muscles rivaled Anderson's. His black golf shirt strained across his massive chest as he reached his hand out, so much so that the Humane Federation logo over his heart was warped. The giant man looked more like a bodyguard than an animal safety rep, but given that he was responsible for the well-being of creatures ranging from mouse to elephant on various movie and TV shoots, she could understand how his size was an asset.

"Hi, I'm Malcolm Franklin," he said, taking her hand in his massive one. "Great to meet you."

"I'm Justine Becker and this is Spencer, also known as Ford."

Malcolm turned sideways and squatted down near Spencer. He muttered a few soft words and Spencer gave him a half-hearted wiggle.

"I've been watching him," Malcolm said as he petted Spencer. "Is he nervous?"

Caught. Justine swallowed hard.

"No, he gets really carsick and we had a two-hour drive. He should snap out of it soon."

"Are you going to do that drive every time he's needed?"

Justine nodded.

"Have you tried herbal remedies? A calming wrap?"

"We've tried everything. But don't worry, we'll figure it out."

"You a trainer?"

"Not professionally." Justine squirmed. Maybe it made sense to start saying she was, since Spencer's role on the show made it sort of true?

"He's a good-looking dude. Unique." Malcolm gestured to Spencer. "Does he get a lot of work?"

"This is our first series, but he, uh, we do mainly live work." Justine knew she had to pad Spencer's résumé so that no one would question how they ended up on the show. Ted had already fired one dog; she didn't want to give any hint that perhaps Spencer wasn't qualified either. And besides, doing tricks for customers at the shop was basically a live performance.

"Huh. First timer. Should be interesting," Malcolm replied. "Anyway, as you know, I'm here for *him*. I've seen all the scripts and I've already raised a few concerns about the action they want, especially that off-leash location shoot. But I need you to keep me informed too. If something feels wrong, tell me. Got it?"

Justine nodded, thankful to have such an important ally who was just as invested in Spencer's safety as she was. But she also knew that if anything about her coaching or Spencer's performance didn't feel right to him, he could have them pulled from the production. There were several organizations that looked out for animal actors, and based on her research the Humane Federation was the toughest one to please.

"Thank you, I will." She shot him her brightest smile.

"Looks like we're getting started," Malcolm said as people began sitting down throughout the room. "Nice to meet you two."

They started to walk away, but Spencer stopped in his tracks and hunched over with his head close to the floor. His whole body heaved once, twice; then an awful gurgling cough echoed around the room. A few people turned to watch as he vomited the contents of his stomach onto the shoes of the second-most important person on the show.

"Oh my God, he's still . . . I'm so sorry . . . let me get . . ."

Malcolm held up his hand to stop her and pulled a roll of paper towels from the backpack she hadn't even noticed he had on. "It's fine. Bodily fluids are a hazard of the job. But you need to get this under control, okay? We can't have him like this on set."

"Of course, it won't happen again. I'm really sorry. But are you sure I can't . . ." She made a cleaning gesture in the air.

"I'm fine, don't worry. Feel better, Ford."

Justine ducked her head and settled in a chair at the back of the room on the end of a row so that Spencer had space to spread out. She felt a tap on her shoulder.

"Justine, welcome," a quiet voice said.

It was Ted Sherman, looking dressier than usual in a navy blazer and button-down, paired with his ubiquitous black base-ball hat.

"Ted, hi!" She was still processing the vomit, so she put on a fake smile. "We're so excited to be here, thank you again."

"And we're thrilled to have you both. But we need you up front." He pointed to the long table where Anderson, Claire, Tay-lor, and the rest of the cast were settling in and flipping through the script.

"Really?"

He nodded. "Spencer is an integral part of the premier. We want him close for this. Come." Ted beckoned Justine to fol-low him.

"Well, Spencer has a ton of skills, but he failed reading

comprehension . . ." She trailed off as she gathered her bag and Spencer's leash. She glanced down at her dog as he skulked behind her.

"You're right over there," Ted said, pointing to a tent card at the end of the table, next to curly-haired tween star Noah Ryland, who was playing Anderson's son.

"Cute dog," Noah said as Justine settled next to him. "But he's got something . . ." The boy gestured to his chin.

Justine looked down at Spencer and saw the twin trails of slobber coming from his mouth, so thick that they almost looked like they were made of gelatin. She fished through her bag to find a tissue, but Spencer plopped onto the ground and lowered his head so that the drool pooled around him like modern art.

She spotted an '80s soap opera actor her mom had always loved making his way to the dais. Then she looked down the line of actors next to her and into the crowd of people on folding chairs in front of them.

Only then did it hit her that she and Spencer were *way* out of their league.

chapter fourteen

"Hi, Griffin, it's Justine."

"What's wrong? Is Leo okay?" His voice sounded worried.

"He's fine." She glanced in her rearview mirror and saw that he was resting his head on the door, staring out the window as if he knew the uncomfortable feelings were about to begin again. It was too cold to be outside, so they were sitting in her car in the parking spot around the corner from the warehouse. "I'm lying. We just had our first meeting for the show and he was really carsick the whole time. He puked on the Humane Federation guy's shoes." She closed her eyes and leaned her forehead against the steering wheel. She wanted to just blurt out the big ask and get it over with, but she couldn't find the nerve.

"Oh no," Griffin said. "That *sucks*. I'm sorry to hear it."

"Yeah, we're sitting in my car getting ready to head back and I was—"

"You're shooting in Red Hook, right?"

"How did you know that?"

"I did some Anderson recon and found out. You're really close to my favorite pub."

Justine's stomach rumbled at the thought of getting something to eat before they headed back. She'd been too nervous to eat a bite during the table read. "Do they do takeout? I can get some food and eat it in the car on the way home."

"You're hungry? I could go for an early dinner, too. Want to meet me there? I'd love to see Spencer while you're in the neighborhood."

Justine stopped fiddling with the enamel dog on her key chain. Did Griffin just ask her out? Hot or not, she was sticking to the promise she made to herself to avoid getting involved with anyone until she had her own weirdness figured out.

"But how can we go to a restaurant with Spencer?"

She heard his tail whip against the seat at the mention of his name. He was a solid reason *not* to go to dinner with Griffin.

"That's why it's my favorite—they allow dogs! And everybody knows Leo there—I mean Spencer. They'll be psyched to see him."

Justine quickly tried to come up with another excuse about why she couldn't meet him, but there was no way out. "Okay, I guess we could meet for a quick meal while I wait for the traffic to die down . . ."

The call to Griffin was supposed to be just two minutes of groveling, then asking to stay in his apartment on shoot days. But here she was getting dragged into family reunions at his local hangout. Maybe paying for his meal would make the ask less painful?

"Perfect. It's called the Yard Bar, on Conover. Plenty of parking on Reed, right around the corner. I'll be there in fifteen minutes."

She could hear him moving around his apartment as he spoke, like he was eager to walk out the door.

She checked the map. "It's a three-minute drive from where I'm parked, so I guess I'll beat you there. You're sure it's okay for Spencer to go in there? Do I need to wait for you to show up?"

Griffin laughed. "Trust me, they're going to roll out the red carpet when they see him. Just grab a table and enjoy the free round."

"Oh my fuggin' gawd, it's *Leo*!" the bartender shouted when Justine and Spencer walked in the door at the Yard Bar. "Griffin told me someone found him!"

The half-dozen people in the bar turned to look at Justine as they walked in the door, and she saw a few smiles of recognition. Spencer bounced on his front paws excitedly while Justine gripped the leash. "Hi, yeah. I'm Justine and he's called Spencer now."

She realized too late that inviting her to his local bar was another bit of psychological warfare. She'd have to spend the meal explaining why Leo had a new name and why it was going to stay that way. She thought about making a quick exit, but she didn't want Griffin to think he intimidated her.

Plus, she needed his damn apartment.

The white-haired bartender came out from behind the bar wiping his hands on his apron. His hunched posture made him look ancient, but his long hipster goatee and suspenders helped him fit right in with the too-cool crowd, like he was their porkpie-hat-wearing grandpa who was a bouncer at CBGB back in the day.

"Hey, doggy boy! Hi there, Leo!" The man surrendered to Spencer's kiss attack with laughs and hugs. "Welcome home."

It was a charming reunion, and as hard as it was imagining Leo happily living his old life, she could appreciate the fact that everyone loved him.

"Anthony, didja see?" the old man called to a bald man seated in the back corner of the small bar. "It's Leo!"

"No way! Welcome back, dog breath!" The guy gave Justine a quick elevator-eyes glance. "You Griff's girlfriend?"

"No!" she shouted. "Just a friend. Long story." She waved her hand to imply he wouldn't want to hear it.

"I'm Wendall," the bartender said. "Is Griff coming to meet you?"

"He is. He told me to get a table."

"The one up front is his favorite, right by the window. I'm going to bring you a drink on the house since you saved Leo. What are you having?"

"Surprise me. Whatever you like on tap."

"All righty, one Mastiff Milk Stout from Lost Dog, coming your way. Griffin's favorite. And a bowl of water for the good boy."

Justine shrugged off her coat and blazer and settled into a chair at the table by the huge front window. Somehow it made sense that Griffin's local was an unpretentious, dimly lit, brick-walled space with a ceiling-high wall of liquors behind the bar. She couldn't tell if it was a new bar made to look old, or if it had been in the neighborhood for sixty years.

Spencer camped out at her feet, panting happily and watching everyone around them, seeming perfectly at home. Exactly fifteen minutes later, Griffin walked in, bringing a blast of cold air and a round of hellos with him.

"Hey there, you," he said, smiling his giant dimple-cheeked smile at Spencer, who leapt up to greet him. "Looking good, buddy! No gum's gonna get you down, right?" He wrapped his arms around Spencer as the dog jumped up to hug him, causing Justine to squirm in her seat. It had taken her months to teach him not to jump up on people.

"Hey, you order food yet?" He unwound his scarf and pulled off his leather moto jacket. She scanned him quickly and was disappointed to realize that even in a basic T-shirt and jeans he looked amazing.

She shook her head. "I was just making my choice, but I'm open to your suggestions. Popcorn shrimp, perhaps?"

"Oh, no debate," he replied, waving at Wendall behind the bar and making the universal "bring me a pint" gesture. "Onion rings to start; they're as big as your fist. Then cheddar and Gruyère béchamel mac and cheese."

"That sounds amazing. But are they small portions? Because I'm *starving*."

Griffin grinned at her. "You actually eat?"

"Do I? Just watch me." She took a gulp of her beer, then grimaced. "Although my appetite might be off since this is like eating a loaf of bread."

Griffin hunched over so his hands were on Spencer beneath the table. "Did Wendall buy you that round?"

"Very sweet of him." She nodded. "I guess you're a *regular* regular here? Everybody knows your name?"

"Kind of." He shrugged. "When I'm in town I'm here quite a bit. But not, like, alcoholic levels or anything," he backpedaled.

She realized it was the perfect in for her request.

"Speaking of being out of town . . ."

Wendall delivered his beer and took their food order, forcing her to stop the request and continue to feel weird about it.

"You were asking me about being out of town?" he asked once they were alone again. He had a habit of staring into her eyes that made her want to look away.

"I told you how bad today was for him, and I'm worried that trying to commute into the city is going to make being on the show really hard for Spence." Her eyes flicked down to where Griffin's hands were massaging him, and she forced herself to ignore it. "So . . . I was wondering if—"

"You want my apartment," he interrupted. "Of course. That's why I offered it. Happy to let you guys crash there."

Her heartbeat slowed a measure.

"Are you sure it's not going to screw up your Airbnb schedule?"

"Not at all. I don't do it all the time because it pisses off my neighbors. I'll just take the listing down for a bit."

Justine finally exhaled. "I can't tell you what a relief that is! Thank you. He was *so* sick today. You have no idea."

"Oh, but I do." He gave her a quick smile. "I remember it very well."

In an instant she was reminded of what she was putting at risk by opening herself up to him. But it was too late to take it back.

The door whooshed open again and a skinny guy in a red knit cap, '70s glasses, and jean jacket walked in and surveyed the room like he was waiting for a round of applause.

"G-man," he shouted, spotting Griffin. "And *Leo*? What the hell?" He looked at Spencer and laughed. "What is going on, man?"

Spencer came out from near their feet with his hind end wagging.

"Danny, hey," Griffin said with a slight frown that only Justine caught. "Long story. How you been?"

"Oh, amazing, man. I've been out in Sedona working on my shit." He finally acknowledged Justine. "Hey, I'm Danny."

"Justine," she replied with a wave. Based on Griffin's cool response she could tell he wasn't a Danny fan.

"You guys mind if I join you?" he asked as he pulled up a chair to their table.

Griffin's mouth went into a tight line for an instant. "Be my guest."

"Leo, man," he replied, his head bobbing as he slapped Spencer on the back. "Never thought I'd see this dude again."

"Same." Griffin shot Justine an apologetic smile.

"Hey! Let me show you some pics of the sweet new deck I just painted for Justin Bieber."

"I never knew there was such a thing as a skateboard artist," Justine said as she and Griffin stood outside the bar under a streetlight with Spencer sitting between them.

"Oh yeah, there is. To my eternal frustration, there is."

"Is that his full-time job? Custom painting skateboards?"

Griffin snorted. "No, his full-time job is being a trustafarian. His daddy started a hedge fund, so Daniel Chase the Second doesn't have to work." He shook his head. "Must be nice. Me, I'm hustling every damn day, but all that guy has to worry about is if his monthly allowance has cleared the bank yet."

"Hey, you're doing okay," Justine replied. "You've got a great job and a fantastic apartment. *I'm* the bigger hard-luck case. I'm so poor I can't even pay attention."

"Whoa, dad joke. Nice." He shoved his hands in his jacket pockets. "Sorry the meal got ruined by him. He never stops talking about himself. And we have some, uh, history that he's conveniently forgotten, so it's not like I enjoy hanging with him."

"He was entertaining," she lied. "And dinner was delicious. Awesome recommendation."

"You didn't have to pay."

"Ah, the old 'pretend you have to go to the bathroom and slip the bartender your credit card' move. Can't beat it."

It felt shockingly like a date, standing in the cold night air with Griffin closer than he should've been given that it *wasn't* a date. It was the first time she'd bothered to acknowledge his lips. There was no symmetry to them. The bottom one was much larger than the top, and she found herself mesmerized by it.

"Are you okay to drive home?" he asked, startling her back to reality.

"Of course. I only had one. Couldn't stomach another of those." She shuddered.

"Yeah, but you scored a bunch of points with Wendall for finishing it."

Justine watched a cab pass by them slowly. "I should probably hit the road. Rush hour is over."

"Rush hour never ends in New York, you'll see."

She felt a tingle of excitement when she realized that she was going to get to pretend to be a local a few days a week.

"When do you want to do the key handoff?"

"How about right now?" Griffin reached into his pocket and pulled out a single key on a narrow brown leather strap.

"Wait, you brought a spare key? How did you . . ."

He smiled, unleashing his dimples just for her. "I had a feeling that's why you reached out today. And if you didn't ask, I was going to offer again. It makes sense for both of you."

Not only was the gesture genuinely kind; it was also a little psychic.

"Griffin, thank you," Justine said.

Her gratitude overwhelmed her, and for a moment she wanted to step around Spencer and pull Griffin into a quick hug, but that would make the not-a-date moment feel even more like one.

"You know where you're going? Need me to nav you out of here?"

"No, I'm good." She nodded and glanced down at Spencer. "He's asleep standing up. Time for us to leave. I'll text you with my schedule for next week."

"Perfect."

Griffin took two quick steps toward her and wrapped her in a hug before she realized what he was doing. She was still holding Spencer's leash and she couldn't reciprocate with both arms, so she flung one behind his back and leaned into him as he pulled her close. He felt solid and warm, like he'd just been sitting in front of a fireplace. Her cheek ended up against the soft leather on his shoulder for a few seconds, and she tried to process exactly why she wanted to raise her face and wait for the kiss that would inevitably come if it were an actual date.

Which it wasn't.

He released her almost as quickly as he'd grabbed her. "Sorry, I'm a hugger."

"Yeah, same. No problem." She had a hard time looking at his face, but he didn't seem to have the same issue. Since she'd already determined that he was a little psychic, it was possible he could tell what she was thinking. Things like imagining his pillowy bottom lip on top of hers. Or pretending to trip over Spencer's leash in the hopes that he'd grab her arm and pull her close. It had been months since she'd felt that electric flicker of want, and he was exactly the wrong person to be on the receiving end of it.

"Let me walk you to your car."

She wished she'd had trouble finding parking. "It's right there." She pointed to the red Mini Cooper peeking around the corner.

"Oh, okay," he said softly. He leaned down and gave Spencer a kiss on the head. "Bye, Spence, hope you make it home without puking."

"I'll text you the photographic evidence either way," Justine said over her shoulder as she walked to her car.

"Perfect, can't wait."

chapter fifteen

Spencer kept his pace close to Justine's, occasionally glancing up at her to check in. They were at mile two of four on their first outdoor run in forever, falling into the rhythm she hadn't realized how much she'd missed. She filled her lungs with the cool fall air and understood that there was no way the treadmill came close to the feelings she got when she ran outside. She needed it, and she was angry at herself for not getting out more often, especially with winter weather on the way.

They were on the "promenade path," the easy, flat trail that bordered soccer fields, parks, and homes. It felt like all of Rexford was outside enjoying the global-warming day, which made Justine relax and focus on her breathing and form. Spencer was her athletic idol; his grace put hers to shame.

When her legs started to itch, she unconsciously reached into the pocket of her hoodie for her headphones to distract herself, only to remember that she didn't have them with her. Running without music was torture, but plugging her ears was a risk she wasn't willing to take.

Yet.

The fact that she was still stopping herself from doing something she loved made white-hot anger rise in her chest. She was strong; there was no reason to let fear change her habits. She had every right to bliss out on the trail, lulled into a dance-trance by Beyoncé. She didn't have her music with her but there was another way she could prove that she was the same old Justine.

This run was going to be more than just exercise.

It was one step closer to reclaiming her badassery.

"Spence, this way."

He glanced up at her and seamlessly shifted his direction. When he recognized where they were heading, he picked up his pace.

"Yup. Let's go!"

Justine broke into a sprint when she saw the trailhead. She knew she needed to slow down because the route she was choosing to take was long and required focus, and focus adds to exhaustion. But she was doing it.

The trees bordering the path were an explosion of bright yellow and orange, like they were wearing their most cheerful gear just for her. Everything felt right for the first time in ages; the fit of her sneakers, the crisp air, the unmistakable smell of leaves piling on the ground, Spencer's joy. The crunch of the rocky ground was louder than she realized without her headphones in, but she found a way to turn the rhythm of her feet into a metronome. She started a chant to keep time.

My. Trail. My. Trail.

They ran farther up the incline to where the trail narrowed. Spencer seemed thrilled to be back, rationing his pee so that he could reclaim every tree. He gave a little whine and Justine unclipped his leash to let him run at his own pace. Spencer dashed ahead and buried his nose at the base of a log.

The farther in they went, the denser and darker it became, but it was fine because Justine could do hard things. She refocused on her foot placement since her balance was lacking. Treadmill running couldn't touch trail running when it came to a total-body workout, and she could already feel the burn in her shoulders and core.

But she felt happy. And strong. And braver than she'd felt in ages.

Was it the lifeline that *The Eighteenth* was going to provide her? Sure. Of course. The thought that she'd be able to pay her bills and Sienna without worrying was enough to make her want to start singing at the top of her lungs. And it wasn't just the money. It was the adventure.

She looked down at her feet, watching for rocks and roots. Her eyes flicked up to scan the horizon, just as she'd learned to do when she started cross-country in high school. A flash of light through the trees momentarily slowed her, and her brain automatically flipped through her fight-or-flight options until she realized the enemy in the shadows was a bird.

"Spence?"

He crashed through the overgrowth to the edge of the trail and paused with one paw up, a quizzical look on his face.

"Okay, we're good. Go sniff."

He turned and disappeared again.

Spencer. Leo. She chanted the names as she ran. Spencer. Leo. Spencer. Leo.

Griffin.

She envisioned his face and smiled even though her calves

were starting to burn from the run. He wasn't a bad guy after all, despite his shitty first impression. He loved Spencer, and Spencer loved him back, which probably carried more weight than anything. And *obviously* he was attractive. Justine rolled her eyes and puffed out a breath at the understatement. Hot. Yes, obviously.

When her mind drifted to the hug they'd shared, she changed her chant.

Not. Happening. Not. Happening.

The endorphin hit came out of the blue. A fizzy feeling radiated from her belly and her mind felt clearer than it had been in weeks. She felt . . . lighter. It was the giant reset button she'd been craving.

She was back.

Something crashed through the trees in the distance and she fought off the adrenaline rush that shot through her chest by imagining what it could be. Deer. A coyote. A black bear. Bigfoot.

Those she could handle.

Her phone rang and she clutched at her pocket to grab it like it was a lifeline, her sweaty hands almost causing her to drop it on the dirt. It didn't matter if it was a telemarketer offering her timeshare deals; she was going to answer. Relief flooded her body when she saw Sienna's number.

"Hi," she panted, still running. "What's up?"

"Hey, where are you? You sound weird."

"I'm out for a run." Justine tried to keep her sweaty cheek away from the phone.

"No way, that's great!" Sienna cheered. "Where?"

"Lockwood Overlook." She knew the two words would shift the rest of the conversation.

"Oh, *wow*. Wow, Justine! Good for you! Is everything . . . okay?"

"Yup, all good. No biggie. Just a quick run. I'm heading back now." She turned in the middle of the trail and began the descent. "What's going on?"

"Oh, yeah, sorry. I'm closing and the register software is acting glitchy. When's the last time you rebooted?"

She couldn't remember when she'd done it. Yet another housekeeping task that had fallen off her radar.

"It's been a while. You can go ahead and reboot. That should fix it."

Spencer crashed through the underbrush and joined Justine on the trail, slowing himself down to match her pace.

Sienna recited the reboot steps. "Okay . . . F10 . . . click 'yes' . . . hit escape . . . save all files . . . and done. I should be fine from this point on. Do you want to stay on the phone with me?" she asked.

Justine wasn't sure if Sienna was asking in case the register acted up again, or to be a support as she made her way back to civilization.

"We're fine," Justine answered vaguely.

And for the first time in a long time, she knew she was.

chapter sixteen

Justine hoisted her overstuffed silver suitcase up the stairs slowly while Spencer ran in place beside her. She'd packed in a hurry, filling a suitcase large enough for a week away with every combination of cute but comfortable clothing she could possibly need for their first day on set. Justine could tell Spencer wanted to bound up the stairs to his old front door like he used to, but she wanted to help him remember his manners, especially with so much riding on his ability to listen to her the next day.

Griffin's flight to Miami was scheduled to depart before she got into the city. As much as she would've liked to cross paths with him "accidentally," there was no reason for her to take even more time off from Tricks & Biscuits to make it happen. Although she had managed to sneak away earlier than she actually needed to.

By the time she reached Griffin's floor she was panting with exertion, and a little sweaty under her black parka. She dropped Spencer's leash, then tucked her hair behind her ears as she unlocked his door. Spencer strolled in like he owned the place, which he sort of did.

She dropped her keys on the table by the door, where the red file lived, and a feeling of ease settled over her despite it. Even though Griffin's apartment had as much personality as a high-end hotel room, there was something about it that felt familiar to her. The lights were on, and for a moment she thought it was Griffin's tiny gesture of welcome. But then she heard the shower and saw steam rolling out from under the bathroom door.

"Spencer!" she whispered, desperate to get out of the apartment before Griffin or whatever Airbnb-mix-up guest was currently using the shower saw her. "Come on, Spence, let's go!"

He stared at her, then juked toward the bathroom door in a single graceful leap. He was still recovering from the drive into the city, but the thought of seeing Griffin seemed to clear his woozy feelings away. He let out a bark and raked his paw down the bathroom door.

The water turned off a few seconds later and Justine rushed to grab Spencer's leash and pull him away from the door.

Griffin came out of the bathroom soaking wet with a navy towel clutched around his waist.

"Well, hello. Fancy meeting you here." The weaponized smile plus the naked torso were almost more than Justine could take. She focused on Spencer so it wouldn't look like she was staring even though she totally was.

"My flight was delayed." He headed for the stairs to the loft. "My clothes are upstairs." He gestured to his naked torso. "Sorry."

Justine wasn't.

She'd already been briefly introduced to the abs, but the

swimmer's shoulders were new, as were the cuts at his waistline that dipped beneath the towel.

Spencer saw Griffin going upstairs without so much as a hello and ripped the leash from Justine's hand. He headed for Griffin like a tornado of paws, as if they were being reunited for the first time again. Justine hovered between being jealous about how Spencer was acting and being fascinated by Griffin's damp body.

"Hey, Spence, ouch! Watch it!"

Griffin tried to withstand the barrage of kisses and leaps while clutching his towel.

"Sorry, he knows better than to jump up," she said but silently blamed Griffin for encouraging him to jump up the last time they saw each other. She knew she needed to grab Spencer's leash in order to stop the assault, but she wasn't sure what would happen if she got too close to a half-naked Griffin.

"Dude, *Leo*, enough," he said, using his free elbow and twisting his body to keep the dog from gleefully maiming his chest.

Justine didn't bother to correct the name.

Spencer alternated between dashing in ecstatic circles and bouncing off Griffin like he was doing parkour. Justine was surprised by how well he was rallying after the drive, but then again, all the rules changed when Griffin was around.

Frustrated that he wasn't getting enough love back from Griffin, Spencer let out an accusatory bark and jumped almost high enough to kiss him on the mouth. Once he hit the ground he latched on to the towel, lowered himself, and gave it a powerful tug-of-war yank.

"No!" Griffin and Justine shouted in unison.

Spencer shook his head and made playful growling noises as

Griffin attempted to back up the stairs without losing the towel. Justine ran forward a few steps, then stopped when she realized that Griffin was barely holding on to the towel in front of his groin and half of his right butt cheek was exposed. She couldn't stop staring. It was the roundest ass she'd ever seen, and she reconsidered her initial guess that he was a swimmer because a butt that perky would definitely lead to water drag.

"Can't you call him away?" Griffin sounded like he was begging, doubled over and holding on to the towel with all his strength as Spencer yanked. "You said he was trained now."

The desperation in Griffin's face made Justine want to burst out laughing. He looked so helpless, so panicked, so . . . hot.

"Spence, out," she said, stifling a giggle.

Spencer immediately dropped the towel and Griffin scrambled to keep himself covered while he adjusted it. He flicked the end of the towel in the air as he looped it around his waist, but the woosh of the towel in the air was too much for Spencer to bear. The dog dropped into a play bow, latched on to what he considered to be the world's best tug toy, and wrenched it completely off Griffin with a powerful head shake.

"Nooo," Griffin shouted, folding himself in half and covering his groin with his hands. Spencer shook his head and whipped the towel back and forth just a few steps beyond him, but Griffin seemed to realize that he'd need to move one of his hands away from his junk in order to grab it. He stood frozen, hunched over with one foot on the stair behind him, and seemed to weigh his options.

"I'm, uh . . . I'm going to . . ." Griffin stammered as he started to back up the stairs slowly, trying to maintain his cool while completely, gloriously, unabashedly *naked*.

"Spence, out," Justine said, trying to keep from staring at the carved-marble perfection that was Griffin's naked body. She'd never been a leg woman, but the muscular grooves along the sides of his thighs had her mesmerized. He had to be a runner.

She knew that if she laughed Spencer would amp up his performance and start parading the towel around the apartment like he was a lion with a dead antelope in his jaws. Spencer looked at her for a moment, towel in his mouth, and seemed to contemplate his next step. Normally at home he'd have listened to her immediately. Spencer was so good at "drop" and "out" that he'd done it with chicken bones on the sidewalk and the slow squirrel he'd managed to snatch off a branch. But once again, the rules were different in Griffinville. Spencer was back in his old hood and up to his old tricks. Walk fast, play hard, and it seemed he'd added a new one: ignore Justine.

"Spencer Aloysius Bartholomew Becker the First. Are you being serious right now? *Out.*"

Justine never yelled at her dog, but on the rare occasions when he had trouble focusing on her she broke out his full name. It did the trick; he dropped the towel at the base of the stairs and trotted to her.

"Nice one," she whispered to him as she gave him a quick rubdown. "Keep him on his toes, okay?"

Griffin carefully pivoted sideways, squatted lower, and grabbed the towel, then wrapped it around his waist. He marched upstairs without a word.

Justine did a quick anatomy roundup of his back as he went up. Yup, there were the traps, delts, and lats, all present and all perfect.

She tucked her suitcase next to the couch and pulled out her phone to get a quick store-status check from Sienna. She responded with a photo of the daily total so far, and Justine sighed and shoved the phone back in her pocket.

Griffin barged down the stairs five minutes later as if nothing had happened, looking travel ready in a Black Watch plaid button-down. She was happy she'd worn her slim-fit jeans and fanciest Athleta hoodie.

"So, your flight was delayed!" Justine said in an attempt to ignore the accidental nudity they'd just shared.

"Yeah." He ran his hand through his still-damp hair. "Sorry I'm still here. I didn't think you were getting in until later."

"Please, it's your place. Whatever!" She giggled and hated the sound of it.

"I'm actually glad we're here at the same time."

"Really?"

"Yeah, there are a few quirks in this place, so I can show you them rather than making you read my anal-retentive guestbook. Follow me." He beckoned her.

"First, the light switches." He pointed to the panel by the door. "None of these work. I always try to leave that little lamp over there on when I go out at night, because otherwise you're walking into total darkness when you get back."

He pointed to the end table he'd pulled his red Spencer file from the first time they met. She wondered if it was still there or if he'd moved it to his safe-deposit box.

"Got it. Little lamp."

"The TV is right there." He pointed at what looked like an abstract print of black-and-white splotches on the brick wall opposite the couch, then picked up the remote. "This button controls everything.

"Kitchen next," he said, continuing the tour. "This entire building has waste disposals that we absolutely cannot use. I repeat, do not use this thing." He pointed in the sink. "The super has promised to get the system fixed for months, but no luck yet. He sucks." Griffin pointed at the switch. "It's taped over, just in case you come home wasted and forget."

She smirked. "Not likely."

"Bathroom." He pointed at the door. "Nothing too quirky in there, but the knob is weird. You have to turn it and lift up at the same time; otherwise it sticks." He demonstrated the secret knob handshake.

"Okay, got it." She nodded.

Griffin pointed to the stairs. "Loft next."

He followed Spencer up the metal stairs and she took the opportunity to stare at his ass. His Levi's fit exceptionally well.

"My bed."

She swallowed hard. Why did he make the two words sound like a command? Spencer seemed to agree and jumped on.

"Weird," he said as Spencer rolled around on top of his gray duvet. "I didn't allow him in bed when he was with me."

"You didn't? You missed out on some prime snuggling. This guy spoons like a pro. Was it a germ thing?"

The corner of Griffin's mouth kicked up and he paused. "No, it was because not all of my houseguests liked threesomes."

It was his first mention of other women, and Justine felt her face go hot.

"I'll have clean sheets on when you come," he continued. "All I ask is that you strip the bed before you leave."

Strip. Bed. Again with the commands.

"Of course."

"Last thing is the temperature control." He pointed to the thermostat near his bed. "Stupidest place to put this thing up here, but whatever. Obviously with a high ceiling and this being a small space it's hard to regulate the temperature for the whole place. I have it programmed, but if you need to override it you have to push the reset button twice."

Griffin kept talking and Justine zoned out. He obviously knew computers and technology and it struck her that he might have cameras hidden around the apartment. She'd seen the reports about Airbnb owners who secretly recorded their occupants. Was he a creeper? Or would he be using the footage to compile evidence against Justine for ownership of Spencer? She continued nodding along as Griffin gave her a lengthy programming lesson, peeking in the corners of the apartment to look for cameras whenever he turned back to the thermostat.

"Got it?" he asked.

"Yes, of course." Justine nodded. "Very straightforward."

Spencer stopped rolling on the bed and let out a little whine.

"He needs to go out," Justine said.

"His signal hasn't changed."

For a second Griffin's face looked sad, like he was remembering what life used to be like when Spencer was Leo, so Justine hustled him off the bed.

"Let's go for a walk, bud," she said.

Griffin looked at his watch. "I'll come too; I have time. If you don't mind."

"Sure."

She didn't want to admit that she *did* mind. How many Leo fans were they going to run into during the walk around the neighborhood, and how many times would she have to explain that no, Leo/Spencer wasn't back for good, and yes, she was an ogre for keeping him away from his birth father?

"Wanna go?" Griffin asked Spencer in an excited voice. "Do you wanna *go*?"

Spencer stood up and turned in three rapid circles, then paused in a play bow. It was a reaction she'd never seen, and yet another reminder that Spencer had lived a lifetime with Griffin before he ever found his way to her.

chapter seventeen

Justine zipped up her jacket against the early evening chill. Griffin had thrown on a light gray wool overcoat that instantly made his jeans and plaid shirt look dressy, and for a second she realized that the three of them looked like a happy family going for their evening walk.

"He's not pulling." Griffin gestured to Spencer. "Back in the day we'd be at the end of the block by now."

"That was one of the first things we worked on, because he's *strong.*"

Griffin laughed. "He is. I considered walks with him part of my workout."

They headed down the sidewalk in silence for a few minutes and watched Spencer mark every pole and garbage can they passed. Justine peeked in the windows of the old brick buildings lining his street and tried to keep her envy in check that Griffin lived in such a cool neighborhood.

"How long have you been in Brooklyn?"

"I moved to Manhattan right after college, then made my way out here four years ago. Since I'm not tied to an office in the city I figured I could get more for my money here. What about you? How long have you been in Rexford?"

"Four years." She sighed.

"Why do you sound like you're talking about a prison sentence?" He bumped his shoulder into hers. "Rexford's awesome. And based on my Instagram stalking, so is your shop. Most people dream of that kind of life."

He was right. Visitors came into Tricks & Biscuits all the time and asked her advice about opening shops in their own hometowns.

"Rexford is a magical place. I really like it there."

Griffin raised an eyebrow at her. "Sounds like you left a 'but' off of that sentence."

"But." She nodded and continued. "I know I'm not going to stay there. It's not my forever."

"So, you'll close your shop and do what? And go where?"

"I *hate* the thought of closing Tricks & Biscuits." She groaned. "Can we not talk about it?" The lease was in her office, where she'd left it, still unsigned.

"Okay, without talking about that part of it, what do you want to do next?"

They were walking by a lit basketball court crowded with people of all ages playing. Spencer paused at the gate and watched.

"That's the problem," she answered, staring at the players taking shots from the free-throw line. "I'm not sure. Definitely something with dogs, but I don't know what. Hopefully, this Ted Sherman show will work out. Maybe I can try dog training full-time." She shrugged.

"You're not really a planner, are you?" Griffin mused.

She smiled at him. "It's that obvious?"

"It is, mainly because I've got my five-year trajectory mapped out and my ten-year trajectory in draft form, and I've been making them since I was in high school."

"Impressive. I wish I could do that, but it's not in my DNA. My mom is a free spirit and I guess she rubbed off on me."

"I'd happily take 'free spirit' over 'benign neglect,' but that's a story for another day," Griffin said.

"Yikes," Justine answered, unsure how to acknowledge his candor.

A woman walking a gray pit bull passed by and the dogs gave each other wags of greeting.

"Can I ask what's on your five-year plan? Maybe I'll get inspired to do one."

Spencer found a small grassy patch under a tree and unloaded a pile. Griffin automatically tapped his hands to his jacket pockets for a bag and seemed to realize that he was off doody duty. Justine pulled one from her pocket and he took it from her hand.

"A gentleman never allows a lady to clean up poo in his presence. Allow me."

Griffin took care of the mess and they continued walking.

"Back to that five-year plan," Justine said. She was actually curious to hear what was on his agenda. "Do you have the typical 'get married, move to the suburbs, and live happily ever after' plotline?" Her pulse inexplicably sped up at the thought of him finding his white picket fence.

"Oh no, nope. At least not for a while. I made a commitment to myself that I wasn't going to get seriously involved with anyone while I'm on my trajectory. I don't have the time or, to be honest, the inclination to be in a relationship. Especially with how much I travel. It never works out."

"Got it," she replied. It made their arrangement easier knowing that they were both unavailable in their own ways.

"What about you and that boyfriend of yours?" he asked. "When's the wedding?"

She laughed. "Oh him? Fake, so you wouldn't murder me the first time I met you. I broke up with my last boyfriend a while ago."

"Aha," he said, arching his eyebrow and stroking his chin. "Let the murdering begin!"

Justine laughed. "My bodyguard might have other ideas about that," she said, pointing at Spencer. "I'm still waiting for the specifics of this trajectory thing. So far I'm not hearing anything concrete."

"Okay, okay. My goal is to make director level within the next year, and I'm on track for that, and senior VP by year five. Then I'll move to a bigger place here in Brooklyn. Learn how to ride a motorcycle and then maybe buy one. And before I knew about Leo being okay, getting another dog was in the plan, too."

Once again she was reminded that the Leo love affair wasn't over for him.

"So now that you've seen him, you're *not* thinking about getting a new dog?"

Griffin looked at her out of the corner of his eye. "I don't know, should I?"

She stopped in her tracks. "Hold up a minute. Is all of this being nice to me and letting me use your apartment just a long game to get Spencer back? Because if that's the case, we need to have a serious—"

He took two quick steps so that he was standing in front of her and there was no way for her to avoid looking into his eyes. "No, that's *not* why I offered my apartment." He studied her. "You really don't trust me, do you?"

"Think about the first time we met." Her voice strained a pitch higher than normal. "Should I, based on what you did?"

"Okay." He nodded. "Fair, maybe I came on a little strong when I first found out he was okay. But may I also point out, ladies and gentlemen of the jury, that since then I've bought you a gourmet seafood dinner, offered to pay Spencer's vet bill, and am now putting you up in my crib?"

"Oh, come on, are you trying to buy me off to make up for acting like an asshole? Because it's not just about money," she scoffed.

Griffin laughed. "It's *always* about money."

She felt the simmer turn into a boil. "Seriously? If you feel like that, how much will it take for you to forget about Spencer? What did you pay to adopt him and vet him? I'll give you the money right now, we'll be square, and I'll take him back to Rexford."

"And where will you stay to keep Spencer from getting sick before the show?" he asked calmly, his eyes traveling around her face. "According to what you just told me, you're betting your future on this job."

Justine squinted at him. "I'll figure it out."

They stood in the middle of the sidewalk glaring at each other. Spencer stood between them, glancing up with a worried expression.

"Stop," Griffin said, reaching out to grasp her arm gently. "Justine, I'm not trying to buy you off, or steal Spencer back, or whatever absolutely shitty thing you think I'm up to. I'm trying to help you."

"Why?" It came out in an angry burst.

"Because I love Spencer and I want to help him." He shrugged. "And by association, I guess that means I also want to help you."

They both looked at Spencer, who wagged at them as if trying to fan the tension from the air.

"Do you still want him back?"

"Yes." The word pierced the air. Griffin continued before Justine could respond. "How could I not? I still miss him, every day. And yes, I'll admit that it's hard seeing him with you."

Justine took a step away from Griffin, pulling Spencer along with her.

Griffin moved so that he was right in front of her again, closer than before. "*But* I also see how good you are together. The way he looks at you, listens to you . . . he wasn't like that with me. We were best buddies. You two? You're soul mates."

She cleared her throat and sniffled.

Standing in the half shadow of the streetlamp with his hands in his coat pockets, Griffin looked even more striking than normal. For a moment, the city slipped away, and it was just the two of them in a pool of light on a cold fall night, trying to navigate the parameters of canine custody and other unnamed emotions.

Griffin broke the spell first. "He's empty now, and I've got a plane to catch. Why don't we head back?"

"Yup, okay," Justine said, blinking fast like a hypnotist had just snapped her out of a trance. She stopped walking abruptly and he continued for a few steps before he realized that she wasn't right next to him. "I haven't said thank you yet," she said softly, almost to herself. "Oh my God, that's such a pet peeve of mine. Griffin, thank you so much for allowing us to stay in your apartment."

"You actually did say thank you, about a dozen times. And you're welcome. To be honest, I like thinking of you and Spencer snuggling up at my place. Makes me happy, in a weird way."

"Me too," Justine said, realizing that it wasn't weird at all.

chapter eighteen

Hey, excuse me. See your shadow? Could you move out of the light?"

Justine had Spencer in a sit-stay and was waiting for Ted to give her the cue for a second time. She didn't hear the white-haired man standing near her with the camera strapped to his chest until he had to yell at her.

"Hey, you! Your shadow! What's your name again?"

Justine jumped. "Who me? I'm Justine."

The man pointed to the uneven brick road that Spencer was about to run across. "See how your shadow is coming into that light? You need to find a new place to stand."

She'd only been on set for twenty minutes and was already overwhelmed. The air felt too still, like they were all in a vacuum, and the lighting ranged from shadowy off set to almost blindingly bright in front of the cameras. Every single person in the room was waiting for her and for Spencer to prove they were worthy of being there, and so far they were off to an absolutely shitty start.

Justine had initially been relieved that their first scene was a simple one; all Spencer had to do was run away from the camera and around a corner on the indoor set that looked like a street scene. It was a simple placement trick they'd done millions of times in tons of different environments. But for whatever reason, Spencer kept pausing and turning back to her instead of dashing around the corner without hesitating.

The first time he tried it, everyone on set snickered because he looked so cute when he twisted his head and looked back, and a little hiccup was no big deal. But the second time he did it wrong she felt the room shift, and someone said, "Here we go," quietly.

"Um, they told me to stand here. Maybe I can lean back?" She demonstrated what she meant and watched her shadow move out of the beam of light that was supposed to be the glow of a streetlamp.

"Yeah, that works," the guy said, watching the ground.

Ted walked over to her clutching the little stack of paper that he never seemed to be without. "Is he ready to try again?"

She looked down at Spencer, who had moved into a sphinx-down with his head resting on top of his paws.

"I think so. I'm sorry we messed up the first few shots, it's just that he—"

"It's his first day, don't worry about it," Ted answered in a way that made some of her stress disappear. "We built in a little extra time for him. Let's just see what happens, okay?"

Something banged and clattered behind the cameras, and Spencer jumped up, already on edge.

"Hold the work, people," someone shouted. Several crew members repeated the phrase and it echoed through the building like a game of telephone.

Justine knelt next to Spencer and massaged his forehead.

She saw Malcolm in a gray Humane Federation hoodie a few feet off set punching the screen of his tablet, and she wondered what he was saying about their performance so far.

"Let's go again," Ted said as he settled behind the monitors. He'd told Justine that they were capturing Spencer's performance on two different cameras from two different angles, which meant that she had a limited space to work with him and remain unseen. Add in the shadow issue and she was even more screwed.

Her whole body was tensed like she was waiting for a starter pistol to go off.

"And . . . action!"

"Wait, I'm sorry." Justine squinted past the bright lights to the Ted-shaped outline in the shadows. "Do you mind if I show him where his mark is again? It's been a few minutes and I want him to nail it this time."

"Did she really just call a cut?" the white-haired camera guy muttered.

"Of course, really quickly," Ted said. "Stay rolling, everyone."

Justine hustled Spencer into a stand and encouraged him to run with her to the hidden marker around the corner, half of an index card. As they got closer she stopped moving so he walked the last few steps alone and said, "Spence, place!"

Spencer walked to it like he was heading for the electric chair.

In that moment Justine realized that every single person on the set, which at last count had been more than thirty, was waiting for her and her dog to do their job. She felt sweat beading along her back from the hot lights as well as the stress of not knowing what the fuck she was doing, which everyone else was slowly figuring out as well.

She tried to stay upbeat for Spencer. "You've got this, buddy. I *know* you can do it!"

They jogged back to their starting point. "Okay, we're ready."

"And . . . *action!*"

"Spencer, place!" she said with so much enthusiasm that she felt like a cheerleader. She pointed that he needed to run and smiled at him like a maniac, hoping it would be enough to coax a real performance out of him.

Spencer licked his lips and watched Justine for a moment, then headed for the spot with his head hanging low, as cheerful as a funeral director.

Once he rounded the corner and was out of sight Justine said, "Wait!" so he'd stay in position. She looked back at Ted, who was staring at the monitor.

"Okay, that was great. Nice work. But let's try it again. I need more enthusiasm. Remember, he senses that Anderson is on the way back and he's running to meet him, so he's upbeat. Is he okay to try it again?"

Justine flicked a glance at Malcolm, who was motionless in the shadows.

"Yes, I think he is." She whistled and Spencer meandered back to her.

They repeated the action two more times and Spencer continued to act like he was being tortured. Malcolm migrated closer to the edge of the set with a furrowed brow.

"You know what?" Ted said from his spot behind the monitors. "Let's move on. Can we do his sad reaction shots now? I think he's in the right frame of mind for that kind of action, right, Justine?"

She wanted to cry. They were blowing it.

No, *she* was blowing it.

It wasn't that Spencer was overwhelmed being on set or surrounded by strangers, because he'd been owning the room prior to getting started. It was Justine's nerves that were jamming his signals and impacting his reactions. He knew her so well that he could sense that something was off.

"Yes, he can do those, no problem," Justine said, crossing her fingers. "He'll get those right."

She noticed that Anderson, Taylor, and Claire were standing near the monitors in costume, looking like gorgeous time travelers.

"Moving on," Ted said. "Reset, everyone."

Justine walked off set as the crane camera swooped up and the various camera and sound people shifted positions. She was still learning the lingo, which meant that half of what was said was like a foreign language. She relied on context clues to figure out what was happening. "Reset" seemed to mean get in position for a new shot, so Justine stood in the shadows with Spencer and watched the set choreography out of the way.

"There's my guy," a voice boomed behind her.

Anderson strode up to them with his massive outstretched arms straining the fitted black blazer, his eyes on Spencer. Ever since the cheese make-out moment, Justine couldn't look at Anderson the same way. There were no butterflies being around the biggest action star ever, just the odd memory of him desperately needing to get to second base with her dog.

Justine watched as Spencer shrank away like Anderson was a game warden on a mission.

"What's wrong with him?" Anderson asked as he bent over and put his face right in front of Spencer's. "Where's my wag, buddy? You don't like me no more?" He'd slipped into his character voice.

"He's carsick," Justine lied, worried that Anderson would take Spencer's lack of affection personally. "It has nothing to do with you, I promise."

It was a convenient fib. Nearly everyone had seen his epic puke moment at the table read, so it made sense that it might happen again.

"I watched his scene and he looked miserable." Anderson was petting Spencer gently under the chin, and Spencer wagged the tip of his tail as a halfhearted thanks. "Are you sure he's up for this gig?"

She froze. As an executive producer on *The Eighteenth*, Anderson had the power to have them thrown off the show. If he decided that they weren't right, all he had to do was hint at it to Ted and they'd be out of a job.

"He's definitely up for it; this is just beginner's blues. It won't happen again, we promise."

"Well, all right, then. No screwing up no more, ya hear? Or it's off to the unemployment line for ya!" Anderson said in Izzy's voice, wagging his finger at Spencer.

Justine gulped as she realized that their future was going to be decided in the next scene.

chapter nineteen

O h, Teen. Look at your face. What will fix it, wine? Or tequila?" Ruth asked as she ushered Justine through her
front door.

"Both," Justine answered glumly. "And whatever mood-
altering drugs you have in your medicine cabinet."

Ruth pulled her into a hug. "I'm sure it wasn't as bad as you
think. Sit." She gestured to her couch and Justine trudged over,
then collapsed in a ball. Freida hopped up next to her and scaled
Justine's hip, then tiptoed up to her cheek and delivered a tiny
kiss.

"I'm ready to listen when you're ready to talk," Ruth called
from the kitchen as she rattled glasses.

"Where is everyone?" Justine asked with her head half-
buried in throw pillows.

"Patrick and Dillon are in the basement playing that new
Star Wars game and Alice is at a sleepover." She walked back
into the front room carrying two massive goblets of red wine
and a bottle of tequila with two shot glasses stacked on the cap.
"The doctor is in. Start talking."

Justine finally sat up as she took the wineglass. "It sucked. *I* sucked. I choked! I think the hugeness of what we were doing finally hit me and I couldn't think straight. I did everything wrong. Obviously, Spence could tell, so he was all tentative and weird because *I* was."

"Was he able to pull off any of it?" Ruth asked as she settled in the cozy chair across from Justine.

"Yeah, thank God. They took some close-ups of him doing sad expressions and twisting his head back and forth like he was listening to something, and he did great with those scenes. Then we were done for the day."

"Which means you finished strong."

Justine considered it, then nodded. "If not, I'm convinced they would've fired us. The Humane Federation rep was right there the whole time, and he is so freaking intimidating. It's bad enough that everyone else on set is watching, but Malcolm was, like, *studying* my every move."

"Why?"

"To make sure I'm not forcing Spencer into performing or doing anything unsafe." Justine threw her head back against the couch and closed her eyes. "Ruth, I don't think we can do this. We're not qualified. Or should I say, *I'm* not qualified."

"Okay. Then quit."

Justine opened one eye. "Seriously?"

"Life's too short to have that much stress on a daily basis. Quit." Ruth tucked her leg underneath her and smoothed her pink floral muumuu.

"But . . . it's the chance of a lifetime. I can't just walk away. Maybe it'll be better from now on since I know what to expect? I actually learned a ton, even when it was awful. I think I can

figure out ways to avoid some of the crap we dealt with today."
She paused. "I bet I'll be more relaxed, and Spencer will do so
much better next time."

Ruth raised one eyebrow and took a triumphant swig of
wine.

"*Damn* you! How do you do that?"

"I think that's a record: it only took three words to get you to
step up. You can totally do it. If you quit I'm never going to talk
to you again."

Justine groaned. "Why am I so predictable?"

"Not predictable, consistent. And one of my favorite traits of
yours is a hardheaded inability to back down from a challenge.
Exhibit A: Sienna told me you ran Lockwood Overlook."

Justine scrunched up her face. "No big deal." She waved her
hand to indicate that she didn't want to talk about it.

"It *is* a big deal. We don't have to get into it, but I just want
you to know that I'm proud of you. Here's to many more trail
runs." Ruth raised her glass to Justine, then took a sip. "Back to
the real gossip. How was spending the night at that guy's
apartment?"

Justine hid a smile. Ruth knew almost everything about her,
but not the fact that Griffin was starting to feel like something
other than just "that guy."

"Fine. Aside from the fact that I couldn't figure out the temperature control, so I sweated the whole night. Oh! Speaking of,
I said I would text him about how it went today. Gimme a sec."

She pulled her phone out and tried to figure out a way to
spin their first day on set into a happier reality than what they'd
dealt with. She settled on sending a photo of Spencer grinning
next to Anderson in his Izzy costume.

His reply came a minute later. CAPTAIN ZALTAN AND SPEN-CER TOGETHER! Ahgrhrh! with an exploding-brain emoji. Did it go okay?

Justine looked at Freida curled up in her lap. Honesty, or more spin?

Not great tbh. I screwed up, Spencer did his best.

That sucks. But I bet you'll kill it next time. You 2 are an amazing team. He attached a photo she didn't know he'd taken the night they were out for a walk. It was from behind and she and Spencer were midstride with Justine in profile smiling down at him. His front paws were a few inches off the ground and he almost looked like he was dancing with joy. Most important, her ass looked amazing. It was a great shot.

Why are there flowers here? Did someone send them to you? Griffin texted.

She sent a crying-with-laughter emoji followed with I wish! I couldn't resist bodega flowers to brighten up the apartment. Enjoy.

He texted a photo of his hand flashing a thumbs-up in front of the bouquet of sunflowers.

Justine set her phone in her lap and stared out the window. How refreshing it was to get a message of support after she'd told him about the bad day instead of an inquisition of exactly what she'd done wrong.

"Why are you smiling?" Ruth asked.

"What? I'm not."

"You are. What's going on?"

Justine felt heat flood her cheeks. "Nothing."

Ruth leaned forward and studied Justine. "Oh my God, you *like* him! Sienna called it!"

"I absolutely do not. I'm still on a dating hiatus. Besides, he's not interested in getting involved with anyone because he has a *trajectory*." Mentioning it made her insides twist a little.

"How would you know that?" Ruth's eyes were shining.

"It came up. We took Spencer for a walk and talked a little."

Ruth nodded and squinted her eyes. "Aha, okay. Thus far we've had a candlelit dinner, a romantic walk, and you spent the night at his place. Sounds like the beginning of something to me."

"Excuse me, but there was no candlelight at the dinner but there was an annoying art bro, the romantic walk was actually a potty break for Spencer, and I spent the night at his place . . . alone." Justine mimed a mic drop.

"But *could* you like him?"

Justine shook her head vigorously. "We are so different."

"Like how?"

"Like he's perfect and I'm a total fuckup. He's got a five-year plan; I own a shop that's had two zero-dollar days in the past month. He can pack for a weeklong trip in a carry-on; I drag half my closet for an overnight. He's got abs; I've got this." She patted her tummy.

"Wait, *how* do you know he's got abs? You've been leaving a lot of details out, I think." Ruth tapped her bloodred nails on the side of her wineglass impatiently.

Visions of his accidental free show danced through her head. Normally Justine told Ruth every detail about her life, but she felt weird talking about Griffin.

"Don't get any crazy ideas. That first day I went to his apartment, his shirt came up when he was taking off his sweater. And he is definitely not into me; I overheard him call me a less-cute Reese Witherspoon."

"Oooh, no way! What a dick! He went full Darcy on you. 'Not handsome enough to tempt me.' Does Spencer still love him?"

"Spencer loves everyone, even the guy who let him run away."

Ruth sucked in her breath. "Harsh."

A shout of victory echoed up from the basement.

"How's Dillon these days? I haven't seen him in ages."

Ruth rolled her eyes. "He's a preadolescent nightmare. Please hurry up and marry that guy and have kids so you can experience the joys of parenthood."

"I told you, not happening."

Ruth snorted. "Talk to your favorite local high priestess. She pulled tarot cards on you two. It's happening."

chapter twenty

Ferrets need hats?" Sienna asked, holding up the toy ferret display model wearing a jaunty blue beret.

Justine shrugged. "Not my jurisdiction, but if I had a ferret I'd be down for some hat photo ops."

They were at SuperPet, the annual national trade show for pet retailers at the Javits Center, and Justine was having a hard time focusing on the plethora of pet products surrounding them.

"Good point," Sienna replied. "Speaking of . . . take this." She handed the toy ferret to her and fished her phone out of the pocket of her overalls, then pointed it at Justine. "Smile!"

"Sienna, no, I look gross." She held the toy so it covered her face.

"Stop, you always look good. I'd kill for your cheekbones. Hold it up. Kiss it."

"Gross, who knows where this thing has been."

Sienna sighed. "You have me doing the T&B social media for a reason, so let me do it! A toy ferret in a hat is cute and weird and shareworthy. Do it for the 'gram, okay?"

Justine placed the toy next to her cheek, pointed at it with her other hand, and gave an exaggerated smile.

"Perfect level of cheese. Love it." Sienna showed her the picture and all Justine could see was bad hair and worse lighting.

They walked on through the show, sidestepping overeager sales reps trying to sell them revolutionary kitty litter and organic parrot chew rings.

"I made a list," Sienna said, pulling out her phone again. "This trade show is overwhelming, and I thought it would be best to map out our go-to vendors; then we can float and check out extra stuff if we want to. I also have a wish list of restock items since tons of vendors have sales going on during the show."

Justine pushed down her credit card worries and gave Sienna a side hug as they strolled. "You're amazing, you know that?"

"Aw, thanks!" Sienna squeezed her back. "And you're a great boss."

Sienna paused to admire a waterproof hoodie, not noticing the booth she was next to.

"Wait, stand there," Justine exclaimed. "Don't turn around!"

Sienna was photo-op-worthy herself in her overalls over a tie-dyed boatneck top, with her hair in a high, messy ponytail. The fact that she didn't realize that she was in front of a giant tank filled with live feeder crickets made the image that much better, so Justine pulled out her own phone and snapped a quick photo.

"Look how cute you are," she said, showing Sienna the photo. "This is going up on the employee-of-the-month wall."

Sienna squealed and ran a few steps away when she realized that the wall of bugs was right behind her.

"Speaking of employee of the month . . ." Sienna said once she'd calmed down from the fright.

"What? You actually want me to make a wall dedicated to you? Don't tempt me, because I'll do it."

"No." Sienna shook her head. "But maybe we should talk head count?"

Sienna had asked about hiring someone else in passing before, but each time it came up Justine managed to change the subject to avoid getting deep about it. The thought of more head count led to financial gymnastics and a stomachache. As it was, she was barely paying herself.

They walked on and accidentally turned down the grooming-supplies aisle, nearly running into a standard poodle decked out with rainbow fur and a Mohawk. Between the barking, buzzing from clippers, and chatter from shoppers, the row was mango-scented chaos.

"Wait a sec." Justine stopped in her tracks in front of a booth filled with scissors. "Are you quitting?"

"No, oh my God, no! I love T&B, you know that. Plus, it's a great pipeline for Like Family. Anytime someone mentions going on a trip I slip them a business card." Sienna winked at her. "No, I'm talking about bringing in a floater employee, like for those times when I have a pet-sitting emergency, or when my cycle and the moon cycle are out of whack." She shrugged.

"Okay." Justine nodded. "You're right. It's something I should think about."

Justine swallowed hard. Sienna *was* right, but adding someone new would muddy her decision-making process. She was a few days late looking at her numbers, which she blamed on *The Eighteenth* but was actually because she couldn't bear to deal with them. Her first check from the show was still a few weeks away, and once it came it would allow her to pay down some of her bills and consider making some of the changes that Sienna kept suggesting in persistent emails and text messages. But all she really wanted to think about was polishing up Spencer's performance for their next day on set.

"I can help with interviewing, and then training." Sienna seemed to realize that she was pushing and laughed at herself. "Geez, slow your roll, S."

Justine chose her words carefully. "No, that would actually be great, if the time comes. I think you're better at reading people, to be honest." Griffin's face popped into her head. Dimpled, generous, unknowable Griffin.

"Okay . . . what are the next steps?" Sienna asked.

"Next steps are freaking out about this adorable powder puff," Justine exclaimed, thankful that she could change the subject as she made a beeline for a bichon in a booth whose head was groomed into a perfect white circle. "There's your next photo op, Miss Social Media."

They fussed over the adorable dog and Justine made a mental note to add "figure out WTF you're doing with T&B" to the list in the "Get Shit Done" notebook she kept under the cash register. Her to-do list was pages long, with more items getting added than checked off. But it made her feel good to make a little dot and write something that felt important at the time in her messy scrawl.

"So, should we hit the toy aisles now?" Sienna asked. "Best Boy Toys is doing a buy one, get one; can't beat that."

"Sure, we can look," Justine answered, giving the bichon one more pat.

They continued down the aisle surrounded by people carrying oversized tote bags crammed with catalogs and giveaways. Justine had a single postcard from a dog-themed nightlight company in her bag, while Sienna's promotional tote bag was loaded down with every handout she could grab. It was as if Sienna could sense that she was running interference for her boss, who couldn't pretend to be interested in bold collar patterns for dogs on the go.

"Can I ask you a question?" Sienna said tentatively. "It's kind of personal."

They were standing in front of a booth filled with bespoke beef jerky chews displayed on silver platters, with flavors like Teriyaki and Wellington. The smell was nauseating, which meant the treats would be a hit with the four-legged crew.

"Um, yikes? But okay."

Sienna studied Justine's face. "Do you want to close Tricks & Biscuits?"

"Oh, wow," Justine answered because she couldn't think of anything else to say. "You went there. Huh."

She was convinced that she'd hidden her worries, but Sienna was next-level perceptive to the point where Justine almost believed her when she said she had spirit guides whispering in her ear.

"Excuse me," a chipper male sales rep in a black logo shirt interrupted them, holding out a tray of jerky studded with sesame seeds. "Would you like to sample our Wagyu beef treats? It's premium Japanese beef."

"We didn't bring a dog," Justine said, gesturing to the empty ground in front of them.

"It's human grade!" The rep picked up one of the squares and popped it in his mouth. "Delicious!"

Sienna pointed at herself. "Vegan." She pointed at Justine. "Training-wheels vegetarian."

"Understood! But our dogs aren't vegetarian, so allow me to give you these samples and a Waggy You price list, ladies." He handed Sienna a shiny one-sheet with two cello-wrapped bags stapled to it.

Sienna studied the price sheet as they walked away from the booth.

"Three ounces for fifteen dollars *wholesale*? These guys won't be here next year, that's for sure."

Justine gestured to the cluster of tables off the main show floor. "Why don't we sit for a minute?"

Sienna dropped her overstuffed bag on the table with a thud, sat down, and stared at Justine.

The question Sienna had asked before the beef chat hung in the air.

"Obviously, you still want to talk about the future of T&B," Justine said.

"Sorry if that's not my business!" she blurted out as if she'd been waiting for the invitation to discuss it. "It's just a vibe I've been getting lately." She paused. "Well, not just lately. It's been like a year."

"What have you noticed?" Justine was worried that her regulars could also sense that she was pulling back.

"You don't seem, I don't know, *excited* anymore. I mean, it's obvious you still love your customers, but you spend so much time looking at the numbers . . ." She trailed off and shrugged.

Justine sighed and stared off into space. "Yeah, the numbers."

"Is everything okay?"

She was about to launch into her typical spin but realized that Sienna deserved to know the truth of what was going on behind the scenes. "No, it's not. Things are rough."

Sienna met Justine's candor with wide-eyed shock. "Really?"

Justine nodded. "I'm trying to figure everything out right now. But you know I love the shop, right?"

"I do."

"Our customers are the best. And I love serving our little community. But the truth is I'm not doing the numbers I need."

"Well, what about the stuff we've talked about? Going green, adding an online component, changing the footprint to improve the dog food section? Based on my research that could help."

Justine hunched over the table and stared at her hands. "Okay, here's the *truth* truth . . . I'm not sure I want to keep going. I hate the thought of shutting down Tricks & Biscuits, but I also sort of hate the idea of staying there. I'm ready for . . . I don't know?" She shrugged. "My next adventure, I guess?"

Sienna leaned back in her chair with her arms crossed.

"Is that why you haven't signed the lease?"

Justine nodded.

"But what will you do if you close the shop?"

She shrugged. "I'm working on that part."

"When is the lease due?"

"End of next month."

Sienna nodded and stared at the crowds streaming through the trade show. "Okay, then. Got it."

"I'm sorry that I didn't tell you sooner. You deserve to know what's going on. You've been such an important part of the shop. Hell, I probably wouldn't have lasted this long without you!" She laughed, hoping to get a smile out of Sienna, but all she got was a half grin. "I'm not going to leave you high and dry. I promise from this point on I'll keep you in the loop, okay?"

"Thanks. I need to make plans too, you know?" Sienna's blank expression suddenly shifted. "But I've got some ideas coming to me. . . ." She trailed off.

"Uh-oh," Justine replied. "Watch out, universe."

"Yup, you know it." She stood up and heaved the bag onto her shoulder. "Okay, let's do the toy thing now. The Best Boy Toys reps are all hot and I need some of that in my life right now."

"Oh *really*?" Justine drew out the question with a wicked smile. "Because if you're in the market for hot guys, I know of one who'd fit the bill."

Sienna scrunched up her face in confusion. "What? Who?"

"You know who."

"Stop. Luis doesn't like me; he barely even looks at me when I'm at Monty's. If he liked me he would've asked me out by now."

They headed down the toy aisle, dodging a tennis ball being chased by an influencer pug being chased by a camera crew.

"I thought you were evolved," Justine scolded gently. "You could ask him out, you know."

"Blech, whatever," she replied as she got on her knees to snap a photo of Insta-famous Pepper the pug. "I'm evolved, but I still like to be asked out, and he hasn't, so whatever."

Justine felt relieved that they'd moved on from talking about the store, but the nagging questions remained.

chapter twenty-one

A mazing! Fantastic! We got it! Reset, people."

A few crew members applauded, and Justine blushed at Ted's praise. Spencer had just nailed his third take of the day, an easy shot of him cocking his head, running to peer out a window on his hind legs, and then exiting the set. She could tell that Spencer knew he'd done a great job by the way he wagged and danced in place. Justine shot a look at Malcolm where he stood in the shadows and he flashed her a thumbs-up.

They were *back*.

"Justine, go ahead and give Spencer a quick 10-1," Ted said. "We're resetting for Claire's scene; then we're back to you two for the barking reaction shots."

She headed outside with Spencer. She'd figured out what a "10-1" was based on context clues; when one of the guys who worked on the cabling hunched over and complained about needing to 10-1 it was clear that it was code for bathroom break.

They both were doing better than Justine could've hoped for given their disastrous first day on set. He seemed completely at ease, requesting pats from anyone who got within arm's length.

And when it came time to work he was laser focused on her, to the point where she nearly teared up with pride.

Justine threw on her jacket and they made their way past the line of luxury trailers where the actors got ready to the lot across the street from the set. Spencer made a few deposits and they headed back to the set. She noticed Malcolm in his gray uniform hoodie standing a few feet away from the door leaning against the brick wall with his eyes closed and his face turned up to the fall sun.

"Hey, Malcolm," she called to him. Spencer high-stepped in anticipation of greeting one of his favorite new friends.

"There he is," Malcolm said, his eyes on Spencer. "You pulled it out today, little dude. Saved your ass. Yes, you did!" He bent over and placed a massive hand on Spencer's chest and the dog melted with delight.

"He was good, huh?" Justine asked, knowing full well that she was fishing for compliments.

Malcolm looked at Justine and nodded. "I was worried for you two. You should've seen my report from your first day. I heard that they already canned one dog and thought they were ready to get rid of Spence next. But after what I saw today I think you're going to do just fine." He paused. "I'm still worried about that water scene, though."

Justine had read through the script and made a mental note about the location shoot in Maryland where Spencer had to wade into running water, but it was a long way off.

"He loves to swim; we should be fine," Justine replied. "Have you had bad experiences with water stuff in the past?"

"It definitely adds a layer. I've almost had to pull our credentials because of a few rough ones."

Justine knew how critical the "certification of animal safety" badge was for movies and shows that featured animals, and that Malcolm was the key for getting it for *The Eighteenth*.

"Well, I want to do everything possible to keep Spencer safe, so when you're ready to discuss it let me know."

Malcolm nodded. "You got it. We have a little time, though. Let him get his set legs and then we'll move on to the tough stuff. You got this, rookie."

He gave Spencer another scratch before they headed back to the set. Even though they had a while to wait, she was eager to watch the next scene. As much as she hated to admit it and as hard as she tried to ignore it, she was deep in fangirl mode.

"Anyone have eyes on Claire?" someone shouted. "Eyes on Claire?"

The next scene was the preface to what they'd be shooting with Spencer, with the chief bad guy from a rival speakeasy sneaking into the loading dock to "send a message" to Anderson by threatening Claire. Spencer's frantic barking would scare the bad guy off and save the day.

Claire speed-walked to the set trailed by her dresser and makeup person. "Sorry, my fault," she called out in her crisp British accent. "Wardrobe issue."

She was wearing a simple long-sleeve gray knit top that hit her hips, belted at the waist by a simple circle of black fabric, and a black skirt that reached her knees. Her makeup was subdued to show that she was a workingwoman and not a showgirl like Taylor. Even still, she was luminously beautiful. Spencer wagged his tail when she walked by them.

Ted met Claire on the set with another actor named Peter Meer in a tan Homburg hat, white shirt, and black vest. He had a wide, square chin that made him look like a comic book villain. The three spoke quietly for a few minutes.

"Let's just try it, okay?" Ted said in his reassuring way as he walked off set. "No pressure, let's see what happens.

"About to go for picture, people. Lock it up," he said once he was in position behind his monitor.

Justine sat on the ground with Spencer on her lap at a safe distance from the action but still close enough to see everything. She kept having "pinch me" moments. It didn't feel like a job; it felt like a dream come true.

Spencer sprawled across her legs so that his head was on the ground on one side of her body and his tail was on the other. He seemed perfectly at ease with the commotion around him. Everyone he met was his friend, so much so that when the boom-mic guy leaned down to pat Spencer's belly he wagged his tail and lifted his leg to provide greater scratching surface area without even raising his head to see who was doing the scratching.

Peter paced around the set muttering and making menacing gestures. Claire walked in circles, gently waving her hands in front of her as if she were dancing to music on invisible headphones.

"Last-looks fly-in," someone shouted, and a crew of people wearing aprons crowded with brushes, sprays, and lint rollers dashed to the set and made minuscule hair and wardrobe adjustments. Justine saw a woman pat the air above Claire's shoulders. They scuttled off set in a pack.

Justine had read the script and knew that the confrontation between Peter and Claire was filled with unspoken menace, a dance of a blustery gangster and an unflinching woman. It was tense enough to read it on the page, and she was excited to see how they'd translate the written word to reality.

"Pictures up," Ted shouted. "Rolling, rolling, rolling. Roll sound, roll cameras. Slates in."

A woman walked on set and held up a clapper board bright with electronic numbers, said a jumble of letters and numbers, smacked it, and walked off.

"And . . . *action!*"

"Myrna," Peter said as he strode onto the set with a lilt that sounded anything but friendly. "You alone?"

Claire had her back to the man and jumped in shock when he spoke.

"Bill. Why are you here?" The expression on her face was real, and her upper-crusty British accent had been replaced by 1930s New Yorkese.

"Needed to talk to your man, but if he ain't here, you'll do." He paused and eyed her up and down. "You'll do just fine, Myrna."

"He's . . . he's inside. On his way back out; he just had to fetch something." Claire's voice quivered and she walked farther away from him. Only a dozen and a half words and Justine was already awed by her performance. Spencer was less impressed, opting to doze on her lap.

"Izzat so?" Peter asked as he made a wide circle around Claire with a smooth, predatory walk. "What would it take to get him out here in a hurry? A squeal?" He slid closer to her like a dancer and ended up just a foot away from her.

Claire's entire body jolted momentarily, like she'd been hit by an electric pulse. She straightened her back and met Peter's gaze with an unwavering stare.

"I ain't the squealing type. You should know that, *Billy*."

"Hey"—he grabbed Claire's wrist—"don't call me that!"

He held on to her wrist and they stared at each other. The air on set practically vibrated from the tension, and Spencer slowly sat up.

"Get your hands offa me, Billy!" She wrenched her wrist from his grip and pushed him away with every ounce of strength in her tiny frame, causing him to stumble backward for a step.

Justine felt a flutter of panic. The wrist grab and push were new. They weren't in the script.

Spencer had moved from his half-up position to full attention and was watching the action on set as intently as the rest of the room.

"Hey!" Peter roared, so loudly that Spencer jumped. "You pushin' *me*? You pushin' *me*?" He strode toward Claire with his face contorted in rage and she looked around the room in desperation, trying to find some sort of weapon to fend off the fight to come.

Justine's breath came in short spurts. Spencer placed one paw on her leg but never tore his eyes away from what was happening on set.

"Keep going, keep going," Ted coached in a quiet voice.

Peter wrapped his massive hands around Claire's shoulders, and she seemed to crumple into herself like tissue paper. He hunched over so that his eyes were level with hers. "You push me, I push back harder. Your man needs to know that, okay?" He stared at her for a second longer, then practically picked her up off the ground and threw her across the room. She stumbled for half a dozen steps, but she managed to right herself, her eyes blazing at Peter.

A wave of cold swept through Justine. Spencer stood all the way up with his tail high in the air and his weight shifted forward. They both couldn't look away from what was happening on set even though she desperately wanted to. Spencer growled softly, but instead of checking in with him Justine was focused inward, trying to sit normally instead of curling into a ball and hiding.

"I guess you ain't a squealer after all," Peter said to Claire in a quiet voice as he skulked toward her.

Spencer took a step forward, still growling softly.

"Spence," Justine said, swallowing the bile rising in her throat. She placed her hand against his chest, but she knew they couldn't move away or the scene would be ruined, and the one thing she'd learned was that no one wanted to be the reason why the cameras stopped rolling.

Peter raised his hand high in the air as if he were about to backhand Claire, and it was all Spencer needed to see. He took off before Justine could grab his collar and dashed onto the set with his head low and his teeth bared, barking viciously at Peter, who was frozen in place with a grimace of real fear on his face. Justine finally snapped out of her trance and leapt to her feet.

"Spence, *out!*" She realized that she'd whispered the cue. Her voice wasn't working.

Ted dashed toward the set, then flashed his palm at Justine and shook his head.

Spencer stood on the set a few feet away from Peter, alternating between a low growl and his raise-the-dead bark. His lips were pulled back and every one of his glistening teeth looked like a dagger. Justine could tell that he wasn't going to do anything more than threaten Peter, but she still needed to call him off because he *sounded* like he was about to murder him.

"All right, dog, all right," Peter said, still in character with his hands in the air like Spencer was a loaded gun. "Back off."

"Ford," Claire said in an authoritative voice. "I'm fine. That's enough."

Justine finally stumbled back into trainer brain and made a short high-pitched whistle. It was a cue she'd picked up watching sheep farmers working their border collies around the herd, though she rarely used it because she couldn't reliably replicate the sound. She was shocked she had the pucker to do it properly.

Spencer bobbed his head for a second, then collapsed into a down. It was as if a switch had flipped, and he relaxed into the position with a heavy stress pant.

"And . . . *cut*," Ted said softly.

The room exhaled at the same moment, and people applauded softly.

"That was amazing," Peter said to Claire, and they hugged. "I almost shit my pants, though." He kept an eye on Spencer as he embraced his costar.

Claire looked over at Justine and blew her a kiss. "Wonderful work, darling."

Justine called Spencer off set and took a few deep breaths to try to calm herself down. Spencer seemed no worse for wear. He wagged his tail and smile-panted at everyone as if the outburst hadn't even happened. But Justine knew from her research that his cortisol levels were probably soaring. Dog stress was as real as human stress, and it would take hours before he got back to normal.

And they both had trigger-happy baggage in their shared history.

Ted walked over to her beaming. "That was *amazing*. I told Peter and Claire to improvise and take it a little farther than what's on the page, but I never imagined Spencer would join in too. It was incredible; he hit a mark and we had him perfectly in frame! We'll need to do some pickups for close-ups, but we couldn't ask for a better take. *How* did you work that out?"

"We, um . . ." Justine knew she couldn't tell him the truth, that she'd lost control of Spencer for reasons she didn't want to admit to herself. "It was a moment where, um—"

"Doesn't matter." He waved his hand and cut her off. "From now on I need you to run any improv by me to make sure we have coverage on him. But this one worked out great." Ted clapped his hands softly in Spencer's general direction. "Bravo, young man. Go get yourself some lunch meat from crafty. You earned it."

Justine clipped Spencer's leash on and turned to leave the soundstage. She was so focused on getting outside for a head-clearing walk that she almost ran into the wall that was Malcolm's chest.

"What the hell was that?" he asked in an even voice.

"What?" She widened her eyes at him.

"That was real, Justine." He lowered his voice to an angry whisper. "I never saw you give him an attack cue; he just took off barking like a junkyard guard dog."

"I did give him a cue; it was subtle." She hoped her acting was as convincing as Claire's.

"I need to write this up," Malcolm replied, glaring at Justine. "We can't have a dangerous dog on set."

"Malcolm! He's not dangerous, I swear! You have to see that. He got caught up in the moment and he thought Claire was in real trouble. It's because . . ." Justine stopped herself.

"I'm listening." He tilted his head at her with an eyebrow cocked.

Justine felt like she was holding her breath. "Long story. But I swear it won't happen again. Please. You *know* he's a good boy."

He paused and looked down at Spencer, who was smiling up at him and circle-wagging his tail so hard that he looked like a helicopter about to take off.

"One strike, Justine. I'll minimize it on the report, but you better not let anything like that happen again. The *only* reason I'm not making a big deal about this is because he showed restraint, not because I like him. That doesn't matter. I don't normally look the other way on stuff like this. My ass is on the line too."

"Thank you, Malcolm," she replied. Her heart slowed a measure and she exhaled. She placed her hand on his arm. "I promise."

"Don't make me regret this," Malcolm said as he walked off while banging away on his tablet.

chapter twenty-two

H ey, Justine? You still here?"

Justine screamed when she heard Griffin's voice echoing through the apartment. She ran to the railing at the edge of the loft and peeked over and saw him greeting Spencer with bear hugs.

"You scared me! What are you doing here? I thought you weren't getting back until late tonight."

"I guess you didn't get my text," he said as he wrapped his arms around Spencer and lifted him off the ground while the dog licked his face clean. "I got out of Kansas early due to good behavior."

"Welcome home." She bit her tongue to keep from correcting his naughty behavior with Spencer. "I didn't get your text, which is weird. I'm just packing to head out; we'll be gone in ten minutes max." Justine looked over her shoulder at the chaos of her clothing strewn on Griffin's bed and realized that ten minutes was an ambitious estimate.

Griffin trudged up the metal stairs still holding Spencer like a baby.

"Hey," he said, flashing his dimples at her.

"Hey!" Justine replied as she flipped the mess on the bed so that her underwear was hidden on the bottom of the pile. "How was Kansas?"

Griffin launched Spencer onto the bed and peeled off his coat. "Really good. The staff picked everything up fast, and they seemed to love the software. And they all gave me incredible reviews, so that's a plus for the old trajectory." He made a hand movement like a plane ascending.

"Very cool," she replied as she pulled shirts and jeans from underneath Spencer, crumpled them into balls, and shoved them in her suitcase. It seemed like the only two things that mattered to Griffin were her dog and the damn trajectory.

Griffin sat on the edge of the bed. "You're not a light packer, are you?"

"Not even close. And obviously you are."

"I could do it with my eyes closed. It's an art. I can give you lessons if you want . . ."

Justine shook her head. "I need tips for *re*packing. I can never fit everything back in my suitcase."

"I see that." He gestured to the mess. "I guess my main advice would be *pack less stuff.* You're only here overnight."

"I know, but I can never make up my mind about what to wear! Don't forget, I'm on my hands and knees for most of the day, but I'm also surrounded by some of the most beautiful people in the world. My goal is to look sporty, but cute."

Griffin leaned back on his elbow and let his eyes drift up and down her body. "I think you pulled it off, Becker. The Adidas are cool, the jeans look good, the black T-shirt is basic, but the sweater-thingy over top takes it to the next level. Sporty, check. Cute, double check."

Justine's cheeks went pink at the unexpected compliment. She smiled as she threw her pajama bottoms into the suitcase. "Thank you."

"How did Spence do today?" Griffin reached out and scratched Spencer's belly.

"He did okay." Justine started crumpling and throwing faster. "Depends on who you ask."

"What do you mean?"

She didn't want to talk about how Spencer had acted. The more she thought about it, the more upset she felt, because she'd lost control of his behavior *and* her own. Because the sensory memories caught her off guard and overwhelmed her, and she hated herself for letting them get the best of her. And because Griffin was smart enough to keep asking her questions until she told him the whole story.

"He . . . went off script. He improvised." She tossed her hoodie in the suitcase in a heap. "Luckily, he did something that worked for the scene, but it wasn't anything I taught him to do. And it's not a behavior I'd like to see him repeat, to be honest. Let's just say the Humane Federation rep isn't a big fan of Spencer's improv."

"That surprises me, that he did his own thing. You guys seem so in tune with each other."

"Yeah, that was the problem," she said under her breath as she zippered her suitcase.

"What?"

"Nothing." She shook her head. "I'm all set."

She wrenched her suitcase off the bed, and it landed on the ground with a thud.

"If I hadn't seen the contents with my own eyes I'd swear that thing is filled with boulders. Let me carry it down for you."

"I've got it. Do I look that weak?"

"Not at all, but I like to help when I can. *I've* got it," he said, gently taking the handle from her and heading down the steep stairs with the suitcase.

"Spence, come on. Time to go home," Justine called to him. He was likely still exhausted from the outburst on set, and she hated to think about how it would impact him during the ride back to Rexford. As he jumped off the bed she realized too late that he already *was* sort of home, but both he and Griffin ignored the comment.

"Do you want some water for the road?" Griffin asked as he parked her suitcase by the door.

"Water would be great, thanks," she answered as she grabbed her laptop and various cords.

Spencer stood in the middle of the apartment and glanced from Griffin in the kitchen to Justine packing up. Rather than going to either one of them, he sat down and watched with his head hanging and his ears pressed flat.

"Hey, don't forget your apples. These'll be good for the trip." Griffin pointed at the bowl on the counter filled with massive pinkish red stunners.

"No, those are for you," Justine replied. "We picked them up at the farmers' market yesterday. I figured you'd be hungry if you got in late tonight. I left some goat cheese in the fridge and a loaf of crusty bread too."

He stopped in his tracks. "Justine, you didn't have to do that. Thank you. Why don't you stay and have some before you head out?"

She paused and pulled her phone out of her back pocket. She was hungry and it sounded like the best idea ever, but it was already close to eight. She had to be back behind the counter at T&B the next day, and she wanted to get home for a good night's sleep after the stressful day.

"I should really go. Besides, you're probably tired—you don't need us underfoot here."

"You wouldn't be underfoot. I'd like the company." He shifted gears quickly. "I don't get to see Spence enough; it would be a treat to hang with him."

Spencer perked up at the mention of his name.

Once again it felt like they were tiptoeing dangerously close to Netflix-and-chill territory, which didn't make sense given that he'd blatantly said he wasn't looking for a relationship. But then again, wasn't Netflix and chill, by definition, *not* a relationship?

"Stay," he said, grabbing three apples and expertly juggling them. "I'll cut them into slices, and it'll feel like kindergarten."

She laughed. "You really know how to tempt a lady." But he did, because he looked even more adorable trying to keep the apples in the air and hold a conversation with her at the same time.

"Stay, just for a little bit, so you can drive home with a full stomach. You're wasting away. You need nourishment." He stopped juggling, held a single apple out to her, and deployed the dimples.

But Justine knew exactly what was going to happen if she didn't walk out the door.

He'd get her a drink, and they'd sit at the bar in his kitchen tearing off hunks of bread and coating them in goat cheese, and she'd eat the apple slices he'd cut for her and drink a *little* too much red wine considering she had to drive. They'd talk and laugh, and Spencer would do something silly, and Griffin would do something naughty with Spencer, and she'd scold Griffin, not Spencer, and they'd pretend fight, and it would lead to the perfect first kiss she couldn't stop thinking about every time she was in Griffin's presence.

No.

He had his trajectory; she had her hiatus.

"I can't, I'm sorry. Lots to do at home. Plus, he's tired." She pointed to Spencer, who had curled up in a ball on the floor.

"Okay, no problem. Maybe another time?"

He looked hopeful, so she nodded.

"I'm going to walk you to your car."

"It's a safe neighborhood; you said so yourself. We're fine, honestly."

"Then pretend it's because I want to walk Spence. Let's go." He was already putting on his moto jacket and halfway out the door with her suitcase before she managed to get the leash on Spencer.

Once on the street she wished she'd agreed to stay a little longer. It was a freezing night, and Griffin's cozy apartment was a much better option than two hours in the car with a drooling dog. "I'm down here a block or so." She pointed as they started walking.

Justine rounded the corner and could see the paper tucked beneath her wiper from half a block away. When they got to her car she realized that she had *two* parking tickets.

"Damn."

"Ah, the street sweeping got you. Sorry, I should've told you about that. Give them to me; I'll take care of it."

"Not necessary," she said, standing a little straighter. "But thanks."

She handed the leash to Griffin and maneuvered her suit-case into the Mini's tiny trunk. When she reached out to take the leash back from him he was looking past her, studying her car.

"What's wrong?"

"I hate to tell you, but parking tickets are the least of your worries."

He pointed to her rear tire, which looked like it had melted into the pavement.

chapter twenty-three

"Explain to me how it's safe for you to drive a ten-year-old car without a spare tire?" Griffin asked.

"Minis don't have room for spare tires!" Justine sputtered at him. "Plus, that's a run-flat tire. I think I can still drive on it." She walked over to the tire and pushed at it with her pointer finger.

"No, that's a *flat* flat tire. You're not running anywhere." He sighed and looked up at the sky. "It's getting late. There's no way you're going to find a garage open tonight that has the right kind of tire in stock. Do you have AAA?"

"No. Damn it!" Justine exclaimed. Spencer walked over and bumped her leg with his nose as if he knew that petting him would help make her feel better. "Shit-shit-shit."

"You could take an Uber maybe?" Griffin suggested.

Justine was already scrolling through the app with her eyes wide. "Yeah, that's not an option."

"I'll take care of it."

"Absolutely not; you're already doing way too much to help

us." Justine shoved her hands in her jacket pockets and groaned in frustration. "This *sucks*!"

"Just come back to my place and we'll figure out what to do. It's too cold to stay outside, and staring at your tire won't blow it back up."

"No, that's okay, we'll figure it out. Don't worry about us."

Griffin didn't say anything as he gave her a "you're insane" look.

"Are you sure? I don't want to put you out or interrupt your plans."

"Justine, do you want to know what you're interrupting? Take-out pho and a few dozen rounds of *Robot Wars* on my iPad. Let's figure this out. Sergeant Boltdriver can wait."

She gave him a little smile. "Thank you, Griffin, yet again. I feel like all I do these days is say thank you to you."

"I'll always help Spencer. And you," he added quickly. He turned his attention to the dog and put on a silly voice. "Come on, Spence, I'll race ya." He jogged a few steps and Spencer hopped down the sidewalk beside him.

Twenty minutes later Griffin had Justine set up at the bar with a glass of red wine and she'd prepared a cutting board with sliced apples, bread, and cheese to share. There was no easy way to make it back to Rexford in time to open Tricks & Biscuits the next morning, so she tried to get creative. Both Sienna and Ruth had offered to make the drive into the city to pick her up, but Justine refused to allow them to do the four-hour round-trip.

Griffin was silent for most of Justine's negotiations, tapping away on his computer, until he finally spoke up with a single word.

"Stay," he said quietly.

"Excuse me?" Justine asked, turning around in her chair to face him. The sight of Spencer curled up next to Griffin on the couch and his hand resting lightly on him triggered a tiny spark of jealousy.

"Just spend the night. It's getting late and unless you want to take a sketchy bus that gets you home at midnight, you might as well stay here. I saw that you still have some food here for Spencer's breakfast. You can get a new tire tomorrow morning and head back. If you go back tonight you'll still have to make another trip in to deal with your car tomorrow, which will still mess up your day."

"But where . . ."

"You can sleep in the loft again and I'll sleep on the couch." He didn't look up from his computer. "It's very comfortable. Wouldn't be the first time for me, or Leo either. I mean Spencer."

It made sense to stay, but it still felt like the worst option possible given that all she could think about was that chubby bottom lip of his. For a second she imagined trying to go to sleep knowing that Griffin was just a few feet below her without a wall separating them. Despite the noise from the street outside, they'd be able to hear each other *breathing*.

She hadn't packed cute pajamas, just an ancient white summer-camp T-shirt that was thin enough to be transparent, black leggings with tan paint splotches on them, and a Temple hoodie with a broken zipper. The whole ensemble was comfortable and hideous, and it made her look like a homeless person. Had she known that she and Griffin were going to be in the apartment at the same time she would've packed something effortlessly sexy, but she quickly realized that she didn't own anything that would qualify.

"I know it's sort of weird to be in the apartment at the same time, but I promise you won't even know I'm here," Griffin added, still focused on his computer. "You can go up to bed and I'll keep my headphones on and watch Netflix down here on the couch."

When he said the word "bed" Justine felt an involuntary flutter in her low belly. Once again he made the word flip from noun to verb.

Spencer twitched on the couch next to Griffin and let out a deep, contented snore.

It was no longer a question; they were staying.

"If you promise it's not too much, then yes. Thank you, again and again and again. A never-ending thank you."

"Of course. Glad you'll both be safe," Griffin replied. He never stopped typing.

Justine texted Sienna to see if she could open Tricks & Biscuits the next morning, but rather than face an onslaught of eggplant emojis when she told her why she couldn't make it in, she kept it vague and said she'd explain later.

Exactly *what* she'd be explaining, she had no idea.

"What do you mean you've never seen it?" Griffin asked from the kitchen as he poured them both another glass of wine.

"I mean I've never watched a single episode of *Galaxy Force*." Justine shrugged from the couch. "It's not my thing. I don't really like sci-fi."

"That's it, I'm officially revoking your overnight privileges. Out." He pointed at the door with a stony face.

"Oh, come on, what's so good about it anyway? It's just explosions and space crap."

He froze in place halfway back to the couch. "*Excuse* me?"

"I said what I said."

Griffin sighed and placed the wine on the coffee table in front of her. "One episode. Give me one episode to change your mind."

Justine grabbed her glass, then crossed her legs and pulled her bare feet beneath her. "Okay. One episode."

"We can turn it off if you hate it, you have my word. But I guarantee you won't. It holds up." He turned off the overhead lights. "Sorry, but we need darkness to get into the *Galaxy Force* universe and Anderson's incredible acting."

Justine choked on her wine when she realized that they were going to be sitting next to each other in the dark. Spencer had moved to settle in Griffin's spot the second he'd left to get the drinks, so only the middle section of the couch was open, or the ottoman.

"Thanks, dude," Griffin muttered to Spencer.

"There's room," Justine said, squishing closer to the arm of the couch. She patted the open space next to her. "Sit."

Griffin settled on the couch so that he didn't bump the peacefully sleeping Spencer or the wide-awake and anxious Justine. She glanced down and realized that his thigh was only a few inches away from hers. She pulled her legs a little closer in, just to make sure she didn't accidentally graze him. There would be no cozy behavior during their watch party, because it would undoubtedly lead to something they'd both regret.

He grabbed the remote and scrolled through the options until he landed on the famous *Galaxy Force* logo.

Justine snorted. "The first episode is called 'The Legend Awakens'? That sounds like a total *Star Wars* rip-off."

"I knew we were going to have to have this conversation." Griffin sighed and shifted so that he could look her in the face like he was about to teach her something important. "I won't get too deep, but you need to know that the show is based on a book written in 1964 called *Our Time in Space*, so it predates *Star Wars*. There are endless subreddits that explain how George Lucas lifted themes from the book."

"And if I wanted examples of stuff he stole you could provide them?"

"You know it." He settled back against the couch. "You can't bitch about my show if you don't have all of the facts."

"Can I ask you one more question?"

"Shoot," he replied, putting the remote down on the couch beside him.

"Are you"—she looked around and lowered her voice—"an undercover sci-fi geek?"

"How *dare* you, madam?" Griffin boomed, trying to keep a straight face. "There is nothing geeky about loving *Galaxy Force*. Nothing!"

Justine threw her head back and laughed because she could tell he was a little embarrassed she'd called him out on his not-so-secret obsession. Now that she understood the depth of his fandom she wondered why he didn't have any Captain Zaltan Funko action figures or collectibles in the apartment.

"Okay, are you ready?"

Justine threw her fist in the air. "Galaxy Force is *on*!"

He rolled his eyes. "The line is 'Galaxy Force is go,' thank you very much. But you'll learn, my young cadet, you'll learn."

Forty-six minutes later Justine was sitting straight up with her hand over her mouth as the credits rolled.

"Holy shit, that was *good*! I had no clue *Galaxy Force* had depth. The planetary caste system totally has parallels to race and class in our country. And I'm in shock that half the crew were women. And Anderson! I'm sorry but he was *really* snackable back then." She fell back against the couch and accidentally jostled Spencer awake.

Griffin gave her an indulgent smile. "So, you liked it?"

"Yeah." She nodded. "Much more than I thought I would. Let's do another."

"Seriously?"

"One hundred percent serious." She paused. "And are you still hungry? Because that apple and cheese combo was just an appetizer for me."

"Yeah, I'm starving too," he answered, grabbing his phone. "What are you in the mood for? Because we've got Pho Grand right around the corner, Curry Heights a few blocks down—"

"I know," Justine interrupted and smiled at him. "I'm a local now, remember?"

"So you are." He grinned back. "The country mouse is finding her way in the big city."

"*Psh*, please. You should see me jaywalking."

Justine watched Griffin as he scrolled through dinner options on his phone. Bathed in the blue light from the TV home screen with his hair messy, his button-down rumpled, and slumped against the couch with his hand resting on Spencer's flank, he looked handsome in a totally new way. He looked . . . comfortable. Like he'd be perfect to lean on.

Which absolutely wasn't going to happen.

She squished herself into the corner of the couch like a contortionist and settled on a safe topic. "Can we talk about those canibots?"

Griffin looked up from his phone. "I love them. Tread carefully, please."

"I mean, obviously they're adorable. Who doesn't love a space dog? But if you think about it, they're a major plot hole. They had technology that allowed them to create hyperrealistic robot dogs to be their companions in space, but the rest of the robots looked like tin cans. Why is that?"

"Do you *really* want to know? Because I watched a YouTube video that suggests the DNA samples taken from the remaining life forms on Earth enabled them to . . ." He trailed off when Justine started to giggle. "What? Too much?"

"A *little*?" She laughed and held up her thumb and pointer finger an inch apart.

He ducked his head and changed the subject. "Did you catch the name of the lead canibot?"

"Yeah, Leonidas X, the battle bot." She paused as the realization hit her. "Wait. Leonidas. *Leo.*" Spencer opened his eyes and looked at her when she said his old name. "Oh my God, you named him for the dog in the show." Her heart twisted at the realization. "That's really sweet."

"And geeky," he replied as he scrolled through their dinner options.

"Not at all."

Spencer shifted until his head was resting on Griffin's thigh, and Griffin placed his hand on the dog's shoulder without even glancing his way. There was still so much love between them that Justine considered herself lucky there was any room left in Spencer's heart for her.

chapter twenty-four

Hey."

Justine thought she heard a voice calling to her through the darkness. Something touched her shoulder and she jumped.

"What?" she slurred in a sleep-drunk voice as she looked around the room with her eyes wide, trying to figure out where she was.

"You fell asleep," Griffin said softly. "But you made it through two and a half episodes. I was watching you. You snore."

Justine sat up and realized that she'd taken over more than half of the couch and that her feet were braced against Griffin's thigh. He was pushed up against Spencer. "I'm so sorry," she said, quickly pulling them away. "I guess I was overtired. What time is it?"

"Late," he answered. "Time for bed."

She stared across the room, still half out of it but not enough to keep the word *bed* from bouncing around inside her head.

"Okay. I need to wash up really quick; then I'll head up."

It hit her that Griffin was about to see her without makeup and her hair pinned back with half a dozen bobby pins, and she was about to see him in whatever he wore to bed every night. Which probably wouldn't have stains.

Justine grabbed her toiletry bag and pajamas from her suitcase in the loft and headed downstairs to the only bathroom in the apartment. Griffin was making up the couch with sheets while Spencer stood next to him with a low wagging tail.

Once in the bathroom she took extra time washing and moisturizing her face and brushed her cowlick into submission. The mascot on her too-small camp T-shirt was bound to get a wisecrack out of him, so she fiddled with the broken zipper on her hoodie, hoping that it would miraculously start zipping. It wasn't like she actually needed it since Griffin preferred the thermostat set to "tropical." She pulled the sides of the hoodie across her chest like a wrap dress, took a deep breath, crossed an arm over her chest, and wrestled with the doorknob.

Griffin was sitting on the couch with Spencer dozing beside him, watching the end of the third episode of *Galaxy Force*.

Onscreen, young Anderson was having a moment with the beautiful cadet named Ardala who'd beaten him in a ramjet training race.

"They have great chemistry," Justine said, standing a safe distance from Griffin in front of the bathroom.

Griffin nodded. "The rumor is that he swept her off her feet and stole her away from her husband, then dumped her."

She studied Anderson. "He was so young. It's crazy to see him looking like that."

"Why? Does he look terrible in person now?"

Justine couldn't believe that she hadn't thought of it sooner. It was *perfect*.

"Wanna see for yourself?" She smiled as the idea took shape.

"What do you mean?" Griffin sat up straighter as if he understood what she was saying but couldn't believe it.

"Come visit the set."

"Seriously? Hell yes, Justine! That would be amazing."

She grinned back at him like a dork.

"Perfect. We'll find a day when you're in town and I'll sneak you on." She whistled for Spencer and he picked up his head to look at her, then immediately plopped it back down. He'd picked his bedmate and it wasn't her. She ignored the tiny spark of jealousy.

"Guess I'm sleeping alone tonight," she said before she realized how it sounded. She gave Griffin an awkward wave. "Good night. Thanks again for everything."

"Yup, no problem. Sleep good."

Sleep.

Like that was going to happen.

Spencer joined her in bed thirty minutes later. Justine could still hear Griffin moving around on the couch just below her, probably trying to get comfortable. A heavy exhale. A cough. She tried to keep still just in case he was listening to her noises too. Even though the streets right outside the window were an orchestra of beeps, crashes, and sirens, the silence inside the apartment was louder.

She was wide awake, and based on the sighs and sheet rustling, he was too.

And now she had to go pee.

The second the thought entered her mind all she could do was think about peeing, which made the feeling that much more urgent. But going to the bathroom involved the double whammy of not only going into the Griffin zone near the couch, but also having him *hear* her peeing. But there was a chance she'd suddenly get shy bladder because she knew he was just a few feet away on the couch and wouldn't be able to go after all, and she'd wind up sitting in the bathroom praying the pee would finally come while he wondered what the hell she was doing for so long.

When Justine finally felt like her bladder was going to burst, she crept out of bed and down the metal stairs, hoping that Griffin had fallen asleep in the past four minutes. He was on his side facing the wall, so she tiptoed into the bathroom, did the weird lift-and-turn thing to close the door, and took the stealthiest pee of her life. The flush-or-don't-flush conundrum stalled her for a few seconds, but she opted for flush *slowly*. She washed her hands and checked herself out in the mirror in the dim glow of the night-light.

Sleepy eyes, with a few pillow creases on the side of her face. But totally presentable if he happened to roll over and catch her sneaking around his apartment.

The doorknob was prone to overloud clicks and squeaks, so she came out of the bathroom in a hurry, plotting how she was going to get past Griffin again without waking him up. Her sole consideration was the sound of her feet padding from the tile of the bathroom to the creaky wood floor outside. She was focused downward on her chipped red pedicure, willing herself to levitate silently back to bed, when she plowed directly into Griffin's bare chest.

"Whoa!" she yelped.

"Sorry!"

The glass of cold water he was carrying emptied onto her T-shirt and the oxygen was sucked from her lungs by the shock of it. But the only thing that she could focus on as they collided was not the fact that the water had made her basically topless or the pain of his foot smashing into hers, but how shockingly soft his skin felt beneath her fingertips. Both of her hands were magnetized to him, and she grasped his shoulder and biceps a few seconds longer than necessary, as if she was about to fall and needed to steady herself.

Solid. So solid. In an instant she cataloged the nuances of his torso so she could think about it when she was back in bed, alone. The hard mound of his shoulder under her left palm, the tense curve of his biceps flexing in her right hand. She had to force herself to keep from sliding her hands along the rest of the peaks and valleys of his body.

His free hand was on her elbow, but it felt like it reached all the way up the back of her arm and was leaving a scorch. He didn't let go of her either, and in that instant they both knew they were holding on to each other for way longer than was necessary. And neither one wanted to stop.

Griffin let go first.

"I needed a drink." He held the now-empty glass out. "That went well. Really sorry about your shirt."

She could tell that he was doing everything in his power to keep his eyes locked on hers since the water had turned the white T-shirt invisible, which also prevented her from sneaking a peek at *his* chest. After a few seconds of excruciatingly polite eye contact, Justine started to feel like she was breathing weird, and she wasn't sure if it was from the shock of the cold water gluing her T-shirt to her skin or the fact that she was desperate to find a reason to touch Griffin again. She shifted from one foot to the other so that he couldn't tell that she was trying to slowly inch closer to him.

"Do you need something else to wear?" His voice was low as he gestured to her chest. He never looked away from her eyes.

Justine shook her head slowly. "I've got plenty of T-shirts in my suitcase."

"Of course you do." The corner of his mouth turned up as he said it and he leaned against the wall. "But are any of them as worn in and comfy as"—he finally glanced down at the logo on the front of her shirt—"as Camp . . . wait, *what* does that say?"

"Camp Beaver Basin." She said it in a fast whisper. "Obviously, that's the reason I only wear this one to bed."

Griffin's mouth dropped open. "Please tell me that's a real place."

"My old summer camp," she replied.

"And the mascot is . . ." He broke off to glance at her chest again. "A beaver making a . . ." He moved closer and Justine caught her breath when she realized that Griffin was just a few inches away from her wet-T-shirt-contest-worthy nipples.

"A dream catcher," she whispered, standing still. She swore she could feel him breathing on her.

Griffin was so focused on deciphering the logo that his proximity to her chest didn't seem to register until he jerked up abruptly.

"Are you, uh, are you cold?" He shut his eyes for a moment when he seemed to realize how it sounded after examining her chest up close and personal.

"A little."

"Okay. You should probably change, then." He murmured it,

like it was an afterthought and not something she should seriously consider.

Justine nodded but didn't move. She finally let her gaze drop to his chest and immediately wished she hadn't, because all she wanted to do was flatten her palms against his smooth skin. She looked a little lower, just below the abs she hadn't been lucky enough to touch, and saw the top of his briefs cresting above his thin gray pajama pants. The little strings that sat just below his belly button were barely crisscrossed.

She blinked and softly cleared her throat.

The silence stretched on as they stared at each other in the darkness. They both seemed to realize that any sudden movements or voices above a whisper could jolt them back to tenant and landlord.

Justine shivered and reluctantly crossed her arms over her chest, hoping that Griffin wouldn't notice. Sure, she was cold, but there was no way she could walk away from him. From whatever was about to happen between them.

The silence wasn't uncomfortable. It was a moment of free fall, a pause between the notes.

"Griffin?" Justine finally said softly.

He didn't answer but instead closed the space between them until he was just inches away and looking down on her. He was so close that she could smell hints of something clean and piney around him and almost feel his heat bouncing off her damp chest. Instead of touching her he stood with his arms at his sides and studied her face, staring into her eyes for a few seconds, then letting his gaze drift down to her mouth, then back up to her eyes.

Justine tipped her head back a little, hoping he'd lean down and finally do the very thing she'd been imagining since the first time she saw him in the park. But Griffin continued breathing her in until she started to question if she was imagining the chemical reactions happening between them.

When she couldn't bear the wait another second longer he finally, *finally* reached out and cupped her cheek gently, like she was something precious and fragile. He traced his thumb along her cheek, causing goose bumps to ripple up and down her arms. Then another agonizing wait, staring into each other's eyes, until he lowered his head and gently brushed his lips against hers.

Everything fell away in a jolt the moment their mouths touched. The wet T-shirt clinging to her breasts, the traffic noise outside, Spencer's soft snores drifting down from the loft. How could Griffin's lips be so soft? She trembled more from the sensation of his mouth on hers than the shock of the cold water on her skin a few minutes before.

He was tentative at first, like he wasn't sure how she'd respond to the kiss, but Justine reached up and threaded her fingers in his hair, pulling him closer so that his mouth was crushed on top of hers. She rose up on her toes and locked her arms behind his head so he couldn't slip away, though based on the low groan he let out against her mouth it wasn't likely he wanted to. Griffin's strong arms snaked around her waist and he pulled her closer to him until her wet T-shirt hit his bare chest. He contracted reflexively from the cold, then pressed up against her again.

"You're freezing," he whispered through the kiss.

"No, I'm not," she rasped back at him.

She felt him smile against her mouth, then teasingly nip her lip.

Griffin's hands roamed from the small of her back up to her shoulders as they kissed, sending shock waves everywhere he touched. Justine felt shaky as his mouth slanted against hers, and it was such an unfamiliar sensation that for a moment she wondered if Brooklyn was experiencing an earthquake. If every kiss she'd ever gotten in her lifetime was to be measured against this one, Justine quickly realized that Griffin had ruined them all in the span of a minute.

He tightened his arms around her and lifted her off the floor a few inches, then walked her backward without taking his mouth off hers, until her body was flush against the wall. Griffin set Justine down gently, gazed at her for a minute with a small smile, then hungrily angled his mouth over hers again, like he was claiming her.

When the thoughts started intruding and pulling her focus away from the kiss that was literally making her knees weak Justine batted them down impatiently. All that mattered was not stopping.

But the word *trajectory* bounced into her head as Griffin's hands slipped down her body to graze her ass. And *hiatus*. And the realization that next week when she was back in his apartment he'd be gone again. When Griffin dropped his mouth to kiss her neck she loosened her grip ever so slightly. He pulled away as if he could sense her hesitation.

"Are you okay?" he asked, a little breathless.

Justine didn't answer right away. Everything inside her was screaming to keep going until they both ended up sweaty and satisfied. If Griffin hadn't stopped they probably would've, but giving her the opportunity to think without his lips against her brought everything into a sharp, depressing focus.

She leaned her forehead against his chest and waited for her heartbeat to slow before saying anything. It was also a test to see if she could resist the pull to kiss him again.

"This probably isn't a good idea."

Griffin let out a long, ragged sigh.

"I was worried you were going to say that," he said softly and rested his cheek on the top of her head. He linked his hands together on her lower back, like they were slow dancing in a school gym.

"The timing isn't right for either of us. You said as much."

"That fucking trajectory," he growled softly.

She nodded, and they were silent for a few minutes, still wrapped around each other.

"I think it's best if we stop now and pretend this didn't happen," Justine finally said.

"Well, that's not going to be easy," he whispered into her hair. "I'm going to think about it every time I look at you."

"But you know I'm right."

He didn't respond but she felt him nod. They kept their arms encircled around each other, and even though they were negotiating how to walk away from what had just happened, neither one seemed especially eager to make it happen.

Justine eventually untangled herself slowly and headed to the stairs without looking at Griffin, because if she did she wouldn't be able to resist the magnetic pull back into his arms.

She padded up the steps silently and slid into bed next to Spencer. Griffin's breathing below her kept her awake for an hour before she fell asleep.

chapter twenty-five

I miss her every day," Frank Mancini said as he placed Flossie on the Tricks & Biscuits counter in front of Justine so she could admire the little dog. Spencer hopped up on the edge of it to say hello but backed off the second Flossie raised her lip at him. He knew better than to tangle with the ten-pound terror, so he curled up in his bed behind the counter.

"How long were you married?" Justine asked.

"Fifty-one beautiful years. Today would've made it sixty. I can't believe Ada's been gone so long." He sighed and gave Justine a sad smile. He seemed to hunch over even more, as if the weight of his loss was a physical burden. "I wish you could've known her."

"Me too, Frank," Justine replied and reached out to place her hand on top of his. "I bet she was wonderful."

Frank had been one of Tricks & Biscuits' first customers and went on to become such a regular shopper that he could make product recommendations to anyone who walked in the door. Justine had been shocked to learn that he'd been a fairly popular singer-songwriter in his youth and she'd convinced him to play his guitar at one of T&B's popular Yappy Hours. Whenever he was in the shop with a crowd of people she always made sure to turn on his most famous song and brag to everyone that the white-haired gentleman with the adorable Yorkie was the one singing.

"We met at her father's deli. Did I ever tell you that?"

Justine shook her head.

"She worked the counter. She was the prettiest girl I'd ever seen, but was she ever *mean*." He shuddered. "Never smiled, only worked. I'd try to talk to her every time I went in, but all she wanted to do was slice my salami and get me out of there."

"So how did you win her over?"

"Perseverance," Frank replied with a wink as he took a sip from his coffee cup. "And lots of salami."

They laughed together.

"I haven't seen that Nick in a long time. What's he up to?" Frank asked.

Justine choked on coffee. "'That Nick' isn't around anymore, Frank. We broke up a while ago."

"Oh? Why is that?"

"You know how it goes; sometimes things don't work out." She shrugged and hoped he wouldn't keep asking questions.

"So, you're single again?" He leaned on the counter. "Because I've got a nephew who's single . . . handsome too. Looks like me in my heyday."

"Considering how great you look now, that's really tempting, but I'm definitely not dating at the moment," Justine said with a finality that she hoped could convince Frank as well as herself.

"But why?"

She sighed. "I've got a lot going on. And I'm just not interested in getting involved with anyone." There was no way she was going to dive into the list of reasons why she kept having to force herself to stop thinking about Griffin and the near miss they'd shared.

"I find that hard to believe." He harrumphed. Flossie pranced her way over to the spot where Justine kept the bowl of sample treats and started helping herself. "I bet the boys are beating down your door!"

"Nope, not even close."

She thought of the few texts she'd received from Griffin in the two days since they'd kissed. The morning after, they'd both pretended nothing had happened as they worked to find a garage to change her tire, and their communications since had focused around scheduling the apartment the following week. It was obvious that they both considered what had happened between them a mistake.

"Just promise me this, Justine. When you find one you like, don't make him work as hard to win your heart as my Ada made me work. I look back now and all I see is wasted time when we could've been having so much fun together." He got quiet for a minute. "We did have fun. And now look at me. My dog is my true love." Flossie walked over to Frank and licked his chin, coaxing a quiet chuckle out of him. "Don't waste your time when it comes to your heart, you got me?"

Justine smiled at him. "I got you, Frank. That's good advice."

"Thank heavens for your shop and all of the friends we've met here. This place and the Rexford senior center are the only things that keep us going."

Justine turned away to pet Spencer so Frank couldn't read her expression. It was as if all of Rexford could sense that she was inching closer to her decision about the future of Tricks & Biscuits and wanted to weigh in with as much guilty peer pressure as possible. Someone had posted a glowing Facebook tribute about Sienna's product recommendations, and there was a rumor that the store was going to be up for a major travel blog's Best of the Hudson Valley award. But reviews and prizes didn't change the fact that the shop felt like an anchor that was keeping her moored in Rexford. The money was starting to trickle in from *The Eighteenth*, which meant that her most vocal distributors were getting their payments on time and she could pay Sienna promptly. Working another job just to keep Tricks & Biscuits alive didn't make sense no matter how much she loved her customers.

"When is my girlfriend coming in?" Frank asked. He had a soft spot for Sienna that he didn't try to hide.

"What, I'm not good enough for you, Frank?" Justine teased.

"Sienna slips more freebies in our bag than you do," he replied with a guilty smile.

"Oh, is that a fact? Well, hold on, mister, because I've got a sample that's unlike anything Flossie's ever had. Be right back."

Justine excused herself to run to her office to try to dig up the expensive Waggy You beef treats they'd gotten at the trade show. The giant promotional bag stuffed full of flyers, catalogs, and samples Sienna had collected was probably still sitting in the corner. She hadn't been in her office since the morning before, and when she opened the door her jaw dropped.

For the first time since she'd opened the shop she could actually see the top of her desk. The skyscraper piles of paperwork normally crowding the surface were reduced to tidy folders on the corner of it. The pens and scissors she could never seem to find when she needed them were tucked in a mug with a French bulldog face on it. The filing cabinet's two drawers were completely shut instead of sagging open. The long-dead flowers in a vase on top of it were replaced by the lavender diffuser Sienna had given her but Justine had never taken out of the box. The random broken food bowls and defective toys that needed to be sent back to the manufacturer were nowhere to be seen, likely tucked away in the boxes stacked in the corner.

Justine headed for the trade-show bag and discovered that Sienna had taken the mess they'd collected and put everything in folders with the paperwork divided by product. It took her only a few seconds to find the fancy treat one-sheet with the small treat bags stapled to it.

She headed for the door but stopped when she saw a lone stack of paperwork in the center of her desk.

It was the Tricks & Biscuits lease with a pen placed neatly beside it and a tiny yellow Post-it note with a smiley face on it stuck next to the signature line.

chapter twenty-six

"Y ou two are doing okay, and I'm shocked," Malcolm said as he stuffed the last of his burrito into his mouth. "I mean, be honest with me. This is Spencer's first real gig, right?"

Justine knew it was time to come clean. The rest of the crew was finishing lunch in the craft services side building and heading back to the set, so no one was paying attention to them. She nodded like she was admitting a white-collar crime.

"How the hell are you two nailing every shot?" Malcolm leaned to the side to peek at Spencer underneath the table. "You seem like you know what you're doing, bud."

"Tons of practice and tons of generalizing his training. I mean, a big part of all of this is Spencer himself. He's an incredible dude." Justine slipped him a bit of tortilla. "Plus, I've been watching everything and taking mental notes. I do *not* want to screw this up."

"You might have a future in this. Have you considered it?"

"Yeah, I hope so." Justine nodded and tucked her hair behind her ear. "It makes sense. I'd love to keep working on productions with Spence."

"You've got one more scene today, right?"

"Um-hm, we should be able to get through it fast. It's pretty straightforward."

"That's the easiest way to make friends around here," Malcolm said like he was sharing a trade secret. "Show up on time and get it *done*. The dude with the trained cats that was here yesterday? Those cats weren't trained at all. Took us an hour to get a two-minute clip. That's why Spencer is my guy. One take."

Justine shrugged. "Eh, we don't always make it in one take, but we do our best. Right, Spence?"

Spencer smacked his tail on the ground in response.

"You'll get to meet Adam later. He's been doing the professional dog thing for years."

"I know, I saw the call sheet! I'm so excited to pick his brain."

Malcolm chuckled. "You might not be so excited once you talk with him. Adam knows his stuff but he can be a bit of a diva. Not the nicest person I've worked with, but you didn't hear that from me."

"Spencer will win him over, I bet. Who can resist this face?" she asked as she placed her hand beneath Spencer's chin and gently lifted it up.

Malcolm craned his neck and gawked over Justine's shoulder. "Hey, there's that old model chick. The one in the song? 'Her eyes, I see everything in . . . her eyes.'" He sang it in a raspy voice like the lead singer of the Sonic Dukes.

Justine turned around and saw Monty walking to the set like a queen, with dark sunglasses on her head and trailed by a few people she didn't recognize.

"Yup, Monty Volkov. And sweet Jesus don't let her hear you calling her old. She's Taylor's mom."

"Right, I totally forgot that they're mother and daughter. Man, she's still gorgeous."

"You want an introduction? Because I know her . . ." Justine wiggled her eyebrows at Malcolm suggestively.

He wadded up his napkin and threw it at Justine. "Yeah, like she'd look twice at an animal herder like me."

"Hey, Matt Damon married his bartender; you never know."

Malcom leaned in closer to Justine. "Have you seen any of Taylor's work yet?"

"We haven't been on set at the same time, no. Why?"

He grimaced. "Oof. She's really unsure of herself so she's taking way too much time with her scenes. She keeps asking for extra takes and Anderson isn't having it."

"Oh, that sucks. I had no idea. Taylor and Monty have a house in my town and they're the reason Spencer and I are here. They suggested us to Ted."

Malcolm tipped his head. "Solid hookup. Pays to know people."

Spencer jumped up from his spot beneath the table as three frowning people on walkie-talkies ran toward the set, their devices crackling with shouts.

"Well, that doesn't look good," Malcolm said with a frown. "Trouble on set."

It was the first time Justine had seen a hint of a problem during the shoot. "Like what kind of trouble?"

"You really aren't plugged into the gossip, are you? Probably Taylor and Anderson going at it. They've had a few little fights, which might have led to a bigger fight." He gestured to more people running to the set. "Lemme go do some recon and I'll report back." Malcolm gathered his things and headed out.

Justine was alone in the craft services area. She'd quickly discovered that food was the great equalizer, which meant that when it came time for meals the lowest-level production assistants might wind up in line next to slumming marquee names waiting to get their morning fruit bowls. It was another spot where listening and watching paid in dividends; lunch with the crew was Production 101.

"I fucking hate him, Mom," Justine heard Taylor wail before she came around the corner. "I'm done!"

Spencer squirmed out from under the table again when he heard the shouting, and Justine froze in place. Taylor was heading right for craft services and Justine wanted to give her space as she ranted. They were acquaintances at best, and from the sound of Taylor's voice Justine could tell that some major insider shit was going down.

Taylor was wearing a sleeveless knee-length blue dress with white polka dots, which meant the scene they were shooting was early in the first episode, before her character starts vamping it up at the speakeasy. She paced with her arms crossed, still unaware that Justine and Spencer were a few feet away. Monty caught up to Taylor, swooping her into a hug, and Justine tried to sneak out without interrupting the moment.

"Honey, he doesn't know what he's talking about. You're phenomenal, baby. You're a *star*!"

Spencer let out a happy woof, blowing Justine's chance for a smooth getaway.

"Sorry, guys, I'm leaving. Sorry, sorry!" Justine kept her head down as if not looking at them meant that she hadn't seen or heard the outburst.

"Justine, come over here," Monty barked back in a voice that signified she had no choice in the matter.

Justine and Spencer walked to the pair cautiously. Their casual lunchtime-in-the-diner relationship didn't feel like enough of a connection to be a part of whatever Taylor was going through, but she wasn't about to say no to Monty.

"Have you seen Taylor working?" Monty demanded. "She's amazing, right?"

"I actually haven't been able to watch, I've been so focused on Spencer." She gestured to her dog. "But I've heard she's doing really well." She lied.

"Is that what people are saying?" Taylor asked her with tears streaming down her cheeks, running her period-approved eye makeup. "Just 'really well'? That's it? Oh my God, he *is* right! I suck!" She threw herself back into Monty's arms.

Any delay in the shoot could now be partially attributed to Justine's poor word choice, so she struggled to make up for it.

"No, Taylor! I was paraphrasing. I think someone said, um, *timeless*. And obviously everyone thinks you look absolutely beautiful!"

She sniffled and lifted her head off her mother's shoulder. "R-really?"

Justine nodded encouragingly. "Yup! Hey, can I get you some water?" She was looking for any excuse to back away and give them space.

"No, just come sit with us." Taylor motioned to a table a few feet away. "I want to get your opinion."

She was trapped, but as much as she hated imposing on the important mother-daughter moment, she wanted to learn more about the on-set dynamics. Everything she picked up was useful eventually.

"Anderson said that Taylor is being a diva and that she's not talented enough for the role. What do you think about that?" They both turned to stare at her, and once again Justine realized that her answer could impact how the rest of the day went for everyone on set.

"I think that's crazy. I mean, I haven't watched you, Taylor, but Ted wouldn't have hired you if you couldn't handle it, right? Ted knows what he's doing."

"Exactly," Monty said, smoothing a wisp of hair from Taylor's forehead. "You have to stop listening to men like Anderson. If I'd listened to men like Anderson Brooks I'd still be working retail."

Justine shrugged off the accidental dig.

"What do you mean?" Taylor asked as she dragged her fingertips beneath her damp eyes, changing her look from sad starlet to post-binge druggie.

"Guys like Anderson put other people down to keep them in their place. He's screwing with your head. I don't know, maybe he's worried you're going to outshine him once the show comes out? Everybody loves an ingenue." Monty sounded wistful as she looked at her beautiful daughter. "I can't even tell you how many times men tried to make me feel bad about myself during my early modeling days. Telling me I was too fat when I was barely a size two. That my face was too round. My teeth were ugly. And don't get me started on the physical harassment."

"Really? But you're the strongest person I know," Taylor said.

"I wasn't always," Monty said with a sad smile. "Remember, I was fourteen when I started, and I barely spoke English. So young." She shook her head. "I had no clue how scary the world could be, and little by little, I found out."

A familiar prickly feeling crept along the back of Justine's hairline as Monty spoke. It hadn't been little by little for her. A single sunny afternoon had changed her worldview.

"That's why I never let you go to shoots alone when you were young," Monty continued. "I wasn't being a helicopter parent; I was there to make sure no one hurt you. And it's not going to stop now that you're a grown-up."

"Mom, you can't yell at Anderson Brooks." Taylor half smiled at her.

"Watch me," Monty said.

Ted peeked around the corner at the group, looking like he was afraid to approach the cool-girl table in the high school cafeteria.

"Hey, Taylor, can I borrow you for a sec?"

Taylor glanced at Monty, then cleared her throat and stood up with a determined look on her face. She headed to Ted with newfound confidence.

"There's my girl," Monty said as she stood up and drifted toward them so she could eavesdrop.

"Gunner, *halt!*"

The German shepherd came to a statue-like stop on the street-scene set, then looked over his shoulder at his handler.

"Stay," the man said in a low voice. The dog didn't move even though he'd come to a stop with awkward footing.

"All right, send him to the truck," Ted said from his usual position behind a bank of TV screens.

"Gunner, in," the man called from the shadows to his dog a few feet away on set. The dog looked tentative for a moment. "Gunner! *In!*" He dashed to the car and leapt inside.

"Now get that window look, please," Ted said.

The handler took a half step forward and raised his arm. "Gunner, watch me! Watch!"

The dog poked his head out of the open door, his mouth in a wide pant.

"Keep it there . . . couple more seconds," Ted said. "Annnd, cut. Okay, we'll pick it up when Peter gets in the truck. Take five, everyone."

The room exploded into the usual activity, with people standing up to stretch and chatting among themselves. Justine kept an eye on the handler and dog, because even their break behavior could give her pointers. It was the first time Justine had ever seen a professional dog-and-handler team up close, and she was in awe of them. Spencer seemed just as interested in the handsome German shepherd.

She watched Adam clip a leash on his dog and couldn't help but notice that the dog ducked his head when his hand got close to him.

"I'm going to go introduce myself," she said to Malcolm. "Wish us luck."

Malcolm smirked. "Holler if you need me to save you."

Adam was leaning against the wall on his phone with Gunner resting at his feet. Although on second glance Justine couldn't call it resting, exactly. The dog was in a perfect sphinx-down with his entire body aligned and at attention. When Spencer finished working Justine always let him do whatever he wanted, to shake off any residual tension he might be feeling from acting. Gunner looked like he was still very much on the clock. He didn't even glance at them as they got closer.

"Hi there," Justine said with a little wave as she approached the pair. She stopped a few feet away since she wasn't sure if the other dog was interested in meeting Spencer. "I wanted to introduce myself; I'm Justine, and this is my dog, Spencer, also known as Ford. You guys did such a great job out there! Hey, Gunner, you're a pro!" She didn't even get a wag in return. Gunner had the approachability of a working service dog.

"Oh, you're the one," Adam answered, giving her a quick once-over. He slipped his phone into one of the many pockets on his khaki vest and ran a hand over his thinning gray hair.

"Well, I'm half of the one," Justine replied. She pointed at Spencer. "He's doing all of the work."

"I was pretty surprised when I found out they cast a nobody for such an important part. I have another dog that would've been perfect to play Ford, but for some reason they went with you." His smile looked more like baring his fangs.

"Oh, no way. Well, at least Gunner is here now." She looked down at the dog. "You're having fun, right, bud?"

Gunner finally wagged his tail and Justine took it as a green light. She put Spencer in a stay and knelt a few feet away from Gunner to invite him to interact with her if he was interested.

"*Don't* touch." Adam said it like she was a toddler by a hot stove. Justine backed away. "There's lesson number one for you; when a working dog is working, let him work."

"I'm sorry, I thought since we're on a break I could interact with him. Rookie mistake."

Justine envisioned Spencer accepting petting from everyone

who passed by him, lolling on his back like he was surrounded by a pack of personal massage therapists.

"All of my animals understand that when we're on set they're *always* under my control and command."

She scanned the room trying to find Malcolm. When she finally spotted him, she made a split-second grimace to beg for an intervention. He nodded and headed over to them.

"Nice work out there, Adam," Malcolm said as he joined them. He glanced down at the dog. "Hey, Gunner."

"We aim to please." Adam was slightly less confrontational with Malcolm. "Will you be chained to this soundstage for the entire shoot?"

Malcolm shook his head. "They've done some stuff at a few local spots but nothing with animals, so I haven't been at any of them. We have our first location shoot coming up, in Maryland."

Adam laughed and bared his fangs at Justine again. "Oh, that'll be *interesting*. You're going to have fun. What sort of action?"

"Water," Justine and Malcolm answered in unison.

"At night," Malcolm added.

Adam threw his head back and laughed harder than Justine thought was necessary. "Oh, good luck with *that*. Here's lesson number two for you," he said, focusing on her. "Expect everything your dog knows to go to hell when you're on location. Trust me, I've been doing this for a billion years. Gunner had the audacity to run away from me during a location shoot. Something spooked him. Delayed us for an hour; we had the whole crew looking for him."

The crew started reassembling just in time for Justine to make a getaway.

"Um, okay. Thanks for the tips." She tried to hide her deer-in-headlights expression as she backed away from Adam and his robotic dog.

"Later," Malcolm said, giving Adam a little salute. He caught up to Justine and draped his arm around her shoulder. "Stop stressing. Adam is just pissed you got the role and he didn't. Don't let him freak you out. You've done the work with Spencer, so everything will be fine. And if you're worried about the location shoot, bring an assistant."

As if she had one.

Cue epic internal freak-out.

chapter twenty-seven

Shh," Justine mouthed at Griffin. "The boom is right there." She pointed above their heads to a microphone on a long pole being held up in the air by a guy wearing headphones.

Griffin cringed and mouthed *sorry* back at her. He shifted his stance and nearly stepped on Spencer's paw.

It was their first time seeing each other since their kiss, and Justine didn't want it to feel awkward for either of them. She figured meeting in public surrounded by a million distractions, including Griffin's childhood hero, would smooth over any remaining weirdness.

Or so she thought, until she saw him striding to the warehouse door, hands stuffed in his pockets and his collar turned up against the chill, looking like a modern-day James Dean. When he spotted her, broke into a smile, and unleashed the dimples, she had to remind herself that they were back to being host and tenant and nothing more. Although once she figured out what scene they'd be watching together she realized that the hiatus and trajectory were about to get a PG-13 workout.

The second Anderson walked on set Griffin swatted Justine and made a split-second "Are you seeing this?" face at her. Justine could tell he was trying to play it off and act cool, but he kept biting back smiles as he watched Anderson get ready for the scene. When Taylor joined Anderson on set she heard Griffin exhale in awe.

"Holy shit," he muttered under his breath, and despite feeling a surprising flicker of jealousy, Justine couldn't blame his appreciation of the young actress.

Taylor looked like a goddess. Her outfit reflected her character's transformation from small-town girl to nightclub entertainer in a thin blush satin gown with black beading. Anderson was wearing a vest and a loosened tie, looking like his muscles were about to pop out of his dress shirt. After a quick conversation with the production's intimacy coordinator and Ted's call for "action," they were toe to toe, staring into each other's eyes like they were about to tear each other's clothes off.

"It fits," Anderson said softly in his Izzy voice, running his finger along Taylor's dress strap.

"Uh-huh," Taylor replied, breathless from his touch. She arched her back almost imperceptibly, then flicked her eyes down and raised them again to meet his gaze. "Thank you, Izzy," she whispered in a shaky voice. "You didn't have to do that."

Anderson was still caressing the top of the strap, running his fingers up and down it. He slid his thumb underneath so that his skin was on hers as he moved his fingers along the inch-wide bit of satin. Taylor let out a tiny openmouthed gasp when his thumb briefly dipped beneath the bodice of her dress at the side of her breast. Anderson met her gaze as if daring her to stop him. He continued to slide his fingers up the strap to her shoulder, then let his thumb trail down her skin slowly until it disappeared beneath the satin and grazed her nipple. Taylor trembled and took a step closer to him, her mouth moving toward his, one aching centimeter at a time.

Justine suppressed her own tiny shudder and peeked at Griffin, who was watching the action with wide eyes. They were stuck on the far edge of the set, standing almost shoulder to shoulder, and for a change she realized that the urge to strip off a layer of clothing wasn't because of the heat from the tungsten lights. Griffin glanced at Justine and caught her watching him, and they both immediately jerked their eyes back to the love scene with guilty expressions. She took a half step away from Griffin and exhaled.

Anderson and Taylor were still moving in slow motion on the set, all restraint and silent want. Justine couldn't believe Taylor's furious "I hate him" to her mother had been transformed into believable soft-core action. They moved closer, both panting with desire that *had* to be real, and as their lips were about to touch Justine found herself silently chanting, *Do it! Do it!*

Finally, their mouths crashed into each other. "Annnd, *cut*," Ted said softly the moment they connected, giving everyone in the room a massive case of blue balls.

Anderson reared back from Taylor with a roar.

"She stepped on my line!" he screamed at no one and everyone at the same time. "That girl has no idea what she's doing!" His people ran to try to keep up with him as he stormed away from the set. It was impossible not to hear him ranting about "hiring fucking models" even as he moved out of sight.

Taylor shot Anderson a look of pure hate over her shoulder and headed in the opposite direction with her team fluttering around her.

Griffin was frozen in place at the edge of the set with his eyebrows knitted in confusion. He pointed to where Taylor and Anderson had just been making out. "Wait. What the hell did I just see? They don't like each other? I mean, that wasn't acting. That was real."

Justine shrugged. "Movie magic."

Spencer pulled Justine a few steps to grab a piece of bagel that didn't make it into the garbage can.

"Anderson seems like kind of a dick," Griffin whispered as they walked away from the set.

"No comment. Let's just say everyone is learning to roll with, uh, his *mood swings*."

"Does he have a lot of scenes with Spence?" He reached down and scratched Spencer under the chin, and the dog leaned into him in a trance.

"He does, but he's always really sweet to him. He saves his tantrums for his human costars," she said, smiling down at Spencer.

"I feel like my childhood hero is crumbling before my eyes. Captain Zaltan is a jerk in real life."

"Not always. Mostly when it comes to Taylor," Justine replied. "Now that you've seen how the sausage is made you'll never be the same again." They passed by Taylor being fussed over by a half-dozen hair, makeup, and wardrobe people.

"Hey, did you see me?" she called to Justine as she walked by with Griffin.

Justine flashed a thumbs-up. "I did! You were incandescent!

Absolutely perfect!" Justine had learned to amp up her adjectives when it came to Taylor's work, although what she'd just seen actually *was* perfect. Her fighting with Anderson offscreen led to electricity onscreen. The hate-fuck vibe was working for them.

Griffin slowed down to a crawl when he realized that he was just a few feet away from Taylor Volkov Rand, supermodel.

He leaned closer to Justine and lowered his voice. "Holy shit, Taylor is *right there.* I could just walk right up to her and say hello. She's a goddess."

"Okay, stalker," Justine said playfully while hiding a furrow.

"Is she nice? I mean, you can't be that gorgeous and be *nice* nice, but is she better than Anderson?" Talking about Taylor made him as puppyish as Spencer.

"Would it break your heart if I told you she was a bitch?" Griffin's face fell.

"I'm kidding, she's great. At least one of your crushes is still sacred."

He looked insulted. "I don't have a crush on Anderson."

"I think you do," she teased. "Captain Zaltan and Griffin, *away!*" she sang, altering the words to the show's theme song.

"Please. I don't stan a-holes." They were at the doors and Griffin looked at his watch. "How much more do you have to shoot today?"

"I'm done for the day. And since you were getting home early today, I packed this morning before I left your place, so everything is in my car and ready to go."

"Oh, okay." He rocked on his heels. "Because I'm done for the day too. Obviously, since I'm here and not working."

Neither one said anything, and Spencer plopped into a down

between them as if he knew he was going to be waiting for a while.

"Heading to the store once you get back to Rexford?" he asked.

Justine shook her head. "Nope, just home. My employee, Sienna, has the whole day covered."

"Ah. Gotcha."

The silence stretched on and Griffin knelt to pet Spencer's belly.

"I hope you had fun coming to the set," Justine said.

"I did!" he answered quickly. "I really did. Thanks for the tour. I was hoping to meet Anderson and shake his hand, but now I'm not so sure I want to."

"Sorry for ruining the magic."

"It's not ruined. Nothing can change my feelings about *Galaxy Force*." He sounded like a little boy.

Justine watched various crew members rushing around the periphery of the building. The guy with rolls and rolls of colored tape hanging from a rope on his belt, the crowd of flannel-wearing, black-knit-capped men and women moving as a pack, the prop department intern holding a stack of vintage newspapers. She finally felt like she fit in with them.

"Since I'm done for the day I'll walk out with you," Justine said. "Let me grab my stuff."

"Farmers' market!" Griffin exclaimed suddenly.

"What?"

"It's Thursday. There's a farmers' market a few blocks over from here. Let's swing by." He paused. "If you want to. I know you have a long drive ahead of you."

"I never say no to farm-fresh produce, and I'm sure Spence will be happy to put off the drive a little longer."

The farmers' market was small, just a few dozen tables braving the chilly day, but they were giving it their best effort with a huge display of festive orange and yellow mums and early pumpkins at the entrance.

Griffin was drawn to the table next to the giant wooden apple sign. "Give me apple everything," he said, eyeing the stacks of McIntoshes and Winesaps. "Oh, look at the pies," he practically moaned.

Justine wrinkled her nose. "I'm not a fan of cooked fruit."

"Huh? Is that even a thing?" he asked. Spencer ran his nose along the edge of the table and sniffed. "Who doesn't like *pie*? I sort of have a fixation with it. Apple pie in particular."

"Why?" Justine threw a few Ambrosia apples in a paper bag for the drive home.

"You know how apple pie is supposed to be, like, representative of family? You eat pies on holidays, and everyone gets a warm, fuzzy feeling about them?"

Justine nodded.

"I never had that growing up. Never. My parents worked most of the 'pie holidays' because they got time and a half, so unless I was invited to a friend's house, it was just another day in the McCabe house." He went back to examining the options spread out on the table.

"I'm sorry," Justine said. Holidays with her mom were small but festive affairs, and sometimes they even made the trip to visit her aunt, uncle, and cousins in Nevada. "Where did they work?"

He picked up a jug of apple cider. "My dad was a line worker at a consumer packaging company. They make boxes, so obviously he was always super busy during the holidays. My mom is a customer-service rep for a home security company. They both worked hard when I was young, but we still struggled."

Justine felt a flash of realization. The trajectory. Suddenly it made more sense.

"I try to help my mom out when I can, but she's too proud." He shook his head. "I guess I got my work ethic from them."

Griffin finally settled on a traditional apple pie with a sprinkling of cinnamon sugar on top of the lattice, six Cortland apples, and a quart of apple cider.

"I think I went a little overboard for just one person," he said as they continued walking past stalls displaying jars of local honey, fresh breads, and piles of gourds.

"Does everything you bought make you happy?" she asked.

Griffin paused to consider the question. "It does. Really happy."

"Then you didn't go overboard. Plus, it's good to splurge every now and then."

He laughed. "I'd hardly call eighteen dollars a splurge. Dropping a grand on a new Shinola Runwell? Now, that's a splurge."

Justine gasped. "You've spent a thousand dollars on a *watch*?"

"Well . . . yeah. And sometimes more. Don't tell me you never splurge on yourself."

"Not in a long time." She waved at him. "Hello, small-business owner here, just trying to make ends meet."

"I respect that," he replied. "But let's say you could splurge on anything right now. What would you get? Not just from the farmers' market, I'm talking anything."

"A thousand-dollar limit?"

Griffin nodded.

Justine peeked at an out-of-place table filled with antique toys and vintage lunch boxes. "That's easy. A really expensive pair of running sneakers and a smartwatch so I could track my runs. I'm finally getting serious about my workouts again."

"That's so . . . sensible," Griffin said. "And you'd still have money left over."

"The heart wants what it wants," she said with a laugh. "I'd spend the rest on this guy." She patted Spencer.

"I don't know, I was expecting jewelry or clothing. But now that I think about it, that doesn't make sense for you."

"Exactly." Justine did an inventory of what she was wearing. "Boots, jeans, T-shirt, hoodie." She pulled her hair behind her ear and pointed to her lobe. "Conflict-free cubic zirconia studs I got for nine ninety-nine. Have you even looked at me lately?"

They'd reached the end of the stalls near a cluster of picnic tables. It was too cold to sit outside, so the area was deserted.

Griffin turned to her. "Yeah, I have looked at you. All the time."

Justine felt her heart constrict at the intensity on his face. The playfulness between them shifted, replaced by Griffin's furrowed brow and an expression that looked like deliberation. She held her breath as she waited for his next move. Even Spencer seemed subdued by the change in the air, moving into a statue-like sit and watching them both carefully.

"Why?" Justine fidgeted with the leash and fought off the urge to move closer to him.

"It's hard not to."

She exhaled slowly and met his gaze. Justine could almost feel the shift taking place between them.

An older man dragging a garbage can drifted toward them and Spencer reacted by barking maniacally as he got closer. It was his DEFCON 5 bark, so piercing that it could shatter windows.

"Let's move over there," Justine said over the noise, pointing back to the vendors. "He's headed for the dumpster behind the tables."

Spencer's reaction was typical, since he was convinced that when their neighbors in Rexford brought their garbage cans in they were actually rolling up Trojan horses filled with fireworks and thunderstorms. Justine knew the only way to get him to stop was to put some distance between them and the scary can-man, so she walked him farther away from the commotion.

When the noise finally stopped, there was no hope of picking up the conversation again. In a few minutes they'd be back to talking about cooked fruit or artisanal bread.

Justine met Griffin at the antiques vendor's table, where he was checking out boxed Furbys and ThunderCats action figures.

He glanced down at Spencer. "All good now?"

"All good." She nodded.

"Do you want to grab a coffee or . . ." He trailed off.

Justine looked at her phone. "It's getting late and I hate sitting in that traffic. Plus, I need to feed him. It's not like I can do it before we go."

"Understood," Griffin replied.

They retraced their path out of the market, both silent. Justine felt an inexplicable sadness settle over her as they walked back to her car. Maybe it was the pending drive back, with Spencer panting a soundtrack in the back seat, or the fact that the crisp fall air was shifting into something that felt more like winter.

More likely, though, it was the fact that the last thing she wanted to do was walk away from Griffin.

chapter twenty-eight

I am the architect of flames and the goddess of fire!" Monty said, holding a burning branch above her head. She was wearing a deer-antler headdress accented with moss, crystals, and feathers.

The crowd whooped and cheered, raising their own burning branches and bottles of beer to her. It was the night of the annual Birch celebration, where all of Rexford gathered at a massive bonfire in the open field on the edge of town to drink, listen to live music, wear silly hats, and gossip. The event had been started by a few artists within the community in the '60s, and while it probably had significance when it began, no one quite knew what they were celebrating or why. People had campaigned to move the event from the dicey weather of late fall to spring, but no one was willing to do it for fear of pissing off whatever mystery pagan god they were celebrating.

Justine was freezing and stood as close as she could to the fire without singeing off her eyelashes. She'd actually gotten crafty and made her own crown of twigs and sparkly garland, but she worried that her head would burst into flames if she got any closer to the bonfire. She waved to a few of her creatively hatted T&B customers as she waited for Ruth to show up.

Luis joined her next to the flames. "Hey, stranger, we miss seeing you at Monty's," he said. "When will you and Spence be back in town full-time?"

"Hey, Luis! Soon enough," she replied and felt bad when she realized that she hoped it wasn't true. She quickly changed the subject. "Did you hear your lady is coming tonight? Maybe you two should finally talk or something?"

"Oh, don't you worry about that," Luis said with a smile. "We've definitely been, um, communicating."

"Wait, what? Why didn't she tell me?"

"No, no, it's not like that. Not yet, anyway. But she's been spending more time at my counter and I've been cooking all my specialties for her, so we're basically married now." He bobbed his head, suddenly sheepish. "Do you think I should ask her out?"

Justine swatted his arm. "Why are you even asking me that? She's been waiting for you to ask."

"For real?" His grin was infectious. "Okay, tonight. For you, Jus." He held out his fist and Justine bumped hers against it. He craned his neck and scanned the crowd as he walked away, a man on a mission.

She spotted Ruth and her husband, Patrick, straining to kick two massive tree stumps toward the fire. Ruth was wearing exaggerated black eye makeup and two swirling black horns that started at her hairline and swooped around her ears and made her look like an evil mountain ram.

"Hey, Teen, we brought you a chair," Ruth said, pointing to Patrick as he flipped it onto its wide side in an open space by the fire. "Sit!"

"Where are you going to sit, Patrick?" Justine asked. She always enjoyed spending time with Ruth's husband.

"No rest for the wicked tonight," he answered. "I'm on kid duty; Ruth has the night off. Where are those two anyway?"

Ruth stood on top of her stump, adjusted the curling black horns on the side of her head, and surveyed the crowd. "There. Throwing napkins into the fire. Wait, now Dillon is trying to attach a flaming napkin to a branch. Could you go deal with them, please?" She sighed as she watched him trot away. "How did I get so lucky?"

Justine laughed. "He's the best. But where's his headdress?"

"Oh, you didn't see his nubs? He's got these tiny baby horns glued to his forehead, right by his hairline. Like Pan. Kids have 'em too. They look like little demons, which is very on-brand these days."

"Let me guess; you made them."

Ruth nodded. "Bam, new revenue stream. Cosplayers eat it up! Who knew there's a market for horns?"

"Wait, did I hear you say revenue stream?" Sienna said, sliding in between them. She was the only smart one in the crowd, in a cozy octopus knit cap, complete with tentacles hanging down to her shoulders.

"She's making horns now." Justine pointed at Ruth.

"Ooh, want!"

Ruth and Justine slid over on their stumps to make room for her to join them in the middle.

"How was T&B today?" Sienna asked Justine. She'd had a week off of *The Eighteenth* and it felt strange spending so much time behind the counter again.

"Not bad, actually."

"And have you noticed that it's been a trend lately? A string of not-bad days?" Sienna looked hopeful.

Sienna had been implementing changes at Tricks & Biscuits since she'd been spending more time there while Justine was on set. Little things like switching up the product placement on the floor, adding a sale shelf, and putting bright green fifty-percent-off stickers on boxes of food and treats that were about to expire were simple shifts that seemed to be having an impact.

"I have, and I know you're the reason. What would I do without you?"

"Aww." Sienna bumped her shoulder against Justine. "Thank you!"

"Tell us what's happening next on the show," Ruth said, winding her hair around one of her horns. "I'm desperate for gossip, because hearing about the parking meter swap-out drama ain't cutting it for me."

"What's next is the location shoot, in Maryland, and I'm absolutely shitting my pants."

"Why?" Sienna asked. "I thought Spencer has been doing great lately."

Justine sighed. "Being on location is different. I met an old-timer professional trainer and he said dogs always do worse on location. He told me his dog ran away, and that dog was so well trained he seemed animatronic. Spencer needs to be off leash for the shot, and it's at night. In an unfamiliar place." She shook her head. "Oh yeah, there's also a stream."

A cheer went up on the far side of the bonfire and the flames shot higher.

"Can't you keep him on leash, and then they edit it out?" Ruth asked. She held her hands out in front of her to warm them.

"Trust me, they're not going to waste the budget to do special effects on my tiny little scene. They're expecting him to do it without a problem. My Humane Federation friend said I should bring someone with me to help, just in case. But I know neither of you can do it, so I'm out of luck."

"Wait, what?" Sienna grabbed Justine's arm. "That is *so* weird! I did a reading on you a few days ago, and now it totally makes sense."

"Do I want to know why you're pulling tarot cards on me again?"

"You'll find out soon enough. But there was one card in this reading that I couldn't figure out. Now I understand." A laugh bubbled out of her. "Wow, tarot never lies, man."

"Are you going to tell me?" Justine demanded.

"Right! Okay, it was an upright Wheel of Fortune card."

"I like the sound of that," Justine murmured.

"It's not what you think. In this pull the significance was about being open to support from others around you. It's so perfect now that I see it!" She paused. "Ask *the DILF* to help you in Maryland!"

Justine choked on her beer. "Not possible. He works so much, he can't get away."

But the thought had crossed her mind. More than once.

"I don't know, I think our little witch is onto something. The man gets vacation days, doesn't he?" Ruth asked.

"And what makes you think he'd want to waste one on me?"

"Didn't I tell you about the *last* time I pulled cards for

you?" Sienna asked breathlessly. "They said that the two of you are—"

Justine threw her hand up to stop Sienna. "Ruth did, and it's not going to happen. Trust me, Griffin doesn't want a relationship with me. And I'm still on my hiatus."

"Asking him to go makes a ton of sense, though," Ruth said as she adjusted her position on the stump. "Obviously, Spencer likes him and trusts him, so he would be great to have with you, just in case something went wrong. Plus, you said he's an Anderson fan, so you can use him as leverage."

"Come on, ask him!" Sienna cheered. "The tarot knows what's up! Do it!"

"Can't hurt to just ask," Ruth added. "The worst he can say is no."

Justine sighed. "Oh my God, you are *such* a mom."

"Text him. Right now." Ruth leaned over and started frisking her jacket pockets for her phone.

"Would you stop it?" She slapped Ruth's hands away. "I'll text him when I'm ready. *If* I decide to ask him."

"Promise?" Sienna asked.

"I promise to consider it."

It was enough of a commitment that Ruth and Sienna backed off.

Justine glared into the flames and crossed her fingers that Griffin would say yes.

chapter twenty-nine

Spencer was leaning against the back seat of Griffin's Volkswagen SUV, panting. He was doped up on his usual herbal antianxiety drops and wrapped in an Ace bandage that hit his acupressure points, but he seemed happier than usual to be in a car, probably because Griffin and Justine were side by side in the front.

Justine leaned over and looked at the dashboard. "Since you wouldn't let me drive, I'm paying for gas." She pointed at the gauge. "We should stop soon."

"There was no way I was going to spend three hours with my knees by my ears in that micro-car of yours. And yes, we can stop. I'm sort of hungry, are you?"

"Please confirm that I'm paying for gas. You took the day off to help me; it's the least I can do."

"Okay, all right!" Griffin exclaimed. "Yes, you can pay for gas. I'll put premium in if it makes you feel better. But can I at least get some food?"

"Yes, please. I'm starving. Usually I don't stop because I hate leaving Spence in the car, but since there's two of us we can."

It wasn't just hunger pangs she was dealing with. The butterflies in her stomach had a few different classifications. Some were dedicated to Spencer's responsiveness and the pressure of the shoot, but just as many were due to spending the whole day with Griffin.

She'd texted him the day after the bonfire and he'd called her back immediately. She could tell by the excitement in his voice that he was thrilled she'd asked, which made her feel less awful for needing him. Now that she was beside him it felt even more right that they were doing it together.

Griffin drove to the closest gas station and hopped out of the car before Justine could give him her credit card. He left his keys in the ignition, so she climbed over his seat, nailing her knee on the armrest, and rolled down the window right as he was reaching into his wallet.

"Hey!"

"Whoops, almost forgot," he replied, smiling a giant dimpled fake smile at her. He took the card from her hand and bowed. "Thank you, Justine. I appreciate it."

"Um-*hm*," she said, shooting him another look before she climbed over to her seat.

Spencer whined from the back. He glanced at Justine, then out the window at Griffin pumping gas.

"He'll be back in a sec, Spence. Don't worry."

He whined louder, so Justine leaned over to Griffin's seat again to punch the rear window button. She rolled it down a few inches and Spencer stuck his head out, snuffling loudly.

"Oh, hey, bud," Griffin said, walking over to Spencer. "You doing okay?" He stroked Spencer's head and lowered his voice.

"We're almost there. Don't worry, you're okay." A pause, then a whisper. "I love you, bud. Do you know that?"

Justine continued to hold her phone as though she were reading it but peeked at them out of the corner of her eye. Griffin had his eyes closed and he was kissing Spencer's head. Spencer looked equally drunk in love with his chin resting on Griffin's shoulder and his tail wagging slowly.

"I love you so much," he whispered again. He took Spencer's head in his hands and gave him a final kiss. "My best boy."

The prickle in her nose caught Justine off guard. There was room in Spencer's heart for both of them. Spencer gave a final low wag as he watched Griffin get back into the car.

"Your card," he said, handing it to her as he settled into his seat. "I filled it to the brim with super extra-premium ultra. Now can we grab some takeout over there?" He pointed at a small Mexican restaurant that bordered the gas station.

"Works for me. I'll run in and you can wait in the car with him?"

"Nope, I'll get it because otherwise you'll pay again."

Justine huffed at him, but she knew it was pointless to battle. Fifteen minutes later he came out loaded down with bags.

"How should we do this?" he asked, juggling the bags on his lap and the divider between them. "This is going to get messy and it's a little too chilly to eat outside."

Spencer was already drooling over their shoulders with his eyes on the prize. Justine knew that the meal was going to be a nonstop assault of sad looks and whining because of Griffin's habit of sharing every meal with Spencer.

"I know—let's open the back and let Spencer hang outside on the leash, and we can spread out in back," Justine suggested.

"Works for me," Griffin said, repacking the bags.

Griffin moved the car to the rear of the restaurant's lot to an area bordering a grassy patch. Justine took Spencer for a quick pee break, then put him on the fifteen-foot line and climbed into the back of the car, where Griffin was unpacking the overflowing take-out bags. With the residual heat from their drive keeping the car warm plus her down jacket, it wasn't a bad spot to have a Mexican picnic. She crossed her legs and made room in front of her for lunch.

"How much did you buy? I asked for *a* taco, not the entire menu."

"Well, they gave me free chips and salsa, and I got you three tacos, not one, because the lady said they're small, and I bought myself a burrito for now, and then I got some cinnamon churros for us for later. Oh, and drinks." He pointed at the cups sitting on the wheel well, then positioned himself so that he was against the seat back and his knees were cranked up awkwardly.

"Is it that obvious that I'm not a one-taco kind of girl?" she asked as she unwrapped her first one and took a massive bite.

"Your Honor, let the record reflect that the witness is pleading the Fifth." Griffin bit into his burrito and pointed to his full mouth.

Justine laughed.

They sat eating in silence and watched Spencer nose around the grass.

"He really is the best dude," Griffin said quietly.

"He is. Thanks again for helping us today. Sorry we had to leave so early this morning, but you know he needs time to recover. And I want time to get to know the location."

"No prob. Happy to help Spencer out."

Another car pulled into the lot and parked a few feet away even though the entire parking lot was open. A guy in a baseball cap and windbreaker got out and jogged to the restaurant, running close to where Spencer was standing. Spencer locked in on the man, clocking his every move, then launched into a fit of barking with his tail held high.

"I should've been on top of him." Justine grabbed her taco and hopped out of the car and walked to where Spencer stood freaking out.

"Hey, Spence, you're fine," she said in a soothing voice, even though his reaction left her shaking. She walked closer and got him to look away by feeding him a tiny bite of tortilla. "It's all good. Hey, Spence, watch." Spencer let out one more grumbly woof in the guy's direction but managed to tear his eyes away from the retreating figure and look at Justine's face. She smiled at him and gave him another morsel, punching down the anxiety she felt swirling inside. "Good boy," she said softly.

Spencer's posture relaxed and he started wagging again. Justine gave him one more small bite of taco and a quick massage, then walked back to the car.

"What was *that*?" Griffin asked, looking shocked at Spencer's behavior. "He was never weird about people when he was with me. It's not an option in the city. That reaction was different than the way he was barking at the garbage-can guy. Are you worried?" He paused. "Spence actually looked dangerous that time, like he'd bite if he could."

Justine felt an involuntary shudder pass through her as a vision of Spencer latched on to a man's arm swam into focus.

"Hey, are you okay?" Griffin asked. "Your face is white."

Justine knew she was eventually going to tell Griffin. Back when she was worried that he was angling to take Spencer back, she'd kept the incident in her back pocket, ready to spring the story on him when it was time for the big guns. To prove that he couldn't compete with her bond with Spencer. But now, even though Griffin seemed to gracefully accept that Spencer was hers, she thought he deserved to hear the story of how her dog had saved her.

She cleared her throat. "Something happened. To me. To us, I mean. That's why he did that. They call it 'one-trial learning.' One major impactful incident sets the precedent for the rest of the responses." Talking about it in abstract terms helped. She willed herself to keep going, but just thinking about the day made the words dry up.

"Okay, this is big," Griffin said as he studied her. "You look . . . not like yourself."

She glanced away, embarrassed that her weakness was written on her face.

"Hey," Griffin said softly, tapping his foot against Justine's knee. "What's going on?"

He needed to know. Justine took a deep breath and started talking.

"I'm a runner. I've always loved running. And when I adopted Spencer it was perfect because he loved it too, and we were a great team. It was our thing; we had our little routines, our favorite trails. Rexford is an amazing place for running, and we took full advantage of it." She paused and smiled at the purity of the memory. "With Spencer by my side I forgot that I was RWF."

"What's that?" Griffin had stopped eating and his half-finished burrito sat in his lap.

"'Running while female.' You get catcalled, harassed. It's a thing. All women runners have to deal with it. But once I started running with Spencer, it stopped. He's not a scary-looking dog, but just having him with me changed the way people viewed me. It was like running with a bodyguard. So I got sloppy." She swallowed hard.

"I don't like the way this sounds," Griffin said slowly. "What do you mean?"

"I started running at odd times. Too-late times when it was getting dark. Or I took trails that not many people knew about." Justine nodded as if she was accepting the blame for her actions. "It was stupid, but Spencer made me feel invincible."

They both looked out at the dog, who was standing with his head back and his eyes closed, inhaling the wind.

"I'm talking too much. This is dumb." She waved her hand to signify she'd finished. "Whatever, I'm fine."

"No, *not* whatever. Please keep going, I want to know."

She'd only had to tell the whole story a few times; to the police, to her mom, then to Ruth and Sienna. When people asked her about the incident, she deflected everything to Spencer, which was enough to derail most conversations to something she could cope with.

Justine took a deep breath, then exhaled slowly. She was going to tell Griffin everything.

"Okay. One day, one *night*, actually, we're out for a run on my favorite trail. It was just getting dark, and I was finishing up, heading back down the hill. By then Spencer was doing better off leash so he was in the brush doing his own thing. He always darted between me and the woods as we ran. I trusted him to explore. I had my earbuds in, and I was totally in the zone." She gestured behind her head. "I used to have really long hair. I'd wear it in a braid." Her face fell and she stopped talking abruptly.

"Are you okay to keep going?" Griffin asked gently.

She nodded and sat up a little straighter, as if reclaiming some of her power. "I always wore my hair in a braid. I loved the way it felt, hitting my shoulders. It kept me in rhythm. So that night, I'm coming down the hill, all up in my brain as usual, and I feel this *yank* on the back of my head. And it scared the *shit* out of me; it almost took me off my feet. It hurt! I whip around and there's this guy standing behind me, smiling, like he'd just done something funny."

Griffin's jaw clenched and he shook his head slowly.

"I take my earbuds out and I'm like, 'What the hell was that?' And he just stands there, grinning at me. And that's when I realize that it's nearly dark and I'm alone on the trail and this guy isn't right. He was in a baseball cap but he wasn't in running clothes or even trail clothes. I remember he had on, like, *business* shoes. He was this hillbilly-looking guy, jacked-up teeth . . ." She took a shuddering breath. "I tell him to fuck off and walk away thinking he's just some weirdo. But then he runs up behind me again—and I can *still* hear the way his footsteps sounded in those stupid dress shoes—and he grabs my braid again, only this time he doesn't let go."

"Justine, I'm so sorry." Griffin reached out and put a gentle hand on the top of her sneaker, the only part he could reach without contorting himself. "This is awful."

Spencer made his way back to the car and stood on his hind

legs, surveying if there was enough room for him to jump in back with them.

"Hey, Spence," Justine said, placing a grateful hand on the side of his face. It was all the invitation he needed, and he leapt in back in a single bound. Griffin quickly put the remnants of their lunch into the plastic bags as Spencer tried to find room to lie down.

Having him near gave her the strength to keep going. Justine cleared her throat and continued. "The guy is holding on to my hair, pulling me backward, and I start screaming. I think I was just screaming 'Help' at first, but then I started screaming for Spencer." Hearing his name made him look up at Justine. "The word is barely out of my mouth and he's crashing through the forest as fast as he can. Oh my God, he sounded like a bulldozer." Justine's eyes filled with tears as she gazed at her dog. "And then Spencer saved me."

"What . . . what did he do?"

A tear slid down her cheek, but she still managed to smile at the memory. "What didn't he do? Spencer came out of the woods and fucking *launched* himself at the guy. He looked like one of those trained attack dogs. He grabbed on to the guy's arm and all I can hear is Spencer growling and the guy screaming. Obviously, he let go of me and I back away, and Spencer is just . . . *dangling* off of him, like his arm is a toy. There's blood on the guy's arm, and I remember thinking, *Good, better his blood than mine.*" She shook her head. "I just wanted to run away as fast as possible, so I scream, 'Out!,' which is Spencer's drop cue when we're playing tug. And he lets go of the guy and then comes sauntering over to me like he'd just been gnawing on a rope toy. But he's got blood on his mouth."

"Holy shit, Spence saved you," Griffin said in a quiet voice. He leaned forward and placed a gentle hand on Spencer's back. "I can't believe he did that. I mean, I can believe it but . . . holy *shit*. He *saved* you."

She nodded. "He did. We ran down the trail as fast as we could. Spencer wouldn't leave my side. The police came, they took my statement, they called Spencer a hero, and they never caught that motherfucker."

The air in the SUV was cold.

"Wow." Griffin paused. "I don't know what to say. I'm speechless." His eyes were soft as he took her in. "I'm so sorry that happened to you, Justine."

"Me too." She let out a strained laugh. "I barely run anymore. I'm so out of shape."

"Stop. You look amazing."

Griffin was gazing at her with the same expression he'd had in the hallway in his apartment. And at the farmers' market. And lately, *any*time he looked at her.

Like she was precious.

Spencer interrupted the moment by asking Justine to pet him by crashing his paw into her cheek, causing her to whip her head back and bump it against the window.

"Ouch, Spence. Thanks." She rubbed her head.

"We're not off to a great start on this trip, are we?" Griffin asked as he activated fifty percent of his dimples.

"We can stop talking about it. Now you know everything about the two of us. It's not something I like to talk about, obviously, but I thought you should know." She shrugged. "I'm still working on Spencer's dude-in-a-cap reactivity. He's usually fine, but certain things still set him off. The guy's running was probably what did it this time." She didn't tell him about Spencer's guy-making-threatening-gestures-at-his-costar reactivity.

"Hey, I don't want to move on from what you just told me yet. Are you, like, talking to someone about it?"

"Therapy? Yeah, until the woman said I need to consider how my actions put me in jeopardy." She snorted. "I've beaten myself up enough about it; I don't need to pay someone to pile on. And my boyfriend, Nick, did the same thing."

"What did he say?"

"Initially he also sort of blamed me too, and then he started making me question *everything* I did. Like I couldn't be trusted to make any good decisions. Which kept reinforcing the idea that I was to blame for what happened on the trail, and anything else bad that happened to me. Even if it was just a low-dollar day at Tricks & Biscuits."

"Fuck him," Griffin said angrily. "And fuck that therapist. They're not all like that, though. Maybe you should think about trying again, with a new therapist? I've heard that people can have PTSD from stuff like what you went through." He stopped talking with a sheepish look on his face. "Sorry, I shouldn't be telling you what to do."

"You're not telling me what to do; you're suggesting. And you might be right. Maybe I should find someone new." She shoved the taco wrappers in the bag.

"Hey."

"Yeah?" Justine stopped cleaning up the lunch mess.

"If you ever need to talk, I'm always here. I just want you to know that."

"Thank you. That means a lot to me."

The three of them got out of the back of the SUV and

stretched and yawned as if they needed to shake off whatever darkness had settled over them. Spencer took one final pee on a pole and they all climbed back into the car.

"Ready?" Griffin asked, searching her face like he was looking for residual sadness.

"Ready."

chapter thirty

A h, hell," Ted muttered as he watched a playback on his tablet with Anderson beside him.

It was the angriest thing Justine had ever heard Ted say, which
meant the location shoot was going very badly indeed. She
cocked her head to eavesdrop harder.

The rest of the crew had been there since early morning, shooting the scenes where Anderson met up with the bootleggers,
whose liquor-loaded car had broken down on the way into the city.
The combination of missing equipment, vintage cars that didn't
work when they were supposed to, and unexpected air traffic that
they had to wait to pass set the entire day hours behind schedule,
which meant that Justine, Malcolm, Griffin, and Spencer had
nothing to do but sit in a nearby tent under heat lamps in their
jackets and hats, drink too much coffee, and watch the bad moods
around them percolate. They'd been on set long enough for Griffin
to flip from wide-eyed fan to jaded critic, although he did stand
taller every time Anderson came within twenty feet of him.

"I can't keep giving it to you at this level, Ted," Anderson
grumbled. "I'm exhausted."

"I understand you are, and I apologize. This has been a rough day for all of us," Ted replied. He sighed and rubbed his fingertips against his eyes. "Lighting is still having some issues, so it's going to be a while before we're ready for the river run. Take five in your trailer."

Justine knew that "five" probably meant "fifty-five."

Malcolm leaned over and stage-whispered, "If the trailer is a-rockin', don't bother knockin'."

"What do you mean?" Justine asked.

"Taylor's been in Anderson's trailer all day."

"What?" Justine practically shrieked. "When did that happen?"

Griffin did a double take. "Wait, she's *here*? Taylor is with Anderson? But I thought they hate each other."

"Set life does strange things to people," Malcolm said. "Everybody knows about it, but no one's talking about it. If you ask me, it's just a way to pass the time."

Justine considered how Monty would take the news that her daughter was sleeping with a man old enough to be her father. It wasn't going to be pretty.

Based on the schedule, Justine had told Griffin they'd be done by five o'clock at the latest, and it was already creeping toward six without an end in sight.

Malcolm blew out a long puff of air. "Gonna be a late night, friends. You regret coming along?" He leaned forward in his chair to catch Griffin's eye.

"Who, me? Are you kidding? This is fascinating! But I am getting a little bored with all the downtime."

"Welcome to the glamorous world of entertainment." Malcolm chuckled and shoved his hands in his jacket pockets.

"Have you been doing this a long time?" Griffin asked.

"Too long," Malcolm answered. "This job breaks people, but I'm still here. Good thing I'm single."

"But there's got to be some fun parts," Justine added. "You get to work with people like me, after all." She grinned at him.

Malcolm watched the various crew members in headlamps moving equipment. "Yep, the people can be the very best part or the very worst part. I've seen it all."

"Okay, give us some gossip!" Justine clapped her hands together and startled Spencer, who was resting at her feet working on a food-stuffed Kong she'd brought to help him cope with all the waiting. He'd already gone through a full bowl's worth of meal ration in the big red rubber toy.

"Yeah," Griffin added. "Who's the most famous person you've met?"

"Tom Hanks," he answered without even pausing.

"Very cool."

"What was he like?" Justine asked.

"Consummate professional. That man knew how to *work*. Nailed his lines every time. Plus, he remembered everyone's names and was generally a decent human to all of us. And let me tell you, that's not always the case." He raised an eyebrow.

"Come on, you can't put that out there and not tell us who's an asshole," Griffin said with a smile.

"Okay, don't repeat this." Malcolm looked over his shoulder and lowered his voice. "Rebecca Dawson."

"What?" Griffin and Justine screamed in unison.

"But that's my girl," Justine said. "She's America's sweetheart."

"Try America's cokehead."

"No way!" Griffin said in disbelief. "But she seems so down-to-earth."

Malcolm shrugged. "That's what publicists are for, I guess. But she was surly as hell to everyone on set. Her character had a kitten in the movie, and she wanted nothing to do with it. I mean, what kind of freak doesn't like a *kitten*?"

"You've just crushed my fandom. She's off my list," Justine said, making a swiping motion in the air. "Malcolm, I could listen to your gossip all night."

"The way this day is going you might have to. But enough about me. I want to know about this dude over here." He pointed to Griffin. "What's your story? You a trainer too?"

Justine snorted softly.

"I'm just a boring corporate drone. I don't have any exciting stories, unless you want to hear about being a thought leader in my company's post-sales life cycle."

"Wha . . . ?"

"I'm kind of a corporate trainer. Once top-tier clients buy our customer-relationship-management software I embed with them and help with the deployment and training."

Malcolm nodded. "I get it. You travel a lot?"

"I do."

"Do you like it?"

"Yeah, but it can get tiring."

"How'd you two meet?" Malcolm asked.

Griffin and Justine glanced at each other and he raised an eyebrow that asked, *Do we really want to go there?*

"A mutual friend," Justine answered. Griffin looked down at Spencer and winked.

"Okay, that's always a good way to start off. And how long have you been together?"

Heat spread on her face. "Oh, no, no. We're not dating. Just friends."

"Really?" Malcolm drew the word out. "Um-hm, okay. And which hotel are you *friends* staying at tonight?"

Justine sat up straighter, ignoring the innuendo. "We're not staying."

"Mistake number one," Malcolm replied. "This is going to go even longer than we thought. Water adds time in the best of circumstances. Add an overtired crew and you're looking at two more hours at least." He settled back in his chair. "You negotiate for overtime?"

She shook her head. "Day rate."

"Well, this ain't day." He pointed up at the dark sky. "They got you for a steal. Better luck next time."

A production assistant in a wool poncho ran into the tent. "We're getting close. Can you swap out Ford's collar now?"

"Oh really? Okay, great." Justine took the brown leather collar out of her pocket, Spencer's costume when he was having adventures with Izzy. She made a kissy noise and showed Spencer the collar, and he stood up, ready to get dressed and go to work.

"What can I do?" Griffin put his coffee cup down and hopped out of his chair.

"Legally? Nothing," Malcolm answered for Justine. "You're not even supposed to be here."

"But I signed all of that nondisclosure paperwork. I think I agreed to donate blood on one of those forms."

"Doesn't matter. You're not assigned as his handler on this project, so as far as my paperwork goes, you don't exist. She's Spencer's sole handler." He pointed at Justine.

A flicker of disappointment flitted across his face. "Okay, I guess I'll wait here, then."

"Malcolm, he can at least walk to the starting location with me, right? Before we roll?"

"That's fine, but he needs to get back here before they start."

"You got it."

Justine pulled on her hat, and the three of them walked out of the bright lights and warmth of the tent. Luckily, it was one of those weird fall-weather spells when the evening felt warmer than the day. She switched on a flashlight and they made their way to the spot near the river, where the crew was putting finishing touches on the lighting. The area was probably beautiful in the summertime, but in the dark the bare branches over the rocky terrain looked skeletal. It was the sort of place where you might stumble upon a dead body washed up from the inky, bottomless river.

Or run into a crazy guy in dress shoes.

"How deep is it?" Griffin asked.

"About six inches. It's not like he's going to be swimming; they just want the look of the water kicking up as he runs through it."

"Are you nervous?"

"Not anymore. This isn't a hard behavior; that trainer just got in my head. I'm happy we had a chance to do some practice. Thanks for helping."

They'd spent time after they arrived working on Spencer's recall on the long line, taking turns calling him back and forth in an open field that was close to where they'd be shooting. It felt good to play together after the heavy conversation, watching Spencer run between them like a gleeful dork.

"You have nothing to worry about, Justine," Griffin said in a way that made him sound like the authority on Spencer's training abilities. "He's got this." He paused, then looked over at her, his eyes locking on hers in an unblinking stare. "And you do too. All of it."

On the surface it was a simple vote of confidence in her training abilities, but his expression brought her back to their conversation in the car. Griffin was telling her the one thing she needed to hear more than anything.

You are still strong.

chapter thirty-one

I don't know if he can do it," Justine said to Malcolm in a panicked voice. She clenched Spencer's leash. "We didn't work on
that behavior."

"It happens all the time. They just don't get it," Malcolm replied, not hiding his frustration. "Dogs can't handle last-minute
script changes."

"Unbelievable." She looked down at Spencer, who was focused on the action around him. "He was going to *nail* it as
scripted."

The requested behavior change seemed simple to everyone
but the two of them. Instead of running through the water after
Anderson, they now wanted Spencer to wade into the river first,
pause in the middle and look over his shoulder at Anderson
trailing behind him, then continue running to the other side. It
wouldn't have been an impossible behavior to quickly map out
in the controlled environment of the studio set, but attempting
it in a dark and unfamiliar spot after hours of waiting around
felt dicey.

"What should I do?"

"Are you concerned about his safety?" Malcolm asked. "Do you want me to speak up and call it for you?"

"No, no, it's not that. It's totally safe. I'm just getting flash-backs to his first day on set, when everyone was waiting for us to get it right. The tension gets me all freaked out, and then it trickles down to Spence and everything goes to hell. And he doesn't even know that run-stop-look-run sequence on land, let alone in the water. I'm not sure how to coach it."

"Well, I'm a little concerned about the water temperature if Spencer can't nail this behavior quickly. It's fine for a few min-utes, but any longer than that and it starts to feel pretty damn cold."

Justine went silent, playing out the various training scenar-ios in her head.

"No, we have to at least try. Give us ten minutes to practice. Stall them for me if you can, please."

Justine walked Spencer to an area just beyond the lights and started the pep talk, hoping she could convince both ends of the leash that the impossible was possible. "We need to try some-thing, okay, Spence? You got this." She reached into her coat pocket and pulled out the thin fifteen-foot line she and Griffin had used to work on the recall and switched out his shorter leash.

She paced in circles, tripping over branches and going over their possible game plans out loud while Spencer trotted be-side her.

"Hey, you okay?"

Griffin stepped out of the shadows.

"Not really. Last-minute script change that we're not pre-pared for. It's not going to go well." She gave him a strained smile. "Good times."

"Oh, come on, you can do this. There has to be a way to cheat it; you've taught Spencer so much. Let's figure this out."

Justine stopped pacing and blinked at Griffin.

"Whenever we have a problem at work we break it down into tiny, manageable steps and chip away at it one bit at a time. Let's try that."

She threw her head back and squeezed her eyes shut. "Ugh, I'm such an idiot! Yes, that's *exactly* how to do it. Dog Training 101. You're better at this than I am."

"Stop. Can I help?"

"Seriously?"

He shrugged. "I did okay working on the recalls with you earlier. Doesn't that give me a little trainer cred?"

She quickly ran through how the scene would go and realized that having Griffin on the opposite side of the river would definitely make it easier on both her and Spencer. And his being a part of the prep work would speed the process.

"Yeah, we could use some support. Thank you, Griffin."

Within minutes Spencer was cheerfully responding to the "away" cue he was already familiar with, dashing from Griffin and coming to a stop when Justine gave him the hand signal. Getting him to continue running to her was simple, but the "look back" part of the sequence kept tripping them both up.

"I have an idea. I didn't train, but back in the day when I used to say, 'Hey, boy,' he'd look at me," Griffin offered. "I forgot all about it."

"Show me," Justine said. "Try it while he's close to me over here."

Griffin nodded, then spoke in a clear voice. "Hey, boy!"

Spencer stopped and whipped his head to look at Griffin, then galloped over to him.

"Whoops," Griffin said as he petted Spencer. "He's not supposed to run back to me. That won't work, will it?"

Justine was silent for a few seconds. "Actually, it might. I think I can cheat it. So, you let go of him when I signal, I'll get him to do a 'wait' when he's in the right spot in the water, then you say 'Hey, boy' and I'll try to override you by giving him another 'wait' cue; then I'll finish the whole thing with a final recall." She paused to go over the sequence in her mind again. "Yeah, we can do it!"

It struck her that not only was it going to be a test of her skills as a trainer; it was also going to be a very public devotion test. Would Griffin's simple "Hey, boy" cancel out her carefully trained "wait" cue?

"Justine," Malcolm said as he strode over to them. "They want you guys now."

She tensed. "No, we're not ready. I want to do a quick practice run in the water."

He shook his head. "I did what I could, but things are getting pretty heavy. I told them there's a chance they won't get what they need. They weren't happy, but whatever. Spencer comes first. You holding up okay?"

"No, not even close." Justine sighed. "Malcolm, I need a favor. I know Griffin isn't officially on my staff, but can you look the other way for this behavior? I really need his help."

"Once again you want me to bend rules for you and put my ass on the line. But okay. They switched things up and now you have to improvise to make it work. It's fine. In the future you have to let me know in advance."

If things didn't work out, Justine wasn't sure that there would be a future.

"I promise. Thank you, Malcolm."

"Thank you," Griffin added. "She's doing all the work; I'm just her backup."

Malcolm leaned over and gave Spencer a quick shoulder massage. "I *believe* in you, Ford! Break a leg." He pointed at Justine. "I'm here for both of you if you feel weird about anything. Don't take any risks, okay?"

Ten minutes later, after a quick conversation with Ted, Justine was pacing on the stones by the river's edge, occasionally shooting looks at Griffin and Spencer on the other side. They had two chances to make it happen. First a practice run with the cameras rolling, then the real thing.

The primary lighting was directed toward the water and she was in the dark, which only made what they were about to do feel scarier. She caught Griffin's eye and he waved at her, like they were just hanging out and not about to do something major. She finally cracked a smile. Nothing seemed to faze him.

She wanted to run and stress-pee in the bushes, but she saw a young woman slate the scene and shouts of "rolling" echoed through the woods. Everything went silent except for the hum of the generators.

"Action."

Justine took a deep breath, then gave Griffin the signal to release Spencer. He looked at her expectantly and she yelled, "Front!" to him, three times louder than she normally would because of the ambient noise. She threw up the hand signal and he took off running toward her through the shallow water. The second he hit the center point where Ted had instructed her to get Spencer to pause, she yelled, "Wait!" and made the hand signal. He stopped with an abrupt splash and waited for her next cue.

She felt like her whole body was shaking as she pointed her other hand at Griffin, and he yelled, "Hey, boy!" As predicted, Spencer turned to look at him, and then everything seemed to slow to half speed. Justine saw the tiniest shift in Spencer's shoulders that meant he was reorienting back to Griffin, but before he could commit to running to him she yelled, "Spence, *wait*!" He froze but seemed torn between staying put and running, so Griffin imitated Justine's "wait" hand signal. Spencer didn't move, his body pointing toward Justine and his head twisted to look back at Griffin.

She waited a beat, then gave Spencer his recall cue and he took off with the water splashing around him, as if he were relieved to have a clear instruction to follow. He barreled out of the river and toward where she was crouching, then danced in place in front of her, acting like he knew he'd earned his liver treat and then some. Justine gave him a handful of treats and held her breath as she watched the figures checking the playback behind the monitors.

"Perfect! One take, we got it, thank you very much, Spencer! You're wrapped for today," Ted's voice rang out. "Moving on!"

Justine wanted to cry with relief.

"You did it! *We* did it!" She clipped the leash on him and headed back over the makeshift two-by-four bridge to where Griffin was waiting for them. Spencer's wagging increased as they got closer to him.

"Nailed it! That was awesome," he said, pulling Justine into a hug that she didn't realize she needed. She clutched him and felt her heartbeat slow as some of the tension finally started to drain from her neck and shoulders.

"Teamwork makes the dream work. I couldn't have done it without you. Seriously. Griffin to the rescue, as always."

"Stop, I was just following the leader. That was all you," he said as they walked back toward base camp. "Are we done now?"

"We're wrapped. Let's get out of here."

Griffin glanced over her shoulder and his whole body seemed to jolt in shock. He leaned close. "There's *Anderson*," he whispered. "He's *right* behind you. Don't move, I'm going to snag a picture."

Justine wasn't about to miss the opportunity, no matter how exhausted she felt. "Hey, Mr. Brooks, do you have a second?"

He turned abruptly toward them with a scowl that magically transformed into a beam when he saw Griffin's deer-in-headlights stare.

"Would it be okay if my friend took a quick picture with you? He's a major Captain Zaltan fan."

"Well, of course, of course, any friend of Ford's is a friend of mine," he replied in his booming fake-happy voice, which Justine now recognized was one hundred percent put on. He still pretended that he was the good-guy everyman with fans not directly involved with the shoot. "Come on over. What's your name?"

He froze. "I'm Griffin. I love *Galaxy Force*."

Anderson let out a booming laugh. "Well, thank you. Come on over here, let's get this picture real quick."

"Go!" Justine whispered, and gave him a shove when he didn't move.

Griffin walked over to Anderson and stood woodenly beside

him. Justine loved that he had a good three inches on his hero. Anderson wrapped his beefy arm around Griffin's shoulders, and Justine snapped a few photos because Griffin kept shutting his eyes and smiling weird.

"Thanks so much, I really appreciate it," Griffin said, almost bowing to him.

"No problem!" Anderson said as he started to walk away. He stopped abruptly. "Hey, Griffin?"

"Yeah?"

"Don't forget to set the course . . . for Galaxy Force!" he said in his Captain Zaltan voice with the character's signature smirk-grin.

"Galaxy Force is *go!*" Griffin replied with the other character's typical reply, wearing a huge smile.

The second Anderson was out of sight, Griffin punched the air. "He was so cool! Wasn't he cool? I can't believe I thought he was an asshole. Did you hear us quoting lines? Can I see the pictures?"

"I did, and you can," she said as she handed him her phone with a bemused grin. "You probably shouldn't have any more set visits, so you can remember this side of him."

"Amazing," Griffin said, scrolling through the pictures without listening to her as they walked toward his car.

"Okay, *that* was a lot." She yawned. "I'm exhausted and Spencer is too. Let's get out of here."

Griffin finally looked up from the photos. "About that . . ."

"What?"

"I think Malcolm is right. We should probably stay over somewhere around here. We're all tired, it's late, and it makes sense to get a good night's sleep and head back tomorrow."

She stopped in her tracks. "Really? But I didn't even bring a toothbrush."

"Think about it. It's three hours back to Brooklyn, then another two hours to get to Rexford. Let's just find a motel and get a good night's sleep."

The idea of being able to put her head down on a pillow within the next thirty minutes made her toes curl with delight. Sienna had Tricks & Biscuits covered the following day, so Justine had no reason to say no.

"I'm in."

"Good! I checked the map and there are a few nearby, but they look pretty sketchy. You okay with that?"

"As long as there aren't visible stains on the sheets, I'll be fine for a night. Let's go."

Fifteen minutes later they pulled into the surprisingly crowded parking lot of the River Lodge Motel, complete with a classic neon-edged sign out front.

"This one allows pets, I made sure," Griffin said as he climbed out of the car.

Justine and Spencer followed him into the ancient blue-carpeted check-in area, which was barely big enough for the three of them. When she saw the ring-for-service bell on the counter, Justine was tempted to ask Spencer to do it, but then she realized he'd worked hard enough already. Griffin tapped the bell and a stooped white-haired man emerged from a back room.

"Checking in?" he wheezed.

"We are, but we don't have a reservation."

"Hrmpf," the man grumbled. "You part of that billiards-league championship thing going on at the Elks Lodge?"

Justine hid a smile.

"We are not," Griffin answered politely with his dimples deployed. "Do you happen to have a few rooms open?"

The man grumbled again and consulted a hard-backed reservation book, running his finger down the page slowly. "The dog too?"

"The dog too." Griffin nodded.

"We have one left. That's it."

"Oh, okay, that's not going to work for us. But thank you," Justine said, turning to walk to the door.

"Young lady, *everyone* is booked," the man scolded. "You damn pool players are spread out all over Aberdeen. And we're the only place that takes dogs." His scowl softened as he leaned over the counter to look at Spencer smiling up at him. "That's a good-looking dog you got there."

"Thank you," Justine and Griffin answered in unison.

"Can you give us a second?" Griffin asked the man.

He turned to face Justine and he lowered his voice. "I'm okay with it if you are. I'll sleep on the floor, or in the tub. I just need to sleep at this point."

He looked as tired as she felt, but the thought of spending the night with Griffin sent a shot of adrenaline through her.

"Fine." She pretended like it didn't matter and like she was bored by the thought of being in a tiny, crappy hotel room with Griffin's chest, which she would undoubtedly see since he probably wasn't going to wear his navy button-down shirt to bed. "We can flip a coin to see who sleeps where. I don't have to automatically get the bed."

"Can we not argue about it here?" He turned back to the old man and handed him his credit card before Justine could even reach into her purse for hers. "We'll take it, thanks."

Her soft harrumph filled the room and Griffin shot her a triumphant grin.

Justine wasn't surprised when the man placed an old-fashioned manual credit-card swiper on the counter and took his time fitting the card and carbon paper in it. He didn't seem to have the hand strength to move the swipe part over the paper, and he struggled with it until Griffin stepped in.

"I can take care of that for you, sir," he said in his business voice with the dimples turned up to eleven.

They were about to leave the vestibule when Justine turned to the old man. "Do you have any toiletries for sale, like a toothbrush and toothpaste? I, uh, forgot to bring mine." She didn't want him to think that they'd picked each other up at the dog park for a quick one-night stand.

"Just take these; they've been in the drawer forever." He threw two sealed plastic bags with vintage-looking toothbrushes and miniature metal toothpaste tubes on the counter along with a key on a diamond-shaped burgundy plastic key chain. "Checkout is at ten. Good night, dog." With that he disappeared into the back.

Griffin picked up the key. "Lucky number fourteen. Ready?" He held the door for her, and Spencer trotted behind Griffin even though it was Justine who had the leash.

"Ready."

At that point, lying was the only option.

chapter thirty-two

"No tank," Justine muttered as she followed Griffin and Spencer up the stairs to the room.

He looked back over his shoulder. "What?"

"Oh, sorry, nothing."

Wearing nine hundred layers for the long day outside was a fine idea, but forgetting to wear a tank or camisole under it all meant that she had nothing to double as a pajama top. Starting from the top, she'd worn her trusty down coat, a cream wool duster, a black-and-gray-camo zip-front hoodie, a thin gray crewneck sweater, and a slim-fit thermal black turtleneck underneath it all. The turtleneck made the most sense to wear to bed, but after dealing with it for fourteen hours she felt like it was strangling her. Her options below the waist were even worse. Jeans, of course, and thin white silk-blend thermal leggings that were essentially see-through and made her underwear look like a piece of wrinkled-up black paper.

Griffin put his key in the knob on the red door and peeked in. "Okay." He held back a smile. "This is our current situation." He stepped back so she could walk in first. "Welcome home."

Justine dropped the leash to let Spencer check it out, and the moment she followed him in she was assaulted by hideousness. The walls were bisected, with wood-paneled wainscoting along the bottom and washed-out burgundy pinstripe wallpaper up to the ceiling. A depressing painting of a barn hung off center on the wall across from the door. Spencer nosed his way on the inexplicable tile walkway that led into the bathroom, which Justine could see had a vanity and sink outside and a powder blue toilet inside.

Then there was the bed. Covered in the most depressing dirt-brown faux patchwork quilt with two speed humps she assumed were pillows, it was a size that hovered somewhere between "college futon" and "department store linen display bed."

"What is that? A twin-plus?" Justine asked as she put her purse down on the dresser. "I've never seen a bed that size before."

"I'd call it a three-quarters of a full. Looks like you're going to have sweet dreams tonight."

"Is this the only light?" She flicked a fluorescent wall light off and on.

"Guess so. The Ritz it ain't."

Being inside the room together made it real. She was spending the night with Griffin again, although this time there was no metal staircase separating them. He'd be sleeping just a few feet away, and they'd both be able to hear every move. Hell, every *breath*.

Keeping busy was the best strategy to avoid stressing about what was about to happen. "I have zero battery left." She fished through her purse. "Dammit, I left my charger in your car. Can I steal your keys and run down?"

Griffin was sitting on the edge of the bed looking at his

phone. "I'm pretty low too. I'll go; you stay here. And while I'm at it I'll take Spence for a quick walk."

"No, I can do that, you don't have to—"

He put his hand up. "Stop. It's no problem, I've got it." Griffin slapped his leg. "C'mon, bud, let's go out."

Spencer dashed to him still dragging his leash and Griffin picked it up and walked out.

The second the door snapped shut Justine fell backward onto the bed. Her exhaustion was tinged with a buzzy feeling that probably was just punch-drunkenness. With Griffin out of the room it was the perfect time to get ready for bed, so she stripped out of her clothes and left them in a pile on the desk, grabbed the toothbrush and one of the thin towels hanging by the vanity, and headed for the shower.

The shower pressure was shockingly good even though the tub itself was closet-sized, so she took her time lathering up with the wafer-thin bar of wrapped soap she'd found on the ledge. She used it from her hair to her toes, and by the time she'd finished she felt so dried out and stripped clean that she swore the soap had sloughed off a layer of skin.

The door to the motel room clicked open and she heard Spencer padding around right as she realized that the towel she was using to dry off was more of a washcloth, and she'd left her clothing outside the bathroom on the desk.

"Hey, Griffin?" She cracked the door open and peeked out, keeping her mostly naked body hidden.

"Yeah?"

"Can you hand me that pile of clothes over there?"

There was a pause. "All of it? You're wearing all of that to bed?"

Was that disappointment in his voice?

"No, not all of it. I'll figure it out."

The stack appeared in front of the door, held aloft by a disembodied hand. Spencer stuck his face in the crack of the door and tried to wedge it open with his nose.

"Just a sec, Spence," Justine said as she tried to keep the dog out while grabbing the clothing. She quickly decided the best combination was the thin sweater, see-through leggings with underwear, and the cream duster to cover the whole mess up until she got into bed. The mirror was still fogged up, so she used her elbow to wipe it away and raked her fingernails through her wet hair. A quick tooth brushing with the vintage toothbrush later and she was ready to face Griffin. She took a steadying breath and opened the door.

"Well, hey there, Mrs. Clean."

Griffin was perched on the very edge of the bed like he knew he was trespassing on her property, with Spencer spread out beside him, taking up more than half the space.

"Hey."

They stared at each other until the silence started to mean something.

"I'm going to, uh." Griffin's eyes traveled down Justine's body. "I'm going to hop in the shower really quick. The TV doesn't work, so I guess it's lights-out and phones. Did you bring earbuds?"

She shook her head.

"Me either." He hopped off the bed and brushed past her to get to the bathroom. "Be out in a few minutes."

The click of the bathroom door locking was enough to remind Justine that they needed to maintain their boundaries, so she walked to the bed and pulled at the bedspread, rolling Spencer from one side to the other to get it off the bed without moving him. The room didn't offer many possibilities to set up a makeshift bed; her options were either sleep on the tile floor beyond the bed or claim the carpeted area right next to it.

Spencer watched as she folded the comforter into thirds and placed it on the floor next to the bed, then threw one of the anemic pillows on top. The minute she settled onto the floor bed, Spencer jumped down off the real one and pawed at her legs.

"It's a tight squeeze, but we'll make it work." She moved closer to the bed and Spencer turned in a circle, then flopped down with his head resting on her hip.

The water turned off in the bathroom and a few minutes later the door opened.

"Justine?" Griffin whispered. "Spence?"

"We're here," she said, rising halfway from the floor on the far side of the bed.

His half-naked body was backlit by the bathroom light as he jumped in shock. "You scared me! I thought you were outside with him. What are you doing on the floor?"

"Trying to sleep?"

Also trying not to stare at the squeaky-clean half-dressed man she was about to spend the night with.

Griffin took a few steps closer and crossed his arms, making his biceps bulge. His jeans hung low on his hips so that the V-shaped cuts peeked out. "Not happening. No way I'm letting you sleep on the floor." He thumbed toward the bed. "Get in bed."

He'd finally said the b-e-d word. Ordered her into it, and for the first time she wasn't just imagining it. Coupled with his nonnegotiable tone, the word sent a predictable tingle down her spine.

"I'm fine, honestly. This is very comfy." She patted the comforter, and the floor beneath it made an audible *thud*. "You paid for the room, I sleep on the floor. It's only fair."

"Okay, if you're not going to sleep on the bed, I won't either." He started ripping the sheets off the bed.

"Stop, stop, stop," Justine said, sitting all the way up and rousing Spencer. "You're being stupid. I'll sleep on the bed."

Griffin smiled triumphantly as he tucked the sheets back in and they scooted around each other, taking care not to touch as they traded places. Spencer watched them both settle into their respective beds and seemed to weigh his options. He decided that on the bed with Justine but with his head hanging off the bed on Griffin's side was the best way to split his affections.

"Ooh, you warmed it up for me," he said as he flicked the comforter over his body and snuggled in. "So comfy."

"Liar." Justine pulled the world's scratchiest sheet up to her chin. "If it makes you feel any better, this mattress is made of plywood."

"Then I guess we're even."

The glow of their phones lit the room as they tried to ignore each other, until Griffin made a frustrated noise.

Justine leaned over the edge of the bed. "What?"

"Work. Schedule changes." He looked at his phone and groaned again.

"Tell me."

He sat up and leaned against the nightstand, which made the blanket fall off and reveal his chest. Justine had to look away because all she could think about was the way it had felt pressed against hers.

"I'm applying for a new job at Vendere."

"Is it part of the trajectory?" She tried to keep the teasing out of her voice. "And what position is it?"

"It's the longest long shot ever. It's like two jumps ahead." He shifted as if trying to find a more comfortable patch of floor. "If I get it I'll be managing all of the people like me on the East Coast."

"Good for you. Way to manifest your future." It was something Sienna always said and it seemed appropriate in the moment.

"Thanks. It's a lot. If I get it everything changes."

"Cha-*ching*."

Griffin laughed. "Well, yeah, that. But it would also mean my whole travel schedule will shift, and then there's the ramp-up period at HQ . . ."

Justine propped her head on her hand. "Can I ask you a question? I've been meaning to ask you this since the first time we met."

"Sure."

"You work a lot, so why did you get a dog if you're never home?" She glanced at Spencer sleeping next to her.

"I've been waiting for you to ask that." He flopped down against the tiny pillow. "My job wasn't always like this. When I started off I was doing the regular nine-to-five thing, but then I got fast-tracked." He shrugged. "I did the best I could with him. He had a few great dog sitters and we made it work."

"Makes sense." Justine fell back against the bed.

"I'm glad I had some extra time with Spencer today before work gets crazy." Griffin paused. "And you."

The two words filled the room with expectation.

"Thank you." It was the only thing she could come up with. "Same."

The silence was broken when the old-timey heater wheezed into action, clicking and hissing like it was about to explode.

Justine leaned over the edge of the bed again, not realizing that Griffin was propped up on his arm, and she wound up almost nose to nose with him. They bounced away from each other, startled by their sudden proximity.

She laughed and played it off. "You're going to get an interview and they're going to fall in love with you and you're going to get the job and then you can check off another career milestone."

"Thanks for the vote of confidence, but it really is a major long shot. Now if I could only get my résumé to upload. They said they didn't receive it." He frowned at his phone.

Justine draped herself on the edge of the bed with her head resting on top of her hands, her still-damp hair falling over her eyes. She watched Griffin tapping on his phone but stopped before he felt her eyes, flopping back onto the bed with a sigh.

The heater let out a death rattle and shut off.

"Hey, Justine?"

She didn't bother sitting up. "Yeah?"

The pause stretched on and she started to worry about what Griffin was going to reveal.

"It really smells like dog piss down here on the floor."

The laugh burst out of her, waking Spencer. He sat up looking confused.

"I think I'm going to go sleep in the tub," he said, standing up and gathering the pillow and comforter.

"No. Stop."

Her voice was so commanding that he obeyed, glued in place next to the bed with the bedding wrapped in his arms.

"You will not sleep in the tub." She gathered her courage and forced the words out. "Just get in the bed, it's big enough for the two of us."

He huffed a laugh. "It's barely big enough for Spencer. You're insane."

She made a show of moving as far as she could to the edge of it, accidentally kicking Spencer. He gave her a disappointed look, then hopped off and into the armchair near the door. "See, even Spencer wants to make room for you."

Her heart thudded as Griffin stood at the end of the bed blinking at her. It felt like it would be an easy decision to make: semi-comfort or cold porcelain. The longer he waited the stupider she felt for offering it.

"You sure you don't mind?"

She sighed and threw back the crinkly sheet next to her. "I don't bite."

"But you do snore." He finally cracked a smile. "I appreciate it, thank you. I'm so tired I'll be asleep in a minute. You won't even know I'm here."

Not true.

He climbed into the opposite side of the tiny bed slowly, like he was getting into an unsteady boat, then turned onto his side facing away from her and pulled the sheet up to his shoulder.

Exhausted or not, there was no way Justine was sleeping. She was on her side with her hands tucked beneath her cheek and Griffin was just a few inches away, facing the opposite direction. She could feel warmth radiating from him. The smell of hotel soap on his skin wafted over every time he moved an inch. Thanks to the turn-of-the-century HVAC unit she was freezing, but Griffin was kicking off thermal energy like an oven. She longed to move a centimeter closer, to steal some of his heat.

He shifted and his foot grazed hers. Justine wasn't sure if the sparks she felt were due to static on the sheets or the fact that Griffin was actually touching her. In bed. She held her breath, waiting to see who would jerk away first, but they both literally held their ground. After all, it was just a foot. They were essentially shaking hands, but with their feet, his warm heel against her frozen arch.

In bed.

When her left arm started to fall asleep, she moved to turn over as slowly as a stalking cat. She adjusted each part of her body individually, starting at her knees, then her hips, and finally her shoulders, until her head was on the pillow.

And looking directly into Griffin's eyes.

She wasn't sure when he'd turned over, but there he was, his adorably crooked nose just a few inches away from hers again, but this time neither one of them moved. Her heartbeat thudded in her ears.

"I can't sleep," he whispered. His eyes traveled around her face. "Can you?"

Justine shook her head slowly. "Not tired in the slightest," she said in a scratchy whisper.

He kept examining her, drinking in every part of her face. Admiring her. She loved how it felt to be trapped in his gaze.

Then, as if a switch flipped, Griffin closed the few inches of space between them and crushed his mouth against hers. There was nothing tentative in the kiss, no questioning brush of their lips like the first time. Justine matched his intensity and suddenly their mouths and hands were frantic on each other's bodies, desperate to explore what they'd only imagined a few weeks before in the darkness.

Griffin hungrily kissed anything he could reach, claiming her mouth and letting his tongue flick along her lips, then breaking away to trace kisses down her neck, then back up to nibble on her earlobes. His urgency made it impossible for Justine to catch her breath, and she struggled to process everything he was making her feel with everything she wanted to do to him. They were perfectly paced with each other, kiss for kiss, touch for touch. Griffin's hands raced over her body, leaving tracks of heat everywhere he touched. He finally flipped on top of her and pulled at the hem of her sweater.

"What are you wearing anyway?" he asked with a frustrated growl. "A chastity sweater?"

Justine laughed and shrugged out of the cardigan, then pulled the sweater over her head with a dramatic sweep.

His eyes went wide at her naked breasts.

"You are *perfect*." He sighed. His urgency seemed to ebb at the sight of her topless on her back beneath him and he let his gaze wander along her body, almost as if he needed a moment to admire her. Griffin trailed his fingertips lightly along her skin, starting at the base of her neck, then slowly tracing a wide circle around her left breast, then her right, sometimes with his fingertips but occasionally taking the weight of her breast in his palm. His touch was agonizingly slow and gentle, and when he raised his fingers away from her with a naughty grin, she arched her back to reconnect with his hand. He teased her with smaller and smaller lazy circles on her skin, sending sparks along her spine, until he was caressing her left nipple with his fingertips, then her right.

Then he lowered his mouth to her nipple and swept his tongue across it as she bit her lip to keep from crying out.

When Griffin was finally able to back away from lavishing attention on her breasts and she came out of the trance he'd put her in, Justine reached down to pop the button on his jeans. He bucked them off as quickly as possible.

"I'm, uh . . ." Griffin paused then settled his body against hers, his naked hardness the only explanation she needed.

"Commando," she said with her lips pressed against his neck. "Brave choice, McCabe."

She realized no boxers meant everything south was fair game, and she traced her hands down his back until she reached his perfect round ass. After daydreaming about it since the first time she'd accidentally seen it, she couldn't resist giving it a squeeze.

He laughed and winced at the same time.

Then she let her hand wander between their bodies and wrapped her fingers tightly around him. He groaned and went still for a few seconds, then continued exploring her body.

"And how do you explain this . . . *situation*." Griffin breathed into her ear as his hand darted beneath the waistband of her weird leggings. She shimmied closer, hoping he'd let his hands dip lower.

She caught herself panting with want. "I . . . I needed them when we were outside, but I don't anymore."

He let his hand slip all the way beneath the leggings again to find her warmth. "No, you don't."

Griffin caressed her through her underwear for a few seconds, and even that was enough to make her shiver.

They found each other's mouths again and kissed greedily, their hands and fingers teasing each other, and for a little while it was all they needed. But they both knew there was more to come.

Justine finally pulled away from his mouth like it was painful. "Did you bring anything . . ." Her voice was ragged.

He nodded.

"Cocky," she said, crashing into his mouth again.

Griffin pulled away. "Hopeful. Desperately hopeful."

They kissed again, knowing that they had the whole night to explore.

chapter thirty-three

Justine studied Griffin's profile as he focused on the road ahead.

"You're talking to yourself."

"What? I'm not."

"You were. It was a full-on conversation, and it looked intense."

He shot a glance at her. "Lots on my mind. It's tough to turn it off."

Justine tried to guess what had him muttering and furrowing as they headed back to Brooklyn. The new job. The trajectory. And maybe how their night together might be impacted by both. She wondered if it kept invading his thoughts the way it did hers. She woke up wanting him again, her body pressed against his, and based on the way the sheet tented up over his midsection it was obvious he did too, but Spencer had other ideas. The first hint of light through the too-short curtains on the picture window had him pacing, and when other guests started stomping by he barked out a warning at them. It wasn't like they wanted to hang out in the depressing room any longer than necessary if they weren't draped all over each other, so they hit the road early.

"Do you want to talk about last night?" he asked without taking his eyes off the road.

Her heart sped up. "Do you?"

"Yeah, I think we should. Obviously, last night . . . changes things."

"Um-hm." She wanted Griffin to take the lead on the conversation, so she'd have some idea about what he was feeling. Because what *she* was feeling was that her hiatus had finally come to an end. But she wasn't going to be the first one to admit that it wasn't just sex for her. Something real had happened between them.

The silence stretched on, punctuated by Spencer's heavy breathing and occasional snorts, which undoubtedly left Griffin's window dotted with dog snot.

"Remember the skateboard artist you met that night at the Yard Bar? Danny?"

"How could I forget? He used the word *architected*."

"Exactly. You could probably tell that I wasn't the biggest Danny fan, but it wasn't just the fact that he's a superdouche."

Justine wondered how Danny played a role in their first sexual encounter but didn't say anything.

"A few years back I was dating a girl named Clementine. We'd been together about two months. It wasn't super serious, but I was into her."

She shifted in her seat. The last thing she wanted to hear about was another woman he was into the morning after they'd had sex for the first time, but she was also insanely curious about his dating history. His social media black hole and lack of photos around his apartment made that part of his life feel off-limits to her.

"My travel was starting to pick up, so we weren't able to hang out as much as I would've liked, but we made it work." He exhaled hard and shook his head. "Or so I thought. Turns out she liked the Yard Bar too and started going there when I wasn't around, and she and Danny got to know each other. And Danny decided that Clementine fit with his vibe—she was super pretty—and he basically swept her off her feet. He doesn't work a real job, so they started traveling together with Danny paying for everything. And Clem ate it up. I had no clue. It was partly my fault because I was working and I wasn't around. I found out they were together when Wendall told me."

Justine quickly replayed the evening with Danny. "Okay, now I understand the bad blood. Why did you let him sit with us?"

Griffin shrugged. "When he figured out what had happened he sat me down, bought me a few rounds, and apologized. Claims he had no clue we were together." He shook his head. "I have my doubts about that, but whatever. What I'm trying to explain isn't about him, or Clem. The point is, when everything went to shit with her I realized that I had a choice to make. Did I want to try to commit to a relationship, or work? Clearly, I chose work."

She knew it wasn't the only reason for his work obsession. He'd said as much to her. A family history of not having enough can do that to a person, but she wasn't about to point out his money obsession to him now that it felt like he was letting her down easy by invoking his stupid trajectory.

"I'm not sure what you're getting at," she replied haltingly. She felt a furnace kick on in her chest, sending an angry heat to her face.

He finally reached over and put his hand over hers again, but she didn't respond. "I'm not great at relationships, Justine. People get lost in the shuffle. I tried dating after Clem, but things always fizzle out because my schedule is so weird. You've seen it firsthand. So I've kept things simple. Nothing serious because I don't have the bandwidth for it."

She let her hand lie limply in his. He *was* breaking it to her gently.

The morning after.

She suddenly felt nauseous, like she'd had too much to drink the night before. She pulled her hand away in disgust and crossed her arms.

"Wait, wait, wait. I didn't explain that right," Griffin said as worry bloomed across his face. "Justine, I told you that because I want you to know about my history, about why I'm gun-shy with relationships. But if you're okay with . . . me . . . and my schedule . . . I'd like to try. With you. With us."

Spencer made a noise that sounded like a combination of a cough and a bark in the back seat.

"How do you mean?" She managed to keep her voice even. She still needed him to spell out what he wanted before she could acknowledge the tiny flicker of hope.

He shrugged. "To be honest, I'm not sure. I don't think I know how to do this kind of stuff anymore. I'm rusty." He paused. "But what I do know is that I'm always happier when I'm with you. Even my damn *apartment* feels happier when you've been in it. I used to dread walking in the door after a trip, but now I love coming home. You left flowers for me. No one's ever given me flowers! And it always still smells like you, even after you're gone. I don't know if it's the candles you burn or just *you*, but the second I walk in the door I get a wave of . . . Justine. It's like walking into the kitchen when someone's baking bread. And then there's the treasure hunt I do. I try to find little things you accidentally left behind." He smiled. "I have your pink cloth headband thing, three of those black hair pins, and a gray sock."

The corner of her mouth quirked up as hope fizzed inside her. "That's where it is. I've been missing that damn sock."

"But, Justine, I need you to know that I can't guarantee anything at this point. Especially now, with this new position on the horizon. Everything could change. But all I know is this feels right to me." He paused. "And now I'd like you to say something because I feel like I totally unloaded on you."

Justine leaned into the doubt and fear she felt mixing in with the bubbliness. He'd said everything she needed to hear, but it was her turn.

"I know all about your trajectory, but you haven't heard about my hiatus," she said, studying his profile while he drove. "I don't want to get too deep into it, especially after everything we talked about yesterday." She swallowed against the lump that formed in her throat. "I haven't dated in a while either. Haven't wanted to. Nick fucked me up royally after the trail thing, and I just needed time to figure myself out. One of the things I realized was that I'd much rather be alone than in a bad relationship. And I haven't met anyone I wanted to take a chance on." She paused. "Until you."

Justine took a deep breath. "Suddenly, I do *not* want to be on hiatus."

He smiled and flicked his eyes to her.

"Does that mean we're giving this a shot?"

"I think we are. I think we have to." She reached over, grabbed his hand, and gave it a squeeze. "And in order to celebrate, we need a naked stopover at your place before I head back to Rexford."

Griffin didn't say a word but punched the gas so hard that Spencer fell over in his seat.

chapter thirty-four

What happened to you?" Sienna asked, her eyes wide as she watched Justine shelving a dog food order.

"What do you mean?" Justine hoisted a thirty-pound bag of wild river salmon kibble onto the shelf.

"You seem different. You look different. Your whole *vibe* is different." Spencer stood nearby eagerly watching the unpacking, hoping that one of the bags had ripped and might spill fishy treasures onto the floor. "Spence, what's gotten into your mom? She's smiling more than usual."

Justine was still holding the secret of her time with Griffin close to her heart. It was something she wanted to savor on her own before she opened it up to Sienna's gloating and Ruth's questions about exactly what they were to each other and how they were going to navigate the future. The truth was, neither of them was sure. But whatever it was felt like the start of something good. Sienna was right: she couldn't stop grinning.

"The shoot is almost over, and I guess I'm feeling nervous about the future. Everyone thinks it's going to get picked up for a full season, but we're still not sure."

"And you're hoping it does?"

"With every bone in my body. I can't believe that I get paid to do it. I love it more than anything."

Sienna's mouth turned down for a split second. "What about T&B?"

Justine threw another bag on the shelf and tried to play off that T&B never even occurred to her. "Of course I love it here. I just think maybe I've . . . I don't know, outgrown it a little?"

Sienna didn't say anything for a few minutes as she arranged the five-pound bags of food on a separate shelf. "Can I talk to you about something?"

"Sure." The bag of food she was about to throw on the shelf instantly got heavier.

"It feels like the right time to have this discussion. Can I throw the BACK IN FIVE MINUTES sign on the door so we don't have any interruptions?"

Justine nodded and tried to read Sienna's body language to prepare for whatever was about to come. Spencer escorted Sienna as she ran to the front of the shop, locked the door, and hung the sign they usually used when they ran out to grab lunch.

"One more sec." Sienna held up a finger and dashed to the office, then came out with a folder. "Okay. Ready?"

"I think so." Justine still had a hard time feeling okay about file folders thanks to Griffin's ominous red one.

Sienna took a deep breath. "Remember how I read cards recently?"

Justine nodded.

"This is what it was about. Because I've noticed you pulling away from Tricks & Biscuits for a while now. I know you still love *parts* of it, but not all of it. I, on the other hand, love everything about being here. Even dealing with the occasional mean customers! This is a really special little store with a ton of potential. And I think you know that I've worked hard to contribute to its success."

"You're amazing, Sienna. I can't thank you enough for all the stuff you do."

She bowed. "Now, that said, I'd like to make you an offer. I have two options for you." She opened the file and handed Justine a spreadsheet. "May I first present option one, my moon shot. It's a lease-to-own plan."

The numbers swam in front of Justine's eyes. "A *what*?"

Sienna cleared her throat and straightened her posture. "I want to buy Tricks & Biscuits from you. Eventually. It's a lease-to-own scenario, so I'd give you a monthly payment."

Excitement tingled along Justine's scalp. "You're serious?"

Sienna nodded. "But . . . our numbers aren't . . . great. I'm sure you've seen it firsthand since you've been spending more time here."

"No, what I've seen is potential. I really believe that moving to more organic stock and opening an online store can turn things around. And adding a second store would increase the buying power with your suppliers. I've run the numbers a million different ways, and I've already taken a quick look at real estate in Valley Ridge for a second store." She handed Justine a few more documents. "Now, once you check out these projections, you might decide that it looks so good that you don't want to sell it to me, and that brings me to option two: hire me to take on this expansion. Bring me in as your partner."

Justine looked closer at the documents. Sienna's research

was impressive. Projections weren't guarantees, but it was a feasible growth plan backed by her uncanny business sense. Justine imagined signing the lease and working with Sienna to update T&B, then watching the little shop's fortunes turn around as a team.

"No."

Sienna cocked her head. "Huh?"

"No, I don't want to partner with you."

A frown flickered briefly across her face. "Okay, I understand it's hard to let go."

"Sienna, no. I mean I want option one. I want you to take over. Without me."

Her jaw dropped. "For real? You want to try the lease-to-own plan?"

Justine nodded. "I think it's time for me to step out from behind the counter. It makes sense for you to own T&B." Her eyes welled up as she said it, partly because it was a fantastic future for the little shop, and partly because she would have to say good-bye to it.

"Seriously?" Sienna ran to Justine and wrapped her in a hug, laughing and sniffling at the same time. "Oh my God, I'm so happy! I can't believe it! Thank you for trusting me with your baby, Justine!"

Spencer barked and jumped at them, offering his own version of a hug thanks to the bad habits he'd picked up with Griffin.

"I'm in shock," Sienna said as she dabbed her eyes. "I'm *doing* this!" She paused and looked at Justine with a confused expression. "But wait, what are you going to do if you leave?"

A slow smile lit up her face. "I'm going to gamble, just like my momma taught me. Like I said, I have a feeling that *The Eighteenth* is going to get picked up."

"Oh my God, you're going to be a momager for Spencer? Perfect! But, I hate to ask . . . you can make enough doing that?"

"Nope." She shook her head, her mouth in a tight line. "Not right away. But I've made some great connections through the show and I'm hoping to keep expanding his work. Doing some commercials and stuff like that. I might even start teaching some tricks classes to people who want to do what we're doing. Plus, there's the gold mine of lease income I'll be making from T&B!"

"Oh my God, please don't put that kind of pressure on me!" Sienna said, holding her hand to her chest.

"Kidding. I'll use what I make from you to buy my coffee every day."

Sienna ran to the front of the shop and unlocked the door, then came back ready to plan. "Our first step is drawing up paperwork and talking to Seth about the lease."

Justine continued loading dog food bags onto the shelves. "Yup. I think we can get it all signed over pretty quickly."

"We have to contact the vendors to let them know. Oh, speaking of! I have a stack of bills and mail you need to look at. Some of it is a few weeks old." Sienna and Spencer ran to the office to grab it.

"Here." She handed Justine a perfectly organized stack of mail. "The parking ticket you got is on the top. They're probably going to jack up the penalty if you don't pay soon."

"Ugh, how much is a ticket in the city? We pay ten dollars in Rexford, so that means it's probably . . ."

"I paid one that was a hundred and fifteen dollars."

"I actually got two on the same day, so why is there only one envelope?" Justine looked closer at it. "And why is it from Kingsford, New York? Do they outsource their tickets or something?"

Sienna shrugged.

Justine ripped open the envelope and pulled out the document. She squinted at it. "Official court summons? Already?"

"That's weird," Sienna replied as she broke down the cardboard shipping boxes.

Justine quickly scanned the letter.

"Wait, *what*? This says that Griffin is taking me to small-claims court. He's suing me to get Spencer back?"

chapter thirty-five

The folded-up summons in the back pocket of Justine's jeans felt like a pebble in her shoe, or a lash trapped on her eyeball. It was the only thing she could think of as she waited for Griffin to get back to the apartment.

He'd been tough to reach as he went through a two-day interview in Chicago for the promotion, and as rattled as she was by the summons, she didn't think it was right to throw him off his game during the stressful process. Rather than texting or calling him to ask about it, she waited until she could talk to him in person and see his face. Griffin had mentioned that he'd be getting back to the apartment as Justine was leaving, so they planned to connect for a quick drink before she left for Rexford. She wanted to spring it on him once they were in public.

She knew he couldn't be serious about it given what they'd shared in Maryland, but she also couldn't figure out why he'd sent it in the first place. Was it a bad joke? It didn't seem like his type of humor. She tried to figure out how she was going to greet him when her excitement about seeing him was overshadowed by the shrapnel in her pocket. And then there was the gift she'd gotten him a week prior, still packed away in her purse.

When Spencer dropped the bone he'd been gnawing on and cocked his head, she knew Griffin was close. The sound of his thundering footsteps a few seconds later made her stomach twist. She wanted to be subdued when he walked through the door, so she could figure out exactly what was going on, but a part of her still wanted to leap into his arms the minute she saw him, summons and all.

Spencer was at the door wagging before his key hit the lock.

"Hey, buddy! Hey there," Griffin said as he struggled to hold on to his luggage and an oversized bouquet of flowers and pet the whirling dog at the same time. "Okay, okay, let me say hi to your mom."

He looked ridiculously, adorably gorgeous, as usual. Her heart surged at the sight of him.

"Hi, you," Griffin said shyly, still bent over and petting Spencer by the door.

"Hi yourself."

Justine restrained herself and gave him the tiniest grin and wave. She watched his face fall in response.

"These are for you," he said quickly, holding a bouquet of sunflowers and yellow roses wrapped in cellophane and green tissue paper.

"Thank you, that was really sweet of you." She took the bouquet and gave him a quick hug. It made her ache to let go after only a few seconds, and his confused expression twisted the pain a little deeper. "I'll put them in water."

She headed for the kitchen and felt Griffin staring at her.

"Are you okay?" he asked, still in his jacket by the door.

She couldn't wait another second. She placed the flowers on the counter and walked back to him. "No, actually, I'm not." Justine reached into her back pocket and thrust the envelope at Griffin.

"What's this?" He unfolded it and stared at it for a moment. "Oh, no way. How did this happen? This was mailed to you?"

She nodded and pointed at the canceled stamp. "It was. Are you *really* trying to take Spencer from me, or is this a crappy joke?" She struggled to keep her voice even.

"No, no, I swear this is just a stupid mistake . . . but I don't know how . . ." Griffin went silent and Justine watched as his face cycled through a variety of expressions until his eyes went wide. "I know exactly what happened! I accidentally left a stack of paperwork at a client's office a while back. They called me to say they had it and that there were some stamped letters with it. One of them was my mom's birthday card, so I asked them to mail everything in the pile for me, and I guess the summons was there too." Griffin looked at the envelope. "Check the post-mark." He sounded triumphant. "It was mailed in California."

She grabbed the envelope out of his hands and squinted at the postmark, and sure enough she could barely make out "Santa Ana CA" in the smudged ink. The twist in her stomach loosened slightly.

"But that doesn't explain why the thing was there in the first place. You went through the steps to start this process to get Spencer back. Why?"

"That wasn't supposed to be mailed. I never intended for this to happen, I swear." Griffin finally took his coat off and draped it on the back of one of the bar stools. "I wasn't in a normal frame of mind right after the first time I met you and got to see Leo again. I mean Spencer. I wasn't thinking. I never meant for it to be mailed. Please believe me."

"But you *did* start the process." Hurt burned through her chest at the thought that he was willing to fight her for Spencer. "You got me to meet you and said it was just to check on him, but you knew then you wanted him back the whole time."

"Initially, yes. I'm sorry I lied to get you to come to the city." His face looked pinched at the memory of it. "But everything changed when I saw how great you and Spencer were together, and when I got to know you. Hell, everything changed the first time I saw you."

"That I don't believe. At all. I overheard you on the phone. You called me a less-cute Reese Witherspoon."

His jaw dropped. "Shit, Justine. You heard that? I wasn't saying that you're not attractive. I meant that you're *beautiful*. Not cute. Beautiful." Griffin paused and his eyes went soft. "God, you're so fucking beautiful I can barely concentrate when you're around."

She didn't respond.

Griffin walked over and gently took the envelope out of her hands, then went to the stove and flicked the burner on. He held the letter and envelope over the flame and let them burn for a few seconds. The paper caught fire quickly and within seconds Griffin was holding on to a mini inferno.

"Ouch, ouch, ouch," he said as he ran to the sink to douse the flame.

Justine bit back a grin.

"Do you believe me now?" Griffin asked as he ran cold water over his fingers. "I just scorched myself trying to make it right.

Justine, I *swear* I wasn't going to pursue getting Spencer back. I don't know what else I can say to convince you."

"Okay. Bodily harm to make a point means something. I believe you."

Now that she had an explanation, Justine was desperate for a real homecoming. She expected Griffin to rush over to her and sweep her into a "this is how nice it is to see you" kiss, but it didn't happen. Instead, his face looked ashen, and he kept his distance in the kitchen. Justine felt like she needed to do something to lighten the mood after accusing Griffin of lying.

"I have a present for you," she said, beaming at him.

"Why would you do that? What's the occasion?"

"No occasion. I saw it and thought of you. One sec." She ran to her purse by the door and fished out the oblong box. Of course Ruth's shop had the perfect wrapping paper: navy blue and dotted with constellations. She'd finished it off with a sparkly silver bow.

"Here." She practically danced in place as she handed it to him. Griffin shook his head, then tore into the package and tossed the wrappings on the counter.

"What the . . ."

The watch was still in its original container, a colored metal bas-relief version of the *Galaxy Force* logo. He ran his finger over the lid with his mouth hanging open.

"Are you kidding me?"

"Open it, it gets even better!"

"No, you don't understand. I *always* wanted one of these watches. My parents wouldn't get it for me; they said it was too expensive. Where did you find it?"

She shrugged. "I have my ways."

Griffin popped the lid, then shut his eyes in disbelief. "You found the Captain Zaltan one?"

"Look closer!" She clapped her hands. "Anderson signed the band!"

Griffin pulled the watch out of the case and inspected Anderson's scrawl in silver Sharpie along the plastic navy band.

"Are you kidding me? This is seriously the best gift I've ever gotten."

Griffin finally pulled Justine into a real hug and her lips found his mouth. She felt herself becoming a little demanding and was shocked when he backed away from her.

"Thank you. I love it, Justine." He made a show of taking off the watch he was wearing and putting the new one on his wrist. Justine tried not to feel insulted that he didn't seem interested in the only type of thanks she wanted.

"Looks good, right?" He held up his wrist.

Justine laughed. "It looks like you're going to a Comic-Con, but if you can own it I'm fine with it."

Griffin stared at the watch for a few minutes and his face shifted back to the worried look he'd had since he walked in. "It's getting late. Do you mind if we don't go out to get a drink? There's some stuff I want to talk to you about."

The knot in her stomach returned.

"Sure, I'm fine to hang out here. I left a six-pack in the fridge for you. And some chips and salsa."

He gave her a half grin. "You think of everything."

Justine made a show of setting out the chips and salsa on the counter while Griffin opened beers for them. At first she worried that he'd been put off by the summons, but she could tell by the way he seemed jumpy that something else was on his mind. They settled on the bar stools and Griffin fiddled with the label on the beer bottle before he started talking.

"I have news. Good news." He paused. "I got the job."

Justine stopped midchew. "Are you kidding?" She accidentally spat out chip crumbs in her excitement. "Boom, *trajectory*! Congrats!" She leaned over and held her beer out to him and they clinked bottles; then she hopped off the stool to give him a peck on the cheek. "That's amazing."

"Thank you." He took a long drink.

Justine studied his hunched posture. "Why don't you seem happy?"

"Oh my God, I am. I'm thrilled. I've been working toward this for such a long time. Better title, more money." He paused. "*Much* more money."

Justine clinked his bottle again. "Cheers to that."

"But I'll be more tied to HQ now."

Justine stuck out her bottom lip. "Aw, poor guy's going to have to commute into Manhattan a few times a week?"

"No. Headquarters are in Chicago. The Manhattan office is a satellite."

She froze. "What does that mean? Do they want you to move?"

"No, they knew that wasn't an option before they even considered me for the position." He frowned. "But it does mean that I'll be spending a lot of time there. I have to head there for training in a few weeks."

"Well, Spencer and I can hold down the fort for you while you're gone. I'm sure I'll be here for a few more shoot days while you're away."

"Justine, it's a monthlong training. They've got me shadowing people and taking meetings out the ass. It's nonstop."

She slid her thumbnail under the label on her beer bottle and tried to get it off in one piece, but it tore irregularly. She smoothed her finger along the remaining part, which now said "Lo Do." Lost Dog, Griffin's favorite import, the kind he'd given her the first time she met him.

"But it's just a month," Justine offered hopefully.

Griffin drained his beer and set it on the marble counter with a *thud* that sounded like it cracked the bottom of it. The noise brought Spencer over to them with the bone hanging out of his mouth like a cigar, as if to make sure that neither one needed his intervention.

"They'll want me in Chicago a lot, plus I'll still have obligations on the road."

Suddenly, everything Griffin *wasn't* saying filled the room.

Not only would they be long-distance; they'd be part-time at best. Justine knew that the joy of their mini reunions would only carry them for so long, and when she needed Griffin to be there for her, or for Spencer, there was a chance he'd be halfway across the country. She realized that he'd probably pulled strings and called in favors to be as available to her as he'd been for the past months, and that with the new job even those small doses of togetherness weren't going to be an option. And most of all, Justine knew her heart well enough to understand that it still wasn't strong enough to weather a Griffin-sized hole.

Unfortunately, it felt like it was too late.

"Your face is scaring me," he said softly.

She shook her head and tucked her hair behind her ear. "Just thinking, that's all."

"About us?"

Justine nodded.

"Don't say it."

She leaned back against the chair and closed her eyes. When she opened them Griffin was staring at her.

"You've thought about it too; I can tell by the way you've been acting," Justine said.

"I have. How could I not?" His voice was raw. "I've been through this before. You get . . . *invested* in someone; then work gets in the way. And it feels like there's no possible way to balance the two. Hell, when it comes to you, 'balance' shouldn't even enter into the equation. You deserve to come first. You should always come first."

Her vision swam, but Justine let out a humorless laugh. "I knew hating you was the better option. You missed a great way out, Griffin. You should've said you *just* sent the summons; that would've sealed this up nice and tidy."

"Damn, if only I were better at being ruthless," he replied with mock disappointment.

Justine caught him swiping his thumb across the watch face, and a heavy silence settled between them. She swore she could hear the seconds ticking away as they each tried to avoid saying the thing they both knew was coming.

She finally spoke up in a voice that was stronger than she felt. "I guess we should pretend like Maryland never happened? I mean, that's what I'd prefer. Everything we talked about in the car on the way home . . . that didn't happen either. It hurts less that way."

The dull ache in her chest made it clear that she was lying.

"Yeah," he said softly, staring at the watch. "I guess you're right."

"Spence and I can find somewhere else to stay. I'm not sure I can handle coming back here, and you probably don't want us around."

He jolted like she'd slapped him. "No, please don't. You and Spencer are always welcome. It makes me happy to think of you guys here."

She felt a chill pass through her, and she hugged her arms around her body.

"There's no chance we could make this work, right?" Justine asked in a nervous rush. "Should we try?"

Griffin didn't answer for a long time, and she felt a spark of hope as she tried visualizing how the two of them could fit into the spaces of each other's lives.

He met her gaze with sad eyes. "You'd get tired of waiting for me to show up."

And in her heart she knew it was true.

Justine choked back the lump in her throat. Crying would undoubtedly lead to comforting, and she worried that if Griffin touched her she'd shatter.

The best course of action was walking out the door, before she could think too much about what she and Griffin were agreeing to. Because seeing him right in front of her made her think that giving up before they even began was a stupid idea.

"We should probably go," she said, standing up slowly.

"If you want to." His eyes were darker than usual, and he had a determined set to his jaw.

But before she had a chance to say anything else, his mouth was on hers, demanding and a little angry, and within seconds they were peeling off clothing and tripping toward the loft. Her shirt on the floor, his button-down on the stairs, still half-buttoned, her bra hanging from the railing. They fought with each other's pants as they hit the top step, barely pulling their lips apart until they were both finally naked. Griffin wrapped himself around Justine and for a little while she was able to forget that it would be the last time.

chapter thirty-six

"We ain't coming back from this," Anderson said as he kicked at a pile of splintered wood. "It's over, Myrna. Stop cleaning."

Claire swept up a pile of glass shards. "Nonsense, Izzy. We'll be fine. Move those for me, would you?" She gestured to the three front bar panels that were strewn across the floor. "They didn't have to be quite so violent, now, did they?"

Anderson shoved his hands in his pants pockets and closed his eyes, overcome by the aftermath of the speakeasy raid. "You never stop, do you? You never stop believing in me, or this place. How do you do it? You naïve? Or stupid?"

The room was silent as Claire gathered her strength for the speech that would end their three-episode run. Myrna was the only character who could stand up to Izzy and live to tell. When she finished speaking, her face was angry, defiant, wounded.

There was a beat as Anderson and Claire stared at each other; then Ted's voice echoed through the silent soundstage. "Aaaand cut. That's a wrap on the first three episodes of *The Eighteenth*, people!"

The room exploded into applause, and more than a few tears. Justine clapped and high-fived a few of the electrical and sound guys she'd gotten to know.

Malcolm crossed the room to give Justine a hug. "Hey, girl, glad you made it today. Where's my dog?" He looked around for Spencer.

"He wrapped right after Maryland, remember? I just wanted to be here for the last scene and say good-bye to everyone. But Spence sends his regards."

The truth was that she didn't feel ready to go back to Griffin's apartment with Spencer. It had been three weeks since the last time they spoke, and she couldn't bear the thought of reaching out to ask for yet another favor. She still wrestled with the idea of staying in his apartment if the show got picked up. It felt weird now that they were back to acquaintances, but it also felt like a tenuous connection to Griffin that she wasn't ready to let go of yet.

Ted picked up a megaphone and walked on set. "Hey, everybody?" The hugging and chatter quieted. "Just wanted to take a minute to thank every single one of you for stupendous work. We've created something beautiful, and you should be proud of what you did." People applauded. "I do want to let you know about a change, though. We're not having a wrap party tonight."

The noise died down and everyone waited for Ted to continue.

"Yeah, we're not having a wrap party because we're not wrapped. FilmFlix green-lit a full season of twelve episodes. We've got a short break and then *nine more episodes*, people!" He whooped.

The room exploded in joyful cheers.

It was happening!

"You and Spence ready for more?" Malcolm asked over the noise.

"One hundred percent," Justine replied as she clapped along with everyone else. The blurry parts of her life were finally coming into focus. At least some of them.

Anderson and Claire pretended to be of the people as they made their way off the set. He clapped backs and shook hands while Claire tilted her head and smiled when people spoke to her, keeping her hands folded gracefully at her waist to prevent contact. He followed behind her almost too closely, until Justine noticed that Anderson had his hand placed lightly on the top of Claire's ass. She scanned the room for Taylor and spotted her on the far side on her phone, surrounded by her minions.

"Hey, you see that?" Justine said to Malcolm, nodding toward Anderson and Claire.

"Oh yeah, you missed it. Taylor's back with that Nigel Young-blood singer guy. Anderson and Claire are fucking now, and everyone is pretending not to notice."

Nothing surprised her anymore.

Without the wrap party Justine realized that she had nothing to do. She needed to get home to Spencer even though he was probably sleeping behind the counter while Sienna plotted her next move at the shop. The handoff was speeding along, and Justine would be officially off the Tricks & Biscuits paperwork by the end of the month. They'd announced the change in ownership on social media and the response warmed her heart; equal parts regret to see Justine stepping away and joy for Sienna's new venture.

Justine chatted with some of the crew as she gathered her

things to head out, and Ted caught her eye and beckoned her to him. His baseball cap was on backward, which looked appropriately celebratory.

"I wanted to talk with you before you leave. Do you have a minute?" Ted's knitted brows immediately put her on edge.

"I do. Is everything okay?"

"Yeah, it is but it sort of isn't." He made a frustrated noise. "I didn't want you to get the next script and discover it on the page without having a conversation first."

Her heart sped up as she waited for Ted to continue.

"Listen, you and Spencer have been phenomenal. I couldn't be happier with his performance. But one of the notes from the bigwigs was that we needed to give Izzy a better reason to seek vengeance on Billy's gang. They think the warehouse fire wasn't enough of a reason. Those kinds of things happen in turf wars." He shrugged. "We need to hit Izzy where it *really* hurts, so he loses his mind, and it triggers his breakdown that propels the rest of the season. They want to go *Game of Thrones*." He paused again. "They want to kill off Ford."

The shock knocked her backward. Her semi-secure future was gone in an instant.

"Wait, really?" Justine struggled to put her thoughts in order. "But Ford is such an important part of Izzy's life. Ford humanizes him and makes him relatable even though Izzy's an awful person. That's really what they want?" She pled her case to Ted even though she knew it was pointless.

He nodded sadly. "I hate the thought of it, but they're right. Viewers are going to destroy us for doing it, but it's the only way to get to Izzy, other than killing off someone in his family. And based on some of the feedback we've gotten, it's probably going to come to that, too."

"How . . . how does it happen? How does Ford die?"

Ted swallowed hard, like he was afraid to tell her. "Billy shoots him. He claims it's self-defense because no one is around when he does it so no one can refute him, but it's in cold blood. Canicide."

"Oh my God," she mumbled. "That's going to be awful. When does it happen?"

"Yeah, that's why I wanted to talk to you, Justine. He dies in the next episode."

The tears sprang to her eyes and she blinked fast to stop them from falling.

"I hate the thought of it too." Ted frowned. "You know what's strange? Remember the first time we met? The two of you showed me a death scene. And now here we are. He's going to do it for real."

"Pretty awful symmetry." She sniffled a few times. "I have to be honest, I'm really disappointed. I was having the best time. We both were."

"I know, it sucks. I wish I had more control."

"I understand," Justine answered agreeably, even though inside she was raging against the news. She didn't trust herself to say more.

"We don't have to get into specifics now, but the final scene is going to be pretty quick; they don't want to drag it out and make it gross. I think we'll be able to get it in a day. We'll send you the schedule soon."

"Of course, no problem," Justine replied.

"Thanks for understanding. You've been amazing. I hope we'll be able to work together again at some point. And I'll vouch for you if I hear of other projects that Spencer might be a fit for."

"I'd really appreciate that, because we're basically out of a job now." She managed a little grin, but speaking the words hollowed her out.

Ted scurried away as if happy to be done with the uncomfortable task, and Justine stood stupidly where he'd left her as the remaining stragglers quickly packed up to leave. No creature was faster than a union crew member at the end of a workday.

She thought about calling Sienna, or Ruth, to tell them what had just happened, but she knew she'd end up crying, and she wasn't ready to unleash the tears during the drive home.

Justine zipped up her jacket and stepped out into the cold, bright late-afternoon sunshine. She decided to walk a bit before heading home to let some of the adrenaline she was feeling drain out before having to sit in the car for two hours. She wished she had her running shoes, because at the end of six miles she'd at least have endorphins to carry her for a little while. Maybe she could go to a bar for a drink? Justine needed mood-altering help, because in the span of just a few weeks her whole life had morphed into something she didn't recognize. Her store, her work on the show, and Griffin, all gone.

Griffin. He was *exactly* who she needed to talk to.

Griffin would understand how hard it was going to be watching Spencer die, and how gutted she was to be leaving the show. Sienna and Ruth had only seen pictures of the set; Griffin had *been* there. He'd experienced it. He'd get it. Hell, he'd probably be just as sad as she was that her run on the show was over.

It struck her that she finally had a real reason to reach out to him. There was nothing manufactured in telling him that Spencer was going to die on the show, and could she please use his apartment once more, for old times' sake and then never again? She vague-texted him are you free now before she could talk herself out of it. She'd make it quick; she just needed to hear his voice. But then again, hearing his voice could likely trigger the tears she'd been holding back.

She considered her soon-to-be-unemployed status while she waited for Griffin to text her and tried not to freak out. She'd put out feelers on a few side projects that various crew members were working on. One was an independent film about a dog who ran a restaurant and the other was a series of veterinary how-to videos about a new flea preventative. Both long shots, and neither one half as cool as working on *The Eighteenth*.

Justine checked her phone. Four minutes had passed with no response. Maybe he didn't realize that she was dangerously close to a breakdown?

She followed up with another text: sorry to bother you, can you talk

The wind was getting to her, daggering across her face and bringing tears to her eyes. She sniffled, then realized it wasn't just the wind.

Her phone pinged and she grabbed at her pocket. But it was from Sienna, a photo of Spencer sleeping upside down with his tongue hanging out of his mouth.

Justine realized that there was no point in her staying, as reluctant as she was to leave the city, so she turned back and headed for her car. Then she admitted why she was dragging her feet; she was hoping that Griffin would text her back and coincidentally be in town, and he'd suggest meeting up so she could cry on his shoulder. For a second she considered driving past his apartment, but there'd be no way for her to tell if he was home or not. Plus, it was creepy.

Still, she gave it one more shot: kind of in a bad place, pls call when you get this.

Her phone finally rang as she was getting into her car, and Griffin's number flashed on the screen. Relief trickled through her. *Finally,* she could share the awful news with someone who would understand. She slid into the front seat and answered.

"Hi, Griffin, thanks for calling." She kept her voice even, but her hand was shaking.

"Are you okay?" he whispered. "Your texts freaked me out. Is Spencer okay? What's going on?"

"Where are you?"

"Work." He stressed the word like she'd asked a stupid question. "I had to sneak out of a meeting, and I have two minutes to talk. What happened?"

In a flash Justine realized exactly why the decision they'd made had been the right one. The visions of having a cathartic conversation with Griffin evaporated the moment she heard his strained voice.

"I'm sorry, Griffin. You're busy, it's nothing. I'll text you the details."

"It was obviously big enough to warrant three SOS messages, so please give me a hint. You've got me live, so spill it."

She weighed trying to condense Spencer's looming death scene and losing her job on *The Eighteenth* to a sound bite and realized there was no reason to involve him after all. He didn't have time for her.

"I, uh, have a scene coming up with Spencer soon and I wanted to check if it's still okay to use your place."

He paused. "I already told you it's okay. You didn't have to scare the shit out of me with all of those texts, Justine. It's fine, my apartment is yours whenever you need it. I won't be back until the fifteenth, so make yourself at home."

She swallowed hard as everything hit her again. Griffin, gone. Job, over. "Okay, thanks. I'll text you the details when I find out."

"Are you sure you're okay? You sound weird."

She grinned despite the tears pooling in her eyes. He could tell. Damn it. He could tell.

"I'm *fine*." It came out in a strained whisper. "Go back to the meeting; we'll talk another time."

"Okay." He cleared his throat and she heard voices echoing behind him. "I'll let you know how those projections look. Fantastic. Okay, bye."

The call disconnected right as she couldn't hold back any longer. Justine put her forehead on the steering wheel and let the tears fall.

chapter thirty-seven

The special effects person told her the blood would wash right out of Spencer's fur, but the huge pinkish red splotch on his side that was still visible after three rinses said otherwise. Justine adjusted her rearview mirror to check on him, and the stain made him look like he was recovering from a maiming. The fact that he had his head tilted back and was panting with his eyes half-closed didn't help.

Justine wasn't ready to think about their last day on set. She'd kept her emotions in check the whole time, even when Spencer staggered and dropped to the ground in his death scene, and when Malcolm gave her a good-bye hug, and when she walked out the green door for the last time. There was too much wild emotion swirling around inside her to set it free.

Staying in Griffin's apartment after the weeks away had been a trial as well. The moment she and Spencer walked in the door the day before, she was smacked in the face by a wall of Griffinness. His essence was thick enough in the air that when she stood still, breathed it in, she was instantly reminded how it felt to be in his arms.

She'd checked around the apartment hoping he'd left something for her. A silly note, the stack of bobby pins he'd collected, even a single apple on the counter just to welcome her back. But it was as sterile and tidy as the first time she'd stayed over, and she tried not to be disappointed. They were missing each other by just a few hours; Griffin had flown back from Houston shortly after Justine and Spencer had left for the set, then was home for a few hours only to have to repack and leave for Chicago in the afternoon.

Her phone rang on the seat next to her and she nearly steered off the road when she saw it was him, as if he could hear her thoughts. Sienna said thinking of someone and them calling out of the blue was "phonetuition," but whatever it was, Griffin calling her in that moment felt right.

"Hey there," she said as calmly as she could.

"Hey, where are you? Are you still at the apartment by any chance?" He sounded rushed and stressed-out.

"No, I just crossed the bridge. Why?"

"Shit." Justine could hear airline announcements in the background. "Something is going on at my apartment and I'm at La-Guardia. One of my insane neighbors called me and said there's water leaking in her apartment. She's in the one below mine, which means something might be going on in *my* place. No one can reach the super, he's worthless. Now, keep in mind, this woman thinks her mailbox is haunted, so I'm not sure if she's hallucinating or there's actually water leaking from my apartment."

Justine clutched the steering wheel as she tried to remember if she'd forgotten to turn off the sink, or accidentally used the cursed garbage disposal. Then she remembered he'd been there after her and breathed a sigh of relief.

"Do you want me to turn around and go check on it?"

He groaned. "I feel terrible asking, especially after a long day, but do you mind?"

She hadn't told Griffin about Spencer's final scene. She hadn't told him much of anything other than the dates she needed his apartment. And the fact was, he hadn't asked her for details. Their communication had been acquaintance-polite and she wasn't about to be the first person to change it.

"Of course I can go back, no problem. Least I can do after all this time letting me stay. I'll call you back as soon as I'm there. When is your flight leaving?" Justine pulled into a parking lot and turned her car around.

"I'm boarding in an hour and a half."

"Okay, I'll make it before you leave."

"Thank you. I owe you." She could hear the relief in his voice.

"Hardly. Call you soon."

Spencer seemed confused to be heading back to Griffin's apartment. He'd gotten used to their normal routine, and coming back immediately after leaving had him swiveling his head over and over as if trying to make sense of why they were speed-walking down the sidewalk again. Justine wasn't thrilled to be back either. She'd said her good-bye to the place knowing she wasn't going to see it again and didn't feel like revisiting it already.

The wind bit through her jacket, so Justine pulled her hat down over her ears and sped up as they got closer to Griffin's building. She'd waited to eat and now she was starving, but she had a half-dozen excellent take-out options all within a few blocks. She was daydreaming about food-truck crepes with Gruyère and caramelized onions as she and Spencer took the front stairs to Griffin's building two at a time. She was almost at the top and reaching into her pocket for the front-door key when her feet slipped out from under her.

Her hands hit the top step hard as she slid down the edges of the stairs. Ice? How was there ice on them? She could hear Spencer's tags jangling along beside her as she tried to regain her footing and her pride. Not only had her purse hit the steps with a wallop, but she'd cried out in shock and then pain as her knees dragged along the steps. She paused before getting up when she finally stopped sliding and quickly tried to assess her injuries.

"You okay?" a guy jogging by paused and asked. Justine shot Spencer a look to make sure he felt okay about the hat-wearing fast-moving stranger, but he seemed more concerned with her. "Miss? Are you all right?"

Justine nodded. "I'm fine, thanks." She waved him on.

Her hands were scratched, bloody, and throbbing. She picked at the little pebbles embedded in her right palm. She felt the same throb in her knees and looked down to discover a rip in her jeans on her right knee with a little ring of blood on it. Her shoulders felt like they'd been knocked out of joint and her right wrist already looked swollen.

Spencer stood beside her watching her intently, ready to give her kisses and wags when she was ready. She took a shaky breath and held up her hands to him.

"Look, Spence, now we're both bloody."

She stood up slowly and made her way up the stairs holding on to the railing gingerly. There was nothing obvious that could've caused the fall other than her own clumsiness, and it made her even angrier than discovering a patch of black ice.

The small lobby was typically quiet, without any evidence of a leak, like buckets, mops, or stressed-out people. Justine paused on each landing to listen for sounds of distress and was met with just the muffled voices from TVs behind closed doors. Spencer did his usual dance routine as he waited for Justine to unlock Griffin's door, and they burst in together like a SWAT team.

Silence. Justine cocked her head to listen for running, dripping, trickling, or gushing water and didn't hear anything but the traffic outside.

She ran to the kitchen and grabbed a sheet of paper towel for her bloody palms, then dashed from room to room trying to ignore the Griffin aura all around her. All sinks were turned off, the garbage disposal was still DOA, and every pipe was intact. The entire apartment was dry.

"Well, that was a worthwhile trip," Justine said to Spencer with a sigh.

She realized she hadn't checked the skylight in the loft. Maybe it had sprung a leak that somehow found its way two floors below? She trudged up the metal stairs slowly behind Spencer, gun-shy from her fall but also because she didn't want to be anywhere near Griffin's bed. She stopped when her eyes crested the floor of the loft and looked up at the skylight. Nothing.

Justine glanced at the bed and noticed something pink peeking out of the top drawer of his nightstand, where he kept his condoms. She leaned closer and realized it was her headband. She was sure the last time she'd used it was in the bathroom to hold her hair back as she washed her face, yet somehow it had migrated to his drawer.

Not an accident.

She hurried back down and texted Griffin a few photos and a thumbs-up emoji.

His text back was immediate. Relief! Thank you so much. Glad it was a hallucination but sorry you had to come all the way back.

NP, safe travels. She kept it short, because there was nothing else to say.

Her hands throbbed and she realized that she needed to clean up before she left. Griffin was bound to have antiseptic and Band-Aids in his vanity. She wasn't one of those nosy people who poked around in other people's business despite spending time alone in his apartment, but now she had a valid reason to do a little recon in the bathroom.

"Spence, please stop. That's disgusting."

He'd followed her into the bathroom and was trying to drink out of the toilet even though his bowl of water was still on the kitchen floor. She ushered him out and banged the door shut so she could tend to her wounds in peace.

Justine didn't even glance in the vanity mirror as she opened it. As expected, Griffin's supplies were lined up soldier-straight. An electric toothbrush, whitening toothpaste, a nail brush, nail clippers, vitamins, spicy deodorant that she was tempted to inhale, an unopened box of cologne, and, tucked in the corner, Band-Aids and Neosporin.

She washed her hands gingerly and powered through the stinging when the soap hit the deeper parts of the cuts. Justine reached over to the towel next to the sink without thinking and ran her hand down it, only to be mortified by the red streaks on the pristine white.

"Idiot." She sighed. "Way to make a good last impression."

Justine had just seen detergent under the kitchen sink and figured she could spot clean the stains before they set in. She grasped the bathroom doorknob without touching her palm to it, gave it an up-and-twist like she always did, then jumped back in shock when the thing snapped off in her hand.

chapter thirty-eight

"He's not answering?" Justine asked as she closed her eyes and rubbed her forehead with her fingertips.

"No, that guy is the invisible man. How can you manage a building when you're never around?" Griffin sounded furious. "I feel so bad, Justine. I'm sorry. Are you okay to wait a little longer?"

She wasn't. Hangry, twenty-five minutes into captivity, and sitting on Griffin's bathroom floor with the knob worthless at her feet made her want to shred the door with her bare hands. Everything she'd been bottling up all day was swirling in her chest and threatening to burst out in a primal scream that would probably freak out the lady downstairs much more than an imagined leak.

"I'm okay."

The line was silent for a minute. "No one else in the building has a key to my front door but him. Damn it! I can call a locksmith."

"No, Griffin, that's not necessary yet. I'll keep trying; it'll work eventually. I'm looking up break-in hacks and reverse engineering them. I'll figure it out. You're getting on a plane in a few minutes. Don't worry about me. Worst case, if I can't get out *I'll* call a locksmith."

Spencer scratched the other side of the door and let out a mournful howl.

"Fuck, I forgot about Spencer! I can hear him," Griffin said. "Was today a tough shoot for him?"

Her mind flashed to an image of Spencer bloody and lying on his side with Anderson wailing above him. The tears poured down Anderson's cheeks as he cradled Spencer in his arms, and he alternated between kissing the dog's face and screaming in anguish. It looked so real that the entire crew was fighting tears by the time Ted called "cut."

Justine's stomach clenched as the oil slick of sadness inside her finally bubbled over. "Today was *awful*." She sobbed. "Spencer died on the show! You should see his fur. And I fell on your stupid front steps, Griffin. I tore up my hands and ripped my favorite jeans, and I bled on your towel, and now I'm trapped in your stupid bathroom and I'm starving and I just want to get out of here and forget everything that happened today." She put her head down and ugly cried into the phone.

"Okay, that's it," Griffin said, his voice determined, like he'd figured everything out. "You're going to be fine; just wait there."

"I don't have a *choice*," Justine wailed as the line went dead.

"What the hell is a hex-key set?" Justine asked Ruth in her tough-girl voice to keep from breaking down again after an hour trapped in the bathroom.

"I have no idea, but Patrick said you should look around under the sink for one." Justine heard a muffled voice. "He said they're L-shaped metal things. Or look for a flat-head screwdriver."

Justine looked under Griffin's sink for the sixth time. "I've got a toilet brush, extra rolls of tissue, and a bottle of moisturizer. That's it."

"Okay, Patrick just offered to drive in and break you out. Or we can call the fire department."

"Stop, I'm not a cat caught in a tree. I'll figure it out." Justine shoved her fingers in the hole where the knob used to be and jiggled. "I feel like something is coming loose."

"Patrick said to check the . . . Hold on, he wants to talk to you."

The phone went fuzzy for a few seconds. "Hi, Justine. Sorry you're trapped, but I think I have a solution for you. Check the hinges. There might be pins in the top and bottom hinges you can pop out, and then—"

"Nope, it's a concealed hinge. I already read about that."

"Damn. I thought I'd be the one to spring you. Do you want me to drive in? I can bring my tools and get you out in two seconds."

"We'd still need a locksmith to get into his front door." Justine sighed. "I have one more thing I can try," she lied. "I'll call you back in a bit, hopefully from the other side."

"Okay, well, I bet I could pick his lock then get in and be your hero, so just say the word and I'm there."

"Thanks, Patrick. Tell Ruth I'll talk to her later."

Justine hung up and stared at the door. She was out of ideas and hacks to get the damn thing open. At least she had water and the toilet if she needed it. She got on her knees and peeked out the crack under the door. Spencer was lying down on the other side.

"Hey, bud. You doing okay?" He whined. "I know, I know. This sucks."

She hadn't heard from Griffin since they hung up. She imagined him running to catch his flight while trying to figure out how to get help to her. Maybe he'd managed to get in touch with the super and he was on his way to get her out? It wasn't like him to leave her hanging without a solution. Griffin was a fixer.

But it wasn't like she was a typical damsel in distress, despite the tears. She needed to rescue *herself.* Justine opened the vanity, grabbed the black plastic toilet brush, then crawled over to the door and jammed the hard plastic in the knob hole. She jiggled it around like she was whipping the world's smallest egg, which seemed to get Spencer revved up on the other side of the door. He let out his wake-the-dead happy bark.

"I know, buddy, I'm trying!" Justine said as she jammed the plastic handle in the hole and Spencer continued barking.

She whirled the handle faster, and either it was working to make the still-intact knob on the other side of the door move or she was delirious from hunger, because she felt the door giving way.

She leaned into it with all of her weight, and the next thing she knew she was outside the bathroom on the floor at Griffin's feet.

"Griffin!" she yelped up at him with the toilet brush still in her hand. "What are you doing here?"

"I thought I was going to save you, but it looks like you didn't need me after all." He held out his hand to help her up while Spencer jumped in circles around him.

It was the first time she'd ever seen him with stubble, and she couldn't stop staring. Griffin was *always* clean-shaven; even the morning after in Maryland barely left him with a shadow on his cheeks. How many days had it been since he'd shaved? And how was it possible that he looked even better with it? Between the new navy wool coat, the gray striped scarf, and the disheveled-chic look, she felt like she was staring at a stranger.

"Are you okay?"

She took his hand gingerly, using just her fingertips so he didn't accidentally hit the scrapes. "I am now. Thank you for coming back, but what are you doing here? You're supposed to be on a plane to Chicago."

Once she was standing he gently flipped her hand over and examined her palm, cradling it in his hand. "Ooh. That hurts. You had a rough day, huh?" He paused until she met his eyes. "I'm so sorry, Justine. That was a lot to deal with."

She sniffled and nodded, leaving her hand tucked in his. "Not my best day, that's for sure."

Spencer leapt up and bounced off Griffin's midsection, and he dropped Justine's hand as he fell backward a few steps.

"Ouch, Spence!" he said as he rubbed his chest.

"You didn't tell me why you're here," Justine said with a frown. "Did your flight get canceled?"

He shook his head. "I rescheduled it. I'm leaving at eleven now."

Justine's heart surged. "Wait, you did that for me?"

"Of course I did. I couldn't let you rot in my bathroom until I got back." A smile played at the corners of his mouth.

"Hey, I found the right tool for the job eventually."

He bent over and picked up the toilet brush lying next to the door. "You did. Very inventive." Griffin disappeared into the bathroom to put it away.

"Now that I'm sprung I guess we should head out," Justine said as she watched Spencer jump up on the couch and start scratching and digging at the fabric like he was settling in.

"Are you hungry? Do you want to grab dinner before you go?" The hope in Griffin's eyes was impossible to miss.

"Probably not a good idea," she answered as she crossed her arms, knowing that she didn't need to explain why.

Griffin's face fell. "Okay. I get it."

"I don't want to keep you, so we're going to go. Hey, Spence, you ready?" She tried not to think too much as she walked back into the bathroom to grab her purse, then brushed by Griffin and past the exact spot where he'd kissed her for the first time. "As of today, your part-time tenants are officially gone. But we really appreciate everything you did for us. I can't thank you enough."

Saying it released a bloom of sadness in her chest. She'd done everything possible to avoid another in-person good-bye with Griffin, yet here they were, living through it.

He blinked and looked confused. "What do you mean? I told you it's fine for you guys to stay here. I'll fix the knob if that's what this is about." He laughed hollowly.

Justine stopped. "I told you on the phone. Today was Spencer's last day on *The Eighteenth*. Didn't you see the fake blood on him?"

"Wait, *that's* what you said? You were hard to understand because you were so upset. When you said he 'died' I thought you meant he had a bad day. They actually fucking killed him off? For good?"

She tensed at the thought of Spencer playing dead and nodded.

"That means you guys won't be coming back here? You don't need the apartment anymore?"

"Nope. Today was the last day."

Griffin raked his fingers through his hair. "Wow. Okay. Holy shit, Justine. I am *so* sorry. Was it . . . something he did? Or didn't do?"

"No, it's a plot decision. I guess it makes sense, but I know for a fact that people hate it when the dog dies. The audience is going to be pissed."

"*I'm* pissed!" he exclaimed. "It's a stupid move. Spencer is amazing on the show."

"Yeah." Justine glanced over at where he was curled up on the couch. "He was." Her lower lip trembled, and her eyes misted.

"Hey, hey, come here." He walked to her with his arms spread wide and scooped her into a crushing hug.

She leaned into him and inhaled deeply, trying to memorize his scent so she could call up the nuances of him in the future. The cold outdoor smell still clung to him, mixed in with the Griffinness she'd grown to love. His coat felt like cashmere against her cheek, and his arms wrapped around her so tightly that she felt like she was about to break. He rested his chin on top of her head as if he didn't trust himself to get closer to her mouth, like she was his best friend's little sister and definitely *not* someone who needed to be kissed by him.

Justine shivered.

He leaned back. "You're cold?"

She shook her head and bit her lip, staring at his chest.

"Hey."

Justine looked up at Griffin as he loosened his grip. He stared into her eyes for a moment, the smallest smile on his lips, then gently placed his hand beneath her chin and tilted her face up toward his.

Even though she knew that kissing him was the absolute worst thing to do, she let her eyes drift shut as his mouth found hers. Her heart simultaneously leapt and shattered as they melted into each other.

He cupped her face and stroked her cheek with his thumb as they kissed. The tenderness hollowed her out and she bounced between desire and despair as their mouths moved together. The longer he kissed her, the less likely it was that they were going to stop. Justine tried to summon up the willpower to push him away but couldn't fight against the tingles of pleasure that rushed up and down her spine as Griffin claimed her lips.

It didn't feel like good-bye.

Griffin made a noise that sounded like a growl and deepened the kiss. Justine leaned into him and her hands found their way beneath his jacket and around his waist, pulling him closer. His shirt was untucked, and she slid her fingers onto the smooth skin just above his waist. He pushed against her with a ragged sigh of pleasure.

And then, as if an unspoken command had passed between them, they pulled apart at the exact same moment.

"This is stupid," Justine whispered, her throat too choked with emotion to manage anything more.

Griffin leaned his forehead against hers, breathing heavy. "'Stupid' isn't the word I was thinking of."

"This can't happen. It's not fair to either of us."

He nodded.

"I'm not doing it again. My heart can't take it." She used every bit of her strength to pull herself out of his arms. "I have to go."

She walked over to get her purse, then whistled for Spencer. He leapt off the couch and ran to her like they were headed out for an adventure.

"Can I at least say bye to him? I mean, this is it . . . for good."

"Sorry," Justine said, quickly dropping his leash. "I keep forgetting this is the last time."

Griffin flinched, then recovered quickly.

"Hey, Spence. C'mere!" It was a modified version of his happy voice, one they could all tell was pretending at the emotion and not really feeling it. Griffin dropped to his knees as Spencer got closer, and the dog ran into him like he was a defensive lineman, knocking him off-balance and onto the ground.

Justine smiled sadly as Spencer pinned him and covered his face with sloppy kisses

"Are you my best boy? Yes, you are." Griffin got up on his knees and lowered his voice to encourage Spencer to calm down. "Look at you, so handsome, even with that red stuff on your fur. My best guy."

Spencer sat in front of him panting with his head tilted back. He scooched closer and closer until his body was flush against Griffin's.

"I'm going to miss you, buddy," he said softly. Griffin wrapped his arms around Spencer and hugged him, and even though Justine knew Spencer wasn't a fan of hugs, the dog seemed to lean into it, almost as if he knew *this* hug mattered. After a few seconds Spencer tilted his head back and licked Griffin's chin.

"I love you too. But I know you're in the best possible place. Stay happy, my good boy."

He finally let go and Spencer stood next to him waiting for information about what to do next. It was as if the air was charged with something unpleasant the dog could sense, and it confused him. Griffin sniffled a few times and looked like he was tearing up.

"Spence, time to go," Justine said softly. Spencer dashed to her and she picked up the leash; then they headed to the door together. "Thanks for everything, Griffin."

Justine didn't look over her shoulder as she grasped the doorknob, because there was nothing left to say, but Spencer paused and gave Griffin one last, long glance before the door clicked shut behind them.

chapter thirty-nine

"You don't like my scallops?" Luis frowned at Justine's plate as he cleared the communal table at Monty's. It was a full moon, which meant that the restaurant was open for one of their twelve special "Full Moon Saloon" BYOB dinners.

"No, they're amazing. And the mushroom risotto is incredible. But I'm not that hungry tonight, I'm sorry." She hoped he wouldn't ask why.

"Bad timing on the hunger strike. We're barely past the second course." He peered at Spencer under the table and Spencer thumped his tail back at him. "I bet he'd enjoy it."

Sienna leaned over to block Luis from clearing Justine's plate. "Don't you dare give this to Spencer. I'm going to finish it for her."

"Okay, all right, I like that spirit, girl." His grin lit up his face and Justine watched as a flicker passed between the two of them. "Glad *someone* likes my cooking."

When he turned his back Justine leaned over to whisper in Sienna's ear. "Um, do you have something you need to tell me?"

Sienna made her eyes go wide in mock shock and she placed a delicate hand on her chest. "Excuse me?"

"You two." Justine bobbed her head in Luis's direction. "Am I picking up a vibe or what?"

"Maybe." She burst out laughing. "Okay, yes. We've hung out a few times and it's been great. I didn't want to say anything because—" She stopped herself.

"Sienna, it's okay. I'm fine."

But she wasn't.

It had been three weeks since the last time she saw Griffin in Brooklyn, and the raw feelings surfaced every time she thought about him. A tiny part wished that she'd stayed one last night with him, to give their final moments together an appropriately melancholy ending. But she knew the pain of the good-bye would outweigh the pleasure of having him.

Justine turned her attention back to the room and plastered on a fake smile when Ruth caught her eye and waved from her end of the table next to Patrick and the kids. Normally Full Moon Saloon night was a shut-down-the-joint party, but all she wanted to do was go home and sleep on her couch with Spencer. She'd spent more time than usual doing her makeup and getting dressed up in an effort to get into the spirit of the night, but the room was too bright, the food tasted bland, and she didn't feel like making small talk with anyone since she had nothing good to talk about.

"Champagne?" An orange-labeled bottle appeared in front of her.

"Oh, no, thanks, Monty." She covered her still-full glass. "I'm good."

Monty squatted down next to Justine's chair. "Taylor showed

me footage of Spencer's last scene with Anderson. Talk about a gut-wrencher. I sobbed."

Justine managed a half smile. "You and me both. Even tough-guy Malcolm cried."

Monty's eyebrows shot up. "That tall, dark, and handsome man you were always hanging around? I wish you'd introduced me."

"Are you kidding me?"

"He looked interesting." Monty shrugged. "So, fill me in, girl. What are you up to these days anyway?"

It was the question she couldn't escape since getting back to Rexford full-time. Everyone wanted to know what she was doing now that she was off the show and no longer at T&B, and the questions chafed her after a while. Sometimes she longed to be anonymous, just another body passing by on the sidewalk.

"I'm working on the curriculum for a canine acting class, so people can teach their dogs how to do what Spencer did. Plus, he auditioned for a dog food commercial, and we've got a conference call with a pet pharma company for some possible print work."

"Look at you, Miss Busy," Monty responded with an approving nod. She held up the bottle again. "You sure you don't want some? Let's party it up tonight, because it looks like we're going to be snowed in tomorrow."

"First storm already." Justine wasn't looking forward to being homebound in her current state of mind. "Thanks, but I think I'm going to head out. Can I settle up?"

"Absolutely not." Monty shook her head so her giant dangly earrings shimmered. "This one is on me because they sacked Spencer. I'm still mad about it."

The small kindness was just what she needed. "Thank you, I appreciate it."

Monty stood up, brushed off the front of her tight black pants, and continued selectively pouring glasses of free champagne for the people in the room that she liked.

"Hey, do you mind if I go?" Justine leaned over and asked Sienna. "I'm not in the right mindset for all of this." She gestured around the room with her nose wrinkled up like something smelled bad.

"Really?" Her eyes went wide. "Are you sure you don't want to stay? Where are you going?" Sienna looked slightly panicked.

"I want to go home. I'm tired."

"Want me to come?" Sienna was already gathering her bag.

Justine was touched by her friend's concern. "No, I have a feeling someone wants you to stick around until closing." She smiled as genuinely as she could and gave Sienna a quick kiss on the cheek.

Justine gathered her things and coaxed Spencer from the spot where food kept mysteriously raining down on him. She blew a kiss to Ruth and struggled to look like she was someone who had her life together and wasn't on the verge of a major breakdown as she wove her way through the tables and out of the restaurant.

It was a freezing night under a dusky, starless sky, so she'd driven the short distance to Monty's. They'd arrived late, so her car was in the back corner of the lot where the trees bordered it.

Spencer stopped walking and raised his head up, sniffing and licking the air.

"What's wrong?" Justine asked.

He let out a muffled test woof and the hair on her arms

prickled. Someone had mentioned spotting a black bear close to the restaurant and she wasn't in the mood to see if it was truth or rumor.

Justine picked up her pace on the way to her car, but Spencer stopped and dug his paws into the ground, then threw back his head and let out a string of high-pitched barks that sounded like a one-sided conversation.

"Spence, come on, let's go." She took a few steps, but he didn't move and didn't stop barking. "What is *up* with you, dude?"

It was like she didn't exist, and Justine realized that his behavior wasn't playful insubordination. Something weird was going on. And it got even stranger when he started jumping up and down at the end of the leash.

"I *really* don't want to get eaten by a bear tonight. Can we please go?"

Spencer gave another high-pitched scream-bark and Justine looked down the street where he was focused.

A shadow was moving toward them. Her pulse sped up as the figure moved into the light of a streetlamp.

It was him.

Griffin, walking toward them with a determined look on his face, like he'd know exactly where to go even if his former dog wasn't barking a frantic welcome to him. She wanted to cry with relief at the sight of him in his perfect coat, walking his perfect walk directly toward them. A smile cracked Griffin's face and he sped to a jog when he realized that Justine had spotted him.

He looked as happy as the first time she'd seen him in the park running toward Spencer.

Only this time he was running to both of them.

He was panting a little by the time he reached her, his cheeks red from the cold. She couldn't believe that Griffin was right in front of her, in Rexford. Her heart turned cartwheels at the sight of him, while Spencer came close to turning literal cartwheels trying to pummel Griffin with his paws. Griffin reached down and gave Spencer a hearty pat and tried to calm him.

"Hi." It was the only thing she could think to say because she was still trying to figure out what Griffin was doing in her town when he was supposed to be off doing trajectory things.

"Hi."

He looked suddenly unsure of himself, like he was crashing her party.

"Where's your car? Why are you walking?" She looked over his shoulder as if his car might be following him like an obedient dog.

How was it possible that she was forming coherent sentences?

"Parked in town, right in front of Tricks & Biscuits. I wanted to see what you built, Justine. I could only peek in the windows since it's closed, but I could see your fingerprints everywhere inside." He paused. "And I needed to walk here, to clear my head."

"But how did you hear about this place?" She gestured over her shoulder at Monty's.

He graced her with half a dimple. "The new owner at T&B is a great conversationalist. A *wealth* of information. She was locking up for the night when I got there, and she recognized me. We chatted for a bit and she said everyone was headed here." Griffin paused. "Let's just say she was very excited that I stopped by."

Suddenly Sienna's worried face when Justine said she was

leaving made sense. Justine could only imagine the flood of tarot card intel she'd probably subjected him to.

They stared at each other, the silence punctuated by Spencer's jingling dog tags and little whines. He jogged a few steps and pulled the leash from Justine's cold hand.

"Spence, stay close," she admonished as he anchored his nose to the ground.

Griffin's face went dark as he reached into his coat and fumbled with something. "I wanted to give this to you in person. I don't trust the mail anymore." He pulled out the red file with all of Spencer's paperwork. "I meant to give it to you a long time ago. Every document is in there. You should keep the vet records, but you can burn everything else. The license, the microchip documentation, the adoption paperwork . . ." He trailed off. "We both know that Spencer has always been yours. Case closed."

Griffin looked ready to turn on his heel and run at the slightest sign of conflict as he passed the file to Justine.

How many times had she imagined opening the little end table in his apartment and stealing the documents? Or stealing only the critical ones and leaving the rest, to make him think he was losing his mind? But now the red file was hers and it was practically burning her fingertips.

"Thank you, Griffin. For this. For everything you've done for us."

What might happen next spun out in a thousand different variations in her mind.

"Did you hear about the storm?" he asked.

She nodded and shoved her hands in her pockets. "Sounds bad. It's definitely going to interrupt your travel for a while."

"Not really."

Justine tilted her head at him.

"I resigned."

"You *what*?"

"From the new gig," Griffin continued quickly. "It wasn't a fit after all. My heart wasn't in it. I opted for a position that got me off the road. A little less money, but lots more peace. Fuck the trajectory."

"Okay. That's . . . major." She didn't know what to make of the change, or the unfamiliar expression on his face.

"It is." He nodded. "We have a lot to discuss, Justine."

There was something in his eyes that she didn't recognize. This wasn't customer-service Griffin. This was Griffin on a mission.

"You sort of picked a bad time for a road trip. The storm is supposed to start soon." The tip of her nose was starting to feel numb and she wished she'd worn a hat.

"Not for another three hours, actually." He cleared his throat. "And it's not going to take me long to say my piece."

Justine didn't know how to respond, so she stood in front of him silently as feathery snowflakes started coming down around them. She pointed. "Guess they were wrong."

The snow didn't seem to register since Griffin's gaze was locked in on her face.

"We made a mistake," he finally blurted out. "We shouldn't have given up on this. On us. Because I'm better when I'm with you, Justine. *Everything* is better when you're around." He paused as if working up the courage to continue. "I started falling for you the first time I saw you with Spencer in the park, and even though I fought against it as hard as I could, all I wanted to do was be near you."

She felt pinpricks behind her eyes and a tickle in her nose.

"And it's so much more than that. Way more. Do you have any clue how much you taught me, Justine?"

She sniffled. "What?"

"You're the bravest person I know. You live life without a net. You take risks. You fight back when things get tough. You can pick a broken lock with a toilet brush, for fuck's sake!" He laughed at the memory. "You showed me how to cliff dive through life and inspired me to take some chances of my own."

Justine tucked the red file under her arm and dragged her fingers beneath her eyes, knowing it wasn't doing any good. She was one more Griffin-confession away from becoming a soggy mess.

"I reevaluated everything I thought was important to me. Justine, even as I was signing on the dotted line I knew I was making the wrong choice. But you have to understand, I had a lot of history to get past. When I used to think about what I needed to be happy, it was all about goals and milestones. Now I know all I need is you and Spencer." He swallowed hard. "If you give me a chance, my only goal will be to make the two of you half as happy as you made me. I choose you, Justine." Griffin took a deep breath then let out a shaky exhale. "Because I love you."

Her tears were falling freely, mixing with the snowflakes that melted on her cheeks. Justine felt dizzy and giddy, like she'd downed all of Monty's Veuve Clicquot.

"Griffin." It came out in a whisper. "I love you too."

Justine took the lapels of his jacket in her hands, pulled him close, and kissed him so hard that he stumbled a step. He recovered quickly and she could feel him smiling against her mouth as he wrapped his arms around her.

She tried to keep kissing him but had to pull back to sniffle and brush away the tears.

"Sorry, I'm all snotty." She laughed and quickly wiped her nose.

"I don't care," Griffin said, looking at her like she was the most beautiful woman in the world. He gently traced the wet tracks on her cheeks with his lips until she forgot they were in the middle of a parking lot during the beginning of a blizzard.

The red file hit the ground as they kissed, and a few sheets of paper blew away. Spencer trotted over to examine what was left of his history.

"You need to pack. Now. Hurry," Griffin murmured against her mouth, suddenly part caveman.

"What do you mean?"

He finally found the strength to step away.

"I'm here to kidnap you two. We're going to beat this storm back to the city and get snowed in together. And I'm going to supervise your packing since we're on a deadline. Let's get moving." He did a wrap-it-up hand signal.

Spencer seemed to understand that they were getting ready to go and started dashing around them over and over, like a border collie trying to close the distance within his flock.

"Hey, Spence," Griffin said, bending over playfully. "What are you doing, you crazy mutt? Get over here!"

He opened his arms and Spencer leapt up to give Griffin a hug.

Justine shook her head as she watched their reunion continue. It was naughty and inappropriate and it drove her a tiny bit insane. There was no fixing the Spencer-and-Griffin manners problem.

But it finally dawned on her; it didn't need fixing.

Spencer and Griffin were perfect for each other, just like she and Spencer were perfect as a team. Different parts of a matched set. The two halves that made her heart whole.

And they were all even better together.

"You two ready to hit the road?" Justine called to them.

For the first time ever, Spencer dipped into a play bow, barked a joyful "yes," and ran to stand next to Justine's car.

Griffin walked over and gently took her hand in his.

"We're all ready. Let's go."

epilogue

I think that was the best day ever," Justine said, resting her head on Griffin's bare chest. The morning sunshine streamed in the two oversized windows flanking their bed.

"Last night wasn't too shabby either," he answered, squeezing her and giving her a kiss on the forehead.

She ran her thumb over the slim silver band on her finger, then glanced over at the heap of white silk and tulle on the chair next to the bed. She sat up abruptly. "Willa is sleeping on my wedding dress."

"Relax, you'll never wear that dress again. And what's wrong with a little cat hair, anyway?"

Justine settled back against his chest. "You'd never think she was so well trained with the way she acts around here. It's her world and we're just living in it."

"You've finally surrendered to your feline overlord." He chuckled.

They were interrupted by a clatter of paws as a tornado of

fur, teeth, and tails leapt onto the bed. Spencer went into a play bow in front of his new little sister, Eunice.

"Eunice, *ouch*," Griffin shouted, pulling the blanket over his chest and doubling over. "How does a dog so small deliver so much pain? I swear, she hits my balls every time she jumps up here."

"Have you ever noticed you're the only one these dogs abuse?" Justine hid a grin and reached over to pat the brindle mixed-breed dog that looked part pug and part Muppet.

They hadn't planned on a double adoption when they visited the Rescue Society of New York, especially just a few months before their wedding. But year-old Eunice and Willa the gray long-haired cat with striking blue eyes had been surrendered as a bonded pair when their owner died unexpectedly. Justine knew how hard it was to find a home for two pets at once. She and Griffin had fallen in love with the duo immediately and she'd been pleasantly surprised to discover that both animals loved learning new tricks alongside Spencer. Shockingly, Willa was already in high demand after a few successful print ads and a hysterical Chewy commercial.

"Did you manage to have fun yesterday?" Justine asked as Spencer and Eunice wrestled at their feet. "Because I did. It was everything I'd dreamed about." She paused. "No, actually, it was better, because no one knew I had sneakers on under my gown."

"It was amazing," Griffin said as he lazily stroked Justine's back. "Spencer nailed the ring-bearer delivery. The food was great, the band was non-fucking-stop. Oh my God, and your *mom*!" He laughed. "She had some moves on the dance floor."

Justine grinned. "Once she figured out Luis could dance she wouldn't leave him alone! Poor Sienna."

"I don't think she minded sitting out. She's huge now."

Sienna and Luis had progressed from courting to forever at warp speed, and they were expecting their firstborn any day. In typical Sienna fashion, they were waiting for the right moon phase after the baby was born to hold their wedding in a field in Rexford.

Justine stared into Griffin's eyes. "I'm so freaking excited. Can we leave? Is it time to go yet?"

"We've got no choice—that Airstream is going to get towed if we don't."

Griffin had called in a few favors with their new neighbors in the brick warehouse with the curved windows and star medallions, getting them to move their cars so he could park the rented Airstream outside until they were ready to leave for their honeymoon. It was going to be a family affair, with the five of them cramming into it and traveling across country for two weeks, making stops to visit friends and family along the way.

"I wish we could take a month off." She pouted.

"I feel lucky we got *any* time off. Especially Spencer. He's busier than both of us."

The matter-of-fact call from *The Eighteenth* show scheduler weeks after Spencer had his last day on set had caught Justine off guard. It seemed that no one wanted to cop to the mistake of attempting to kill Spencer off on the show, so they acted almost as if it hadn't happened. The scheduler gave her a brief overview of the new script direction and a request that Justine and Spencer consider coming back.

It wasn't even a question.

Justine wrapped the top blanket around her and got out of bed. Eunice stopped trying to tear off Spencer's wedding bow tie, and Willa woke from her deep sleep to stare at her. They all seemed to know that wherever Justine went, fun followed.

"Get out of bed, Mr. McCabe," she said. "It's time to start our forever. I'm ready."

"I don't know, Mrs. McCabe," he replied as his eyes trailed up and down her body lazily. He unleashed the dimples. "I think our forever can wait a *little* while longer."

He reached beside the bed to grab one of the millions of dog toys strewn around the loft, then tossed it down the hallway, causing Spencer and Eunice to jump down and tear after it. Then he crawled across the bed, letting the sheet drift off his body, and grabbed the edge of the blanket wrapped around Justine. He gave it a tug and she fell into the bed on top of him, laughing and shrieking.

"You will *always* be my favorite adventure," Justine whispered to Griffin as he kissed her on the nose.

acknowledgments

Knock wood, I rarely suffer from writer's block, but the one exercise where it always hits me?

Acknowledgments.

I want my thanks to be sufficiently appreciative of the love and support around me (and maybe a little bit funny too), but nothing I write feels like enough. I stare at the blank page and get stressed out as the deadline I promised to make slips by. (A week late on this one. Whoops!)

So let's just pretend I've written an eloquent opening paragraph about the writer's process and dive right in!

Endless thanks to my agent, Kevan Lyon, for her ability to navigate my fragile artistic temperament like a therapist. You are my rock! Kate Seaver, my amazing editor, thank you for the epic brainstorming sessions and for bringing clarity to my writing. Your superpower is making sense of the jumble I submit.

My publicity and marketing dream team, Bridget O'Toole, Tara O'Connor, and Dache' Rogers, astound me with their creativity—thank you for being nonstop. And Mary Geren, thanks for always answering my ridiculous questions with kindness. I'm truly honored to be part of the Berkley family.

I have so much love for my everyday crew, the women who lift me up and inspire me in equal measure. First and foremost, my sister Jessica . . . I *still* want to be just like you! Jennifer Buckley (thirty years and counting!), Nerice Kendter, Heidi Bencsik, your support is everything. Helen Little, Jenni Walsh, and Suzanne Baltzar, my Pale Mimosa crew, we'll be back to our in-person four-hour brunches soon. And Linda Facci, thanks for providing the crafty inspiration for a very special character in *Lost, Found, and Forever*!

Hey, bookstagrammers? I want you to know that you're incredible. Thank you for everything that you do to shine a light on the authors you love. I've been lucky enough to be on the receiving end and let me tell you, it's the absolute *best* feeling. I'm humbled by your support.

Big thanks to my wonderful in-laws, John and Mary B., for being my cheerleaders and preorder pros. It's good to have St. Francis on my side!

Lifetime, hall of fame-level thanks to my parents, who wrote the book on being supportive. I love you both so much!

And even though his name doesn't appear on the cover, my husband, Tom, is my secret cowriter. You are my forever brainstorming partner, and my forever Fav.

lost,
found,
and
forever

VICTORIA SCHADE

Questions for Discussion

1. One of the central issues in *Lost, Found, and Forever* is defining the boundaries of pet ownership. Is it based on length of time, the strength of the bond, or the ability to care for the animal? How would you define "ownership" based on your relationship with your current pet?

2. If you were in the same situation as Justine and discovered the person who used to own your pet on social media, would you reach out to them?

3. Justine worries that Spencer loves Griffin more than her. Does your pet play favorites in your household, and if so, why do you think that is?

4. Justine lives in a quaint town but doesn't feel at home there. Why do you think Justine chafes at some of the aspects of small-town life that many people appreciate?

5. Do you think Griffin's offer to let Justine use the apartment was purely altruistic, or did he have an ulterior motive?

6. Justine's work on *The Eighteenth* exposes her to a new world where she's completely out of her element. Have you ever taken a similar huge leap of faith?

7. How do you think Justine's frightening incident on the trail impacted her? Do you think she dealt with it properly?

8. Justine, Sienna, and Ruth are all at different life stages, yet they share a close friendship. What do you think bonds them to one another?

9. Sienna uses mysticism to make decisions and attempts to use it to guide those around her. Do you believe in tarot cards and horoscopes? Does mysticism influence your decision-making process?

10. What obstacles do Justine and Griffin face on the road to their happily ever after? Do they share any similarities, or are they true opposites?

Author photo by Jeff Reeder

Victoria Schade is a dog trainer and speaker who serves as a dog resource for the media and has worked both in front of and behind the camera on Animal Planet, as a cohost on the program *Faithful Friends*, and as a trainer and wrangler on the channel's popular Puppy Bowl specials. She lives in Pennsylvania with her husband, her dogs, Millie and Olive, and the occasional foster pup.

Ready to find
your next great read?

Let us help.

Visit prh.com/nextread

Penguin
Random
House